THE
MANY
LIVES
OF
HELOISE
STARCHILD

JOHN IRONMONGER

WEIDENFELD & NICOLSON

First published in Great Britain in 2020
by Weidenfeld & Nicolson
an imprint of The Orion Publishing Group Ltd
Carmelite House, 50 Victoria Embankment
London EC4Y ODZ

An Hachette UK Company

1 3 5 7 9 10 8 6 4 2

A CIP catalogue record for this book is
available from the British Library.

ISBN (Hardback) 978 0 2976 0823 3
ISBN (Export Trade Paperback) 978 0 2976 0824 0
ISBN (eBook) 978 0 2976 0825 7

Typeset by Input Data Services Ltd, Somerset

Printed and bound in Great Britain by Clays Ltd, Elcograf S.p.A.

www.orionbooks.co.uk
www.weidenfeldandnicolson.co.uk

For Oli and Theo

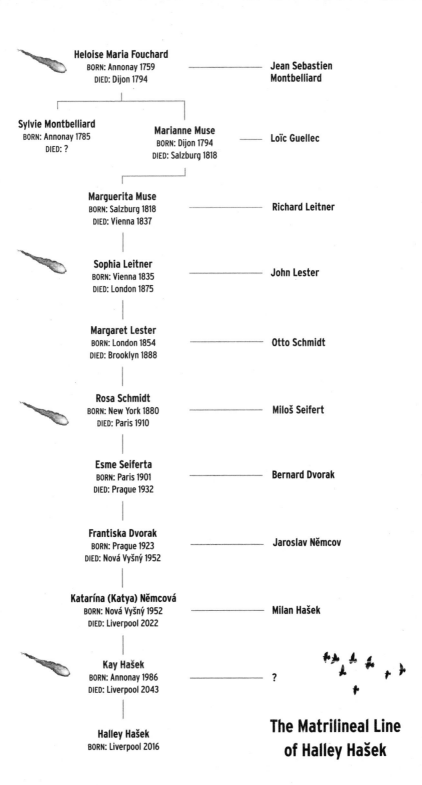

Heloise Maria Fouchard
BORN: Annonay 1759
DIED: Dijon 1794
— Jean Sebastien Montbelliard

Sylvie Montbelliard
BORN: Annonay 1785
DIED: ?

Marianne Muse
BORN: Dijon 1794
DIED: Salzburg 1818
— Loïc Guellec

Marguerita Muse
BORN: Salzburg 1818
DIED: Vienna 1837
— Richard Leitner

Sophia Leitner
BORN: Vienna 1835
DIED: London 1875
— John Lester

Margaret Lester
BORN: London 1854
DIED: Brooklyn 1888
— Otto Schmidt

Rosa Schmidt
BORN: New York 1880
DIED: Paris 1910
— Miloš Seifert

Esme Seiferta
BORN: Paris 1901
DIED: Prague 1932
— Bernard Dvorak

Frantiska Dvorak
BORN: Prague 1923
DIED: Nová Vyšný 1952
— Jaroslav Němcov

Katarína (Katya) Němcová
BORN: Nová Vyšný 1952
DIED: Liverpool 2022
— Milan Hašek

Kay Hašek
BORN: Annonay 1986
DIED: Liverpool 2043
— ?

Halley Hašek
BORN: Liverpool 2016

The Matrilineal Line of Halley Hašek

PROLOGUE

1759

A night unlit by candles. A night of stars.

The man is on a hillside when he first sees it, low on the horizon, the faintest smudge of light against the empty black of sky. There it is, for a second. And then gone. An object as much of his imagination, perhaps, as of the universe.

His heart quickens. He bends to his telescope, squinting in the darkness, pushing so close his eyelashes brush the glass.

Where is it? Has it vanished? He pulls his face away and studies the sky.

There! Between the Twins and the Great Bear. A fleck of white. He aligns the telescope and peers through it again. '*Sacrebleu!*'

He whispers to the woman, beckoning her, as if volume in his speech might frighten the object away. 'See there.' His voice betrays his excitement. 'The comet – exactly as it was foretold.'

She drops her face to the telescope.

'Do you see it?'

He can hear her soft breath in the winter air.

'It is Helios,' she says, 'the god of Athens and Rome.'

'It is.'

'When the ancients saw such a thing as this, they would say, "*Behold Helios circling the world in his chariot of fire.*"'

'Yet we know better,' he says. He blows into his hands to defeat the cold. 'We are modern people now. We understand the mathematics directing this celestial messenger on his endless journey.' A thought has come to him. 'Perhaps if our child lives a long life he may see it return.'

'Perhaps then, if our child is a son you should name him Helios.'

'It would be an unusual name,' he says. 'He would be a child of the stars.'

All of the universe had shrunk to a small, dark circle at the distant end of a telescope, and in that circle a feather of brightness like the softest pinch of down from a dove.

'A messenger of fire from a faraway world,' he tells her. 'What futures might he foreshadow?'

'Futures?' she asks.

'There will be many. Every time he visits he sees how our world has changed.'

The woman blinks. She stumbles slightly, as if startled. Her balance is lost and the telescope swings away. Her hand drops to her belly, she reaches out and takes her husband's hand, presses it to her middle.

'Something has awoken him – he's kicking,' the man says. His eyes shine at this.

She smiles at him. 'Or maybe . . . *she*.'

PART ONE

Katya's Gift

For my part I know nothing with any certainty
But the sight of the stars makes me dream.

Vincent Van Gogh

1

Katya, 1952

It rained like the storms of Genesis the night Katarína Němcová was born. The Tatrzańska River burst its banks, and a tide of mud and debris swept along the dirt lane to the Němcov farm like an avalanche. The midwife's bicycle stuck stubbornly in the mudslide at the top of the track leading down the river valley to the village of Nová Vyšný, and the midwife, unwilling to launch herself on foot into the deluge even for the birth of a baby, was forced to ring her bell furiously to announce her presence. The infant's father, Jaroslav, ran all the way up the track through the mud to collect her, and he carried her back to the homestead over his shoulder like a sack of corn, with no boots on his feet and nothing more than a strip of tarpaulin held over his head to shield them both from the rain.

Katarína's mother had been in labour for fourteen hours. She had been awake for thirty. She had very little energy left. Blood vessels had burst in her eyes.

'What kept you?' Jaroslav asked the midwife.

'Twins in Stará Lesna,' the midwife told him, 'a rainstorm in Poprad, and a stillborn in Vysoké Tatry.'

When baby Katarína (known from that day as Katya) was born, an hour or so later, a tiny grub of an infant, underweight, blue, slick with mucus and blood, her mother Frantiska died. Baby Katya took her first breath as her mother took her last, like the blow and suck of an accordion – out, and in. One soul departed, and the other gave voice to the trauma in a wail, a cry to the gods.

*

In the foothills of the Tatras the rain would often fall as snow in November. In the winter of 1952, the village would say, it fell as tears. Every household sent someone to the funeral of Frantiska Němcová and the weeping was as loud as had ever been heard in the graveyard of the small white church on the hillside where the young woman was laid to rest. Baby Katya's grandfather Krystof (Frantiska's father-in-law) slipped on ice on the morning of the burial, cracked his skull on the cobblestones, and came to the funeral with bloody bandages swathing his head. Six young women from the academy in Štrbské Pleso, friends of the dead woman, wearing white-and-black uniforms, looking cold against the snowscape of the High Tatras, sang a lament that started quietly like a whisper but grew into a crescendo, and the grey-coated crowd around the grave held hands with one another and murmured along with the chant. Many of the women wept. There were so many in the churchyard that latecomers had to stand behind the wall along the roadside, taking shelter under the oaks.

Snow began to fall as the bearers lowered the coffin into the ground.

Baby Katya's father, Jaroslav, like a frozen statue at the grave-side, wore the same black greatcoat his grandfather had worn when he came back from the war in 1918; even stripped of all insignia and colours, and faded from years of wear, it lent him a military bearing. The long-faced priest with heavy eyebrows who swung incense over the mouth of the grave was Jaroslav's brother Paul. He laid a hand on Jaroslav's shoulder when the words had all been spoken, as the crowd pressed forward to throw soil.

Thunk. Thunk. The earth was rocky in the Tatras. It fell onto the coffin like shrapnel.

'She only lived here for nine years, and yet they loved her in this village,' the priest told Jaroslav.

'They did.'

Wiping cold dirt from gloved hands, mourners lined up to pay their respects, blowing lungs of steam as they waited. 'We are so sorry,' they said, each one clutching young Jaroslav's hand, some of them offering a kiss to his cheek. 'She will be missed,' said others. 'God will bless her daughter,' many said.

A woman bent with age, her head buried beneath a black wool shawl, cupped Jaroslav's hand into her own. 'Does the infant have the gift?' she asked, her voice a watery cough.

'She is only five days old,' Katya's father said. His eyes were red from weeping and from the cold. 'How would we know? We will not know for a dozen years or more.'

'Do her eyes shine?'

'Yes, they shine.'

The old crone kissed Jaroslav's hands. 'Then she has the gift,' she said.

'Perhaps,' Jaroslav said. He returned the kiss.

'I pray to God for it.'

'You should not. It did not bring Frantiska joy.'

'But I will pray all the same. It will bring her back.' The woman released his hands.

The priest took the old woman's shoulder. 'Veruska Maria, you should get out of this cold. It will kill you.' He steered her away, her feet crunching on the newly fallen snow.

By the time the line of mourners had shrunk to a straggle, the snow was drifting down in flakes as big as roses. 'We should get inside,' the priest said. 'We should get warm.'

'She shouldn't be buried like this,' complained a farmer from Starý Smokovec. Beneath his coat he was wearing the blue one-piece boiler suit he wore to milk cows at the collective farm. 'All this . . .' he waved an intolerant arm, '. . . all this religion. This chanting. It is not the communist way.'

'Her family was from the West. It is what she would have wanted,' Jaroslav said. His eyebrows hovered low over his eyes.

'Well, it's too late to ask her now.'

9

A man wearing no hat, the tips of his ears glowing purple in the cold, whispered something into Jaroslav's ear, so quietly, Jaroslav had to lean close to hear it.

'Is it true she was in Lidice?' he asked.

The farmer nodded, a faint drop of his head. 'She was.' This reply, too, was a whisper.

'How did she survive?'

'By the grace of God,' Jaroslav said. 'The grace of God and a stubborn will.'

A Russian GAZ-M20 automobile, like an overweight cockroach, was parked at the top of the lane, as close as it would dare come without running into deep snow, and the driver, a jowly man with a Bolshevik *budenkova* cap, sat watching the funeral stony faced without once leaving his vehicle, or turning off the engine.

'Look at him,' Krystof said to the priest, nodding up towards the man in the motor car. 'NKVD.' He spat into the snow as he spoke the words. 'Russian secret police. Just in case Frantiska was a spy. Someone has been telling them stories. What do they imagine she can do, now she's dead?'

A tractor from the collective farm came to sweep away snow but it left a landscape of grey mud beneath its wheels. Mourners found themselves picking their way up the hill to the church hall along a perilous trackway of snow and mire. Jaroslav's sister Marta, wearing impractical high heels, carried baby Katya, swaddled in so many blankets only the infant's eyes showed through. In the warmth of the Tatry Kostol hall everyone wanted to see the child, but Marta was sparing. 'She is sleeping,' she told almost every person who tried to lean in for a closer view.

It was almost an hour before the baby opened her eyes and cried. The hubbub in the hall died away and the cry of the tiny infant rose above the heads of the mourners like the call of a wild bird.

'It's Frantiska,' said Verushka Maria, the old crone, her voice heavy with age, and many heads turned her way. 'It's little Frantiska reborn. I know that voice,' she said. 'I would recognise her anywhere.'

2

Katya, 1965

It had been a hard winter. There were snows still on the Tatras in April, and even on the foothills. The ground in the meadow field had frozen as hard as cement for four months and now, with the thaws of spring, it was as soft as marshland.

'I think my mother's dreams have started,' Katya told her father. 'I've been having them for a month.'

They were steaming the pipes of the milking machine with vapour from an iron kettle. The machine was still a novelty on the small farm. 'Keep the teat cups clean and the cows will be spared infection,' Jaroslav would tell his daughter. It was a lesson the collective had taught him when the device was installed. But the pipes would freeze in the cold barn, and the machinery would fail, and Jaroslav would wonder if the mechanical milker was a blessing or a curse.

'Are you sure these are your mother's dreams?' Katya's father asked, even though he knew the answer.

'Last night I dreamed of Paris.'

'How do you know it was Paris?'

'I just know. It was a gala with lords and ladies in masks and fine dresses. A carriage with twelve white horses. Two men flying high in the sky in a balloon of blue and gold.'

Jaroslav turned his face away. He was occupied coiling rubber piping onto a spool. When he spun an iron handle, the tubes would twist like reluctant snakes. 'Well, those *are* your mother's dreams,' he said, after a while. He put down his spool and took his daughter's hand. His eyes looked sorrowful. 'So I expect you're right. Your mother warned me, long before you were born. She told me if we had a daughter, the dreams would start sooner or later. I had hoped perhaps they wouldn't. They won't always be so bright.'

'I know they're mother's dreams because I remember them,' Katya said. She unwound a strand of hair from her forehead and began to coil it around her finger, first one way, and then the other. 'I know what real dreams are, but these aren't the same. With real dreams I've forgotten them before I climb out of bed. What did I dream about? By breakfast I can never tell. But not these: these are dreams I can't forget. They are part of me. They stay with me. The gala with the fine ladies and the golden balloon might as well have happened to me yesterday. It's as if it was part of my own past.'

'I know,' Jaroslav said softly.

'They're sharp, these memories,' Katya said. 'So sharp that I'd recognise the faces of the people if I saw them in the street. I know their names. I know their voices. The men wore wigs with curls. Monsieur Philippe had a beard like a spear and—'

'Can you speak the language?' Jaroslav asked.

'The language?'

'The language in your dream? *Tu parles français?*'

The girl hesitated. 'I don't know.' She looked puzzled. 'I must have understood the language or else . . . how would I have known what was going on?'

'It will come to you,' Jaroslav said. 'I don't claim to understand it. Your mother spoke five languages and not one of them did she learn in school. You must be strong, little Katya. Your mother would dream up memories that only her mother could have had. And now you can do the same. No one else has this gift, Katya. Just you.'

She was thirteen, Katya, as wiry and slender as a wild deer, a farm girl from her boots to her breeches. She could rise early and slip unheard into the yard, and drive cows into the parlour before her father even appeared at the door with the ashes of his first cigarette. 'She doesn't look a lady,' Krystof would say wryly of his granddaughter, and he didn't mean it unkindly.

13

She had the look of a girl raised by menfolk, badly combed, unpampered, a feral creature, perhaps, not tall, not girlish, not over-bathed or scented, born perhaps of wild things. She had, at thirteen, shoulders that could carry a feed sack, but little in the way of curves. Not a lady then. Yet the straw-coloured curls that framed her face seemed delicate, and her features were small, and when she soaked away the farmyard stains and pulled on one of her mother's vests, or the red linen pinafore her aunt Marta had made for her, she could turn the head of any man in the valley. 'She has eyes as sharp as a kite,' her father would say of her, and this was true. She had an inquisitive expression, and a way of raising her eyebrows in disbelief if anyone tried to tell a falsehood; and she had a fire at her core that could make her very company feel dangerous, precarious, as if something within her was spoiling for a fight. Perhaps this was a teenage thing. 'Take a deep breath,' Jaroslav would tell her, when some injustice or other had raised her hackles. 'It won't help anyone if your face turns our milk to butter.'

'One day I'll take you to Paris,' Katya told her father, confidently. Her face displayed the insouciance of her age. 'I don't care about the party rules, or what the collective says, I shall take you to Paris, and show you the place in my dream where I saw the balloon.' Her face was set in youthful determination.

Jaroslav offered a rueful smile. 'Maybe one day.'

Katya looked down. 'I know her name,' she said. 'I know the name of the woman in my dream.'

'You do?'

'Her name was Heloise.'

'So it was,' Jaroslav said. 'Your mama spoke of her often.' He squeezed Katya's hand. 'They are ghosts, Katya. Ghosts. They are dead and gone. Every day when your mother rose she would say to herself, *These things are past*. You should say it too.'

'These things are past,' echoed Katya. She lifted away her father's arm and swung a fresh bucket onto the iron range. 'These things are past.'

'It is wise not to talk about them,' Jaroslav said. 'Except to me.'

'Would people think me mad?' Katya asked.

'Perhaps.'

According to the files and ledgers of the committee for agriculture of the province of Prešovský-kraj, the Němcov farm should have been a *jednotné roľnícke družstvo*, an agricultural cooperative, owned by the people and run for the people, and managed perhaps by a graduate in dairy husbandry from a city college, answerable to the voice of the people and the rules of the party. But with just thirty-one cows, and only twenty-six in milk, they didn't need a great deal of help from the people to manage it, and somehow the farm had remained a family affair, and no sharp young graduate had ever shown up to take over. The farm had been Krystof's until the day a runaway bullock stamped on his left foot and broke half a dozen bones; Jaroslav had stepped in to run things, and somehow no committee had ever approved this family arrangement nor thought to rescind it. Before Krystof it had been Old Man Gregor Němcov, Krystof's grandfather who had lived at the farm when there were no committees, and no collectives, and a farmer could own his land and sell his own produce, and do what he liked with his fields; and before Old Man Gregor, another Němcov, his full name now forgotten, and before him another, and surely another. There had been Němcovs raising cows in this valley for generations. The soil was in their blood.

Two boys from the nearby city of Poprad came on bicycles every day for the morning milking. They were barely older than Katya. Jordy was lanky and sharp, with a face like a rat and teeth that grew in awkward directions. 'Good teeth to bite a man with,' Jaroslav would say of Jordy. His father was an official in the Štátna bezpečnosť, the state security agency. Everyone would be careful on the farm to measure what they said in Jordy's earshot. He was a reliable worker, and he seemed honest enough, but you could never be too cautious. Who knew what he might report back to his father?

The second boy, Marat, was older but somehow still a baby. He had never taken to schoolwork, had never learned letters or numbers, and he mumbled his words so softly that few, apart from Katya, could decipher anything he said. It didn't seem to matter. Words are not an essential currency in a milking parlour. Both boys were good with the cows, and that, Jaroslav would say, was all he needed. 'The cows know,' he would say, and he would tell Katya, 'We're lucky to have any help at all. All the village boys go to the cities these days. No one wants to milk cows anymore.'

Katya's grandfather, Krystof, would appear after breakfast with a cigarette between his lips and a shovel in his hands, ready to barrow muck out of the byre and spread new straw. On days when Katya was at school, Jaroslav's sister Marta would walk from her job at the telephone exchange to help with the afternoon milking. Katya would help her father and the Poprad boys with the dawn milking, and afterwards she would dress for school while Jaroslav harnessed up the horse, and the boys lifted the filled milk churns onto the dray cart. It was a routine born of practice and economy of effort. In summer months they were smiles and laughter, but in the winter they would muffle up to save precious body heat, and they would pull on heavy leather gloves, and toil in silence as the east winds leaked into the byre. Jaroslav, now forty, stocky with a wide moustache and a sorrowful expression on his face, would wear a one-piece boiler suit, military winter fatigues, and a Russian *ushanka* hat with earflaps that tied beneath his chin. 'These winds come all the way from Siberia,' he would say. He would pull his hat low over his eyes and his cold nose would glow like a beacon.

At eight o'clock in the morning, with every cow milked and the churns all filled, they would stop whatever they were doing to count the chimes from the town hall clock at Nová Vyšný and listen to the echoes of the bells down the river valley, and this would be the sign for Jaroslav to drive the milk cart to the dairy, stopping off just once at the corner of Vodárenská and Fraňa Kráľa so Katya could walk the last ten minutes to school.

'One day,' Jaroslav told his daughter as their old horse pulled them along the six-kilometre trail into town, 'you will dream bad things.'

Katya was silent. She was watching a rat scuttling down a ditch, its sinuous black tail drawing circles in the air.

'Katya?'

The rat disappeared into a hole.

'I know, Father.'

In April the snows of the Tatras were melting. The rivers were deep with melt waters. Katya swung off the dray cart at Vodárenská and blew her father a kiss, stepping over the rebellious stream of cold mountain water that ran alongside the road.

'One day,' Jaroslav told her, leaning from the dray, 'memories will come back to you like a flood. This is what happened to your mother. I know. She would want me to warn you. It won't be an easy time.'

'These things are past,' Katya said.

'They are, they are, my little Káťa. There are good things in your past, and there are bad things. There are good people and bad people. There are dreams that will wake you up with a smile, and dreams that will leave you screaming.'

'You have often warned me of these things, Papa.'

'I know. But it still won't make it easier when the time comes. One day, too, you will learn where Heloise's gold is.' He grinned and blew a kiss.

'Heloise had gold?'

'So your mama told me. Just be sure to tell no one.'

'I won't.'

In the afternoon, when there was no real work to be done, and if the skies were clear, Jaroslav would sit outside on the farm bench with Krystof, his father, both of them looking up towards the mountains as if in search of inspiration from the heavens, and they would smoke together, dark and oily tobacco rolled into papyrosas, until, on a still day, the smoke would hang over them like a cloud. Katya's little terrier dog, Zora, would squeeze onto the bench beside them.

'You should take a new wife,' Krystof would tell the younger man, from time to time.

'Why should I? You never did.'

'Times were different.'

'Times are never different.'

On this day, Jaroslav told his father about Katya's dreams.

'Everything comes around,' the old man said. 'We think it'll be summer forever, but winter is always waiting.'

'What if she wants to leave?' Jaroslav said. He was rolling tobacco between his fingers. 'She is already talking about Paris. She will want to go there.'

'She surely will. But we are Slovaks.' Krystof shrugged. 'This is the East. This is not the West. Where can we go? The gates to the rest of the world are closed.'

'It worries me that she won't be happy here. Not for much longer. Why should she be? She will see too much of the world in her mother's memories. And who knows? She may want to go looking for her gold. Who could blame her? I would want to go too,' Jaroslav said. He looked up to the mountains where the peaks were hidden in cloud. 'I have always wanted to go. Not because of the gold.'

'I know,' Krystof said.

'I have lived without gold for forty years, I can live without it for forty more. But all the same. It would be good to see more of the world than this valley. Good to be able to stand up and speak my mind. Frantsya and I would make all kinds of plans, but nothing would ever come of them.' He rolled the papyrosa between his fingers and his thumb and tamped down the tobacco. He let his voice grow quieter. 'Frantsya wanted to

18

show me America. She wanted me to see New York. She told me I would have been a rich man in New York. I would drive a Cadillac. We would take holidays in California.'

'We all have dreams,' Krystof said. 'Even Comrade Stalin couldn't stop people dreaming. Heaven knows, he tried.'

Jaroslav glanced from side to side. 'They say if you wear black and carry weights to float just below the surface of the Danube River at the Devín Gate, after dark, with a piece of rubber hose held tight between your teeth, you can swim from Bratislava into Austria. The border goes right down the centre of the river.'

'You'd get shot trying,' the old man said. 'Plenty of people do. The Pohraniční Stráž watch the river like hawks. They shoot anything that moves.' He scanned the farmyard to be sure Jordy was nowhere within earshot. 'They're the most ruthless border guards anywhere outside Berlin. They have nets in the river to ensnare you. And spotlights. And dogs.'

'Well then,' Jaroslav said, lighting his cigarette and blowing smoke out between his teeth, 'we could try a different route.'

'We?'

'I would have to go with her. She's only a child. We could cross the Danube further east in Hungary where there are no fences, and we could find somewhere to run over the border into Austria. They say the Hungarian border is less well patrolled.'

'It may be less patrolled,' Jaroslav's father snorted, 'but they have an electric fence 200 kilometres long. And a minefield. No one gets over it. You need to be realistic, Jarek. Katya will not be leaving Czechoslovakia soon, or any time in our lifetime. And maybe not even in her lifetime. Not this one anyway.'

'I have heard there are secret tunnels in Berlin.'

'So secret you'll never find them. And besides, how do you plan to take Katya to Berlin? On the dray cart?'

'How about her dreams?' Jaroslav asked. He held his cigarette in the centre of his lips and drew the black smoke into his lungs. 'How will we manage without her mother here to guide her?'

'You'll manage. You're a good father. And she's tough, your girl. Probably tougher than her mother, and her mother was tough, God rest her soul. She can bear them. Let the dog sleep on her bed.'

'Will it help?'

'I hope so.'

One night in May, Katya woke screaming. 'There was a man in my bed,' she told her father.

Jaroslav knelt by his daughter's side to comfort her. 'What was his name?'

'Miloš Seifert,' she said. 'He had a beard. And he stank of vodka.'

'Relax,' Jaroslav said, and he stroked her hair with the back of his hand. 'It was one of your mother's dreams. He is not the man I warned you about. This one was your great-grandfather, married to Rosa. He was a drinker, that much I know. I suspect he smelled of whiskey. But your mother would tell me he was harmless.'

'Then who is the man I should be frightened of?' Katya was shaking. She sat with her pale legs over the side of the mattress.

'You will meet many men in your mother's dreams who weren't altogether harmless,' Jaroslav said. 'Some women too. None of them can harm you now. They are gone. They are ghosts. And very few will harm you even in the dreams. Some will. One in particular. But you will harm him back. The past is past, my Katerina. All past.'

In June, Zora the terrier had eight puppies. All of them survived. She whelped in the log shed, and Katya insisted they move the whole litter into the house. There were rats in the shed and rumours of a lynx in the valley. 'A lynx could eat a puppy,' Katya told her father.

'There are lynx in the mountains, I have seen them often enough,' Krystof said. 'But they don't often come down into

20

the valley. And even if they did, they are wary of people.'

'But not puppies,' Katya said.

The pups and their mother moved into Katya's bedroom.

In June six of the cows had calves. All were healthy; five were heifers, and only one a bullock. They had never had such a good calving. 'Things are looking up for us,' Jaroslav said.

'You will be a rich man yet,' said Krystof.

In July a delegation from the central committee for agriculture paid a visit to the farm. Five men and two women with clipboards and stern faces stalked from barn to barn, taking notes. 'They can take this farm away from us,' Krystof warned his son darkly, as one of the women screwed up her face at the smells from the slurry pit.

'Why would they take it away? Our family has been in this valley longer than anyone can remember. No one else could farm it as efficiently as we do.'

'They have never liked us,' Krystof said. 'They can take away our farm and send us west to dig coal.'

In August Jaroslav stayed out late one Sunday night in the town of Poprad drinking beers with farmers from the collectives, and on Monday morning, when Katya came downstairs for the early milking, a young woman with freckled cheeks, wearing a cotton cap, and with her hair tucked behind her ears, was in the kitchen boiling water in the kettle. 'I'm Otillie,' she said to Katya, blushing very slightly. 'I'm your father's friend.'

'I'm glad to meet you,' Katya said, pulling on her boots.

'I stayed overnight because it was too far to walk home last night,' Otillie said, turning her face away so her blushes could not be seen. 'And it looked like rain.'

'It's OK,' Katya said, tugging hard on her laces. 'I know what men and women do in the bedroom. It is not a mystery for me. I hope you made my father happy.'

'I think I did.'

'Good.'

3
Katya, 1968

'Dear God, we shall be free. We shall all be free.' The woman in the hallway of the homestead was out of breath, untying the laces of her boots. It was still dark outside. 'We shall all be free!' she shouted into the kitchen. Free!'

'Free of what?' Katya came downstairs to investigate the commotion. 'Good morning, Hana Anya. This is early for you.'

'Is my daughter here?'

'She's with Father. It isn't five o'clock.'

'Call her down.' The middle-aged woman who had burst through their door was glowing like an ember.

'Otillie!' Katya called up the stairs, 'your mother is here,' and then to the new arrival, 'You're lucky. We haven't started milking yet. May I make you tea? A *trdelnik* pastry?'

'Pastry, yes. And coffee. With just a splash of schnapps.'

'What's this about?' Katya steered the visitor onto a kitchen stool, filled a kettle and plonked it onto the iron range.

'Mr Dubček has been elected,' Otillie's mother said. 'Just as we all hoped. First Secretary of the Party.'

'A wonderful thing!' Katya cried.

'Indeed! It means change. It means our borders will open. Mr Dubček has promised to open them. He is going to stand up against Moscow and all their regulations. It couldn't be better.'

'We shall be able to travel,' Katya said, catching her breath as she spoke.

'I shall go to London,' said Hana Anya. 'I have always wanted to see London. And New York. I shall visit my half-sister in West Germany and see my nephews.'

Jaroslav came downstairs in his boiler suit. Katya and Hana

22

Anya had linked arms in a dance around the room. 'Good news,' Jaroslav said, once all had been explained. 'But let's not get too excited. Mr Dubček will have a great deal to do. Don't expect him to worry too much about farmers in the Tatras.'

'He will open our borders,' Hana Anya said, waving an arm in the air as if she were brandishing a flag.

Jordy, the dairyman with the crooked teeth and with the father in the secret service, was crossing the yard with two buckets of milk. Jaroslav glanced anxiously through the window in his direction. 'And our country will be flooded with spies from the West,' he said, loud enough for Jordy to hear. 'Don't misunderstand me, Hana. I want to travel as much as any man. More than most. But I'm a good communist.'

Krystof shuffled into the kitchen in his nightgown and sat heavily at the long table. 'We're all good communists in this household,' he said as if this was something he had said a thousand times before. He started to roll up a cigarette, the first of the day.

'My dreams come every night,' Katya told her father some days later as they slapped the last cow on the rump and sent her out to pasture. 'I start to dream almost from the moment my eyes shut, and when I wake I've lived a dozen years and met a hundred people; I've married and given birth; I've died; I've crossed an ocean. I wake, and it's always a shock.'

'I imagine it must be.'

'Last night I was in New York,' she said. 'I was a schoolgirl. There was a parade in the square. You wouldn't believe it, Father. So many people. Men in hats. Horses. There were huge, tall buildings.'

'Her name was Rosa, the girl you dreamed about in New York. Rosa Schmidt. She was fifteen when she made that memory,' Jaroslav said. 'She was the same age you are now. Your mother told me many of her stories. It was 1895, a Thanksgiving Day parade on Broadway.'

'There were elephants,' Katya said. 'They walked right past me, and I reached out a hand, and one of them touched me with his trunk.'

'And an Irish boy gave you a bottle of liquor and you drank it together under the Brooklyn Bridge.'

Katya laughed. 'I haven't had that dream yet. Perhaps I should look forward to it.'

'Maybe you should.' Jaroslav let a short silence grow between them, then he turned to look at her. 'Have you met Églefin yet? Roderique Églefin?'

'I have.' Katya's expression grew dark. She linked arms with her father, and together they stood and watched the heavy cattle lumbering into the meadow.

'I'll get the boys to clean the machine today,' the farmer said. He swung the door of the byre and slid the iron bolt. 'You get ready.'

'Thank you, Father.'

'Have you seen your gold? Heloise's gold?'

'Yes.' Her answer was quick.

'You come from a very rich family, Katarína Němcová.'

'So I'm beginning to understand,' Katya said.

'We talked about going to find it. Your mother and I. Of being rich,' Jaroslav said. He started uncoiling the pipes of the milking machine, ready for steaming.

'And would you still like it? Heloise's gold?'

'Ahh . . .' Jaroslav gave Katya an apologetic look. 'Would I like it? Would I like to be rich? Once, perhaps. Once I might have liked it.' He hung the rubber pipes on a nail. 'It isn't a question to ask of a farmer, little Katya. You've seen riches. You know what it's like.' He took his daughter's arm and led her across the yard, glancing from side to side in case anyone might be in earshot. 'Yet your mother would say riches aren't made of gold, they're made of flesh and blood. When you're a poor farmer with only one warm coat there is much to be said for being rich. But me? I dream of other things. I dream of faraway

24

places. I dream of a place where a man might hold his head up and walk freely, and speak his mind, where no one will tell him what he has to think, or where he has to work, or what he has to say. I dream of waking without fear – fear they will take my farm, fear they will send me to the mines. So no. I don't want Heloise's gold, little Katya. Besides, you can't grow rich in Poprad. The party would take it from you and leave you poor again. So if we want riches we have to leave. And do we really want to leave this valley?' He swung the field gate closed and together they stood, their elbows on the gate, looking out over the river meadows and the foothills to the Tatras, watching as the cows bent their heads to the tall grass. 'Can we really find riches better than this? That's what your mother would have said.'

'I know, Father,' Katya said.

'I spoke to your grandfather about it many times. He swears we would all be killed if we tried to leave Czechoslovakia.'

Katya smiled. She put her hand on her father's arm. 'Maybe if Mr Dubček opens the borders . . .'

'Maybe.'

The summer of 1968 was one of the hottest in many long memories. It was in the summer of 1968 that Katya found a boyfriend and told him about her gift. It was also the summer of the shooting on the Prešov-to-Poprad road.

It was the summer when everything started, and the summer when so much ended.

An eventful summer.

The sun rose almost every morning out of a clear blue sky and the dark-green pastures and blue-black forests that rolled all the way north from the foothills around the industrial town of Poprad, to the high wall of the Tatras mountains, were lit with a glow that turned golden, as May became June, and as June became July, and the barley fields began to ripen, and then grow dry. One of the Poprad boys, Marat, out on his bicycle, saw the lynx stalking along the lane looking in the ditches for rats. He pedalled furiously to the farm with the news, but when everyone followed him back, the lynx had gone.

The other Poprad boy, Jordy, found a girlfriend, with teeth almost as crooked as his own, in Starý Smokovec, and he started humming rock and roll tunes from America, and grew his hair in a quiff like Elvis Presley.

Katya started dating a boy from the academy at Štrbské Pleso early in July. He was seventeen. 'He is way too old for you,' Jaroslav would grumble. 'And you shouldn't be thinking about boys. You're only fifteen.'

But Katya liked his company. His name was Milan Hašek and, when he wasn't at the academy, he worked in the paper mill on the Tatrzańska River, just a few kilometres downstream from the Němcov farm. He shared a motor scooter with his brother, a Russian Vyatka VP-150 in shiny aquamarine blue, identical (so everyone would tell you) to an Italian Vespa. On the days when it was his turn to ride it – Mondays, Wednesdays, and Saturday mornings – Katya would straddle behind him, letting his hair fly into her face, holding so tight to his shirt that her knuckles turned white. Milan wasn't an especially good-looking boy: he was slight of build, and pale of complexion, and his hair had a tendency to curl; he wore wire spectacles and he tied these around his head with twine to prevent them flying off when he was riding the scooter. But he was earnest, and Katya liked that. 'I care nothing for looks,' she would tell her father. 'I only care about his heart.' Milan read books. He talked politics. He was a party member of the youth league. 'Are you a good communist?' Katya would ask him. 'Of course I am,' he would say. 'Are you?'

'I'm a reformist,' she would reply, and a hint of the fire would appear in her eyes. 'That's the best communist in my book.'

'Maybe it is.'

They dated but in the summer of 1968 they rarely did more than hold hands. Katya would allow Milan, sometimes, to kiss her on the cheek, and once or twice, at the end of an evening, to kiss her softly on the lips goodnight. She was in no hurry to go further, and neither, it seemed, was he. His hands didn't roam. It was a relationship, it seemed to them both, growing out of friendship and not out of lust.

'Have you ever heard the Beatles?' he asked her one day.

'The girls at school talk of them,' she said.

'I have a record,' he told her. 'Do you have a machine?'

Katya shook her head.

'Then you must come with me to my brother's apartment on Záhradnícka. We can listen to it there.'

Milan's brother's apartment was in central Poprad, up seven flights of stairs in the residences of the hospital where he worked as an X-ray technician. It was a single room with a single bed. His gramophone player was a Hungarian wind-up phonograph in an olivewood box case, and he treated this like the treasured possession it was, wiping it with a soft duster into all the corners before he would allow it to play. He held his long technician's fingers to his lips. 'We have to play this quietly,' he whispered. 'These walls are made of paper.'

They huddled over the instrument. Milan gingerly lowered the record onto the turntable and lifted the heavy needle into place. His brother nervously managed the volume control.

The sound of the music was deliciously subversive. The needle went *scratch, scratch, scratch*. A crash of guitars. A kind of smouldering, energetic harmony. Voices in an oddly familiar language. A *thump thump* of drums.

She loves you, yeah yeah yeah . . .

Milan's brother dropped the volume. 'This is not a good tune to play too loud,' he explained. 'They can put you in prison for playing this song.'

It was music that could find its way into your bloodstream and swim among the veins. Katya could feel the electricity in her limbs. It was music that made you hold your breath. It was an infection that entered the body like a parasite through the ears and overwhelmed the brain. 'She loves you,' she whispered to Milan in English, her eyes half closed with the pleasure of it, but he too was in the trance the music created, his head swaying like a willow in a high wind.

Milan slid his hands around her waist and they let their foreheads touch, and they were glowing with the heat from the music. They played both sides, and the songs were curiously foreign but deliciously magnetic and Katya could feel the music in her bones.

'It's English,' Milan explained to Katya. 'English words.'

'I know,' Katya said, and surprisingly she did. 'It means *she*,' and she pointed to herself, '*loves*,' and she pointed to her heart, '*you*,' and she pointed to Milan.

Afterwards, when they had played the record a dozen times, they hummed the tunes together on Štefánikova Street by the river, walking back to the bus stop, and Katya tried to teach Milan the words. '*Yuh yuh yuh*,' he sang. '*Yuh yuh yuh.*'

'How did you understand the English words?' he asked her. He linked his hand with hers.

'There's a lot about me you don't know.'

'Tell me.'

'My father doesn't like me to talk about it.'

'Your father isn't here.'

She smiled at this. 'It isn't a secret in Nová Vyšný,' she said. 'But I don't discuss it much. Sometimes the old women of the village will ask me. They call it my mother's gift.'

'Tell me.'

'I don't think it's a gift. I call it my mother's ghosts.' She took a breath. The sun was high in a perfect sky, not a sign of a cloud. 'There is something odd about my family line,' she said, looking at his face. 'I think it's something that happens to us in the womb. Some sort of curious alchemy or magic. Who knows? Something that happened to me. A strange thing.'

'In the womb? What is it?' He was curious now. They walked together onto the bridge. This was Poprad, a featureless town, a poor community of square, concrete apartment blocks and wide, quiet roads, but the riverbank had some charm, especially in the summer. They stood and looked down the avenue of trees along the water's edge. There were cyclists gliding past with bags on their backs. There was a woman walking a child. They lingered for a while to soak up the view.

Katya hummed the tune. '*She loves you . . .*' She laughed at his reaction. 'I have my mother's memories,' she said, at last. She turned to look away from him. 'Don't laugh. They come to me in dreams.'

'You have your mother's memories?' He sounded uncertain.

'And my mother had *her* mother's memories, so I have those as well. And her grandmother's memories, and back, and back, and back. I have all my mother's lives.' They stopped to lean on the rail over the narrow river. Katya stooped to pick up a pebble and she dropped it into the dark water. *Make a wish*, one of her more distant fathers would say. *Drop a stone in the water and make a wish.*

'Back . . . forever?' Milan asked. He was holding his expression well.

'No, not forever,' Katya said. She was looking far away. 'There was a first . . .'

He raised his eyebrows.

'A woman called Heloise Maria Montbelliard, one of the smartest women of her time.'

'I see.' Milan allowed his forehead to frown very slightly. He tried her name, 'Heloise Maria . . .'

'Montbelliard.'

'Not a Slovak name,' he said.

'No.'

'And . . . she was the first?'

'Yes.'

He looked at her, almost uncertain what to ask. 'And you actually know her name?'

'This is silly. Of course I know her name,' Katya said, a little crossly. 'I have her memories.' She slid an arm around Milan's waist. 'I know this must seem odd to you. It seems pretty odd to me too, and I live with it all the time. But I remember Heloise's life. Not every detail, but it's like a childhood memory, there are bits here, and bits there, and there are bits missing. It's like a jigsaw puzzle where you only have a few dozen pieces and a hundred are lost, but it doesn't matter, you can still understand the picture. You have the important pieces. That's what it's like. Some memories are so sharp, they might have happened to me yesterday. Others are dim, confused. Others ought to be there, but when I go to look for them they're gone. Just like ordinary memories, I suppose. I remember days, and people, and conversations. I remember places. And faces. And meals. I remember gardens, and trees, and my favourite horses. I remember dogs. I remember teachers. I remember friends and enemies. I remember bedrooms, and cold winters, and hot summers. I remember boyfriends, and lovers, husbands, and children. I remember Heloise's past as if . . . well, maybe as if it were my own. And perhaps it is.'

Milan looked unsteady. 'I'm not sure what to say,' he said.

'In the old days,' Katya said, 'they would have burned me as a witch.'

They walked from the bridge to the bus stop on Štefánikova and Milan touched Katya's hand as she boarded the bus. 'To-morrow?' he said. He gave her the soft kiss she allowed him.

'Don't be too freaked out,' she said. 'Or I'll wish I had never told you.'

'Tomorrow,' he said, and he smiled to let her know he was all right.

'She loves you,' she said.

'Yeah yeah yeah.'

How blissful to sleep. On winter mornings, when the dying embers of the kitchen fire had given up trying to keep the house warm, when trails of frost grew up the windows like the maps of frozen rivers, Katya would lie buried beneath woollen blankets and her mother's Barguzin fur wrap, balanced in that sublime world between sleep and wakefulness. Half an hour, perhaps, until Jaroslav's old alarm would ring and summon them all to milking. Half an hour of undiscovered pleasure. She could open and shut her dreams now, like books from the shelf. She could close her eyes and choose, could pick a place to go, a time, a date, a ghost to take her there.

She had eight lifetimes to explore. Or so it seemed. If she closed her eyes she could journey back to any one of them. Relax. Breathe. And the memories would come.

She could see the drawing room of a fine French chateau, could smell the tallow candles and hear the snorting of teams of horses, the click-click of servants' feet on the tiles, and the laughter of guests. A harpsichord would chime. There would be dancing. Wine would come in flagons. The sky was cornflower blue. There were sunflowers growing around the lawns. A great statue of a sea god poured water from his fingertips into a fountain. She could see all this. She could imagine descending the stairs, and there, instead of the cold stone floor, and the bare larder, and the hungry cattle of the Němcov farm, would be maids bearing silver trays with oysters and raspberries and soft cheeses and cold meats. The house would smell of warm baked bread.

She could, if she chose, become Sophia Lester, blonde and formidable, an English lady with a town house in St Mary-le-Bow, and a country house in Stafford, and a lady's maid from Edinburgh, and a husband in the royal court. Ha ha ha – she could hear English laughter, and smell the stink of London drains, and feel the itch of London fleas, and taste the curdled milk in the pudding rice. She could feel the scurrying tap-tap of mice on her bedclothes. She could look from her window and see rainclouds clearing and sunshine peeking through.

She could be Margaret Schmidt, four storeys up in two small rooms of a Brooklyn brownstone with a view over the East

River to New York City. Out on Bedloe's Island in the bay they were building the pedestal for a giant statue (the biggest in the world, they boasted), and Margaret's husband Otto ran a team of construction workers there, and every one of them spoke a different language. 'It's *der Turmbau zu Babel*,' he would tell her, the Tower of Babel. 'We should go back to France and look for my family's gold,' Margaret would urge him, but Otto, like many of the husbands in her memory, was dubious about her gift. 'Tell me where to find it,' he would say, and he would look at her with an expression that spoke of disbelief, 'and I will send some of my men.'

'But I don't know where to send them,' she, Margaret, would protest, not altogether truthfully. 'I will recognise it when I see it. That's all I can say.'

She was Katya Němcova, a farm girl from the Slovak mountains, a dairymaid with hands already hard from toil, with a face becoming weathered from sun and from wind; and yet she could, if she closed her eyes, become Rosa Schmidt, Margaret Schmidt's daughter, who danced the ballet, and travelled from New York to Paris in search of a secret fortune, and married the man she met during a storm on the Atlantic, Miloš Seifert, an importer of liquors; Miloš plied her with rye whiskey, and held her close as their boat fought the storm. Or another day she might be Esme Seifert, Rosa's daughter, a Parisienne belle, who wore broad-brimmed hats and skirts to the ankle. Esme married a Viennese doctor, Bernard Dvorak, a specialist in dream psychology, a man who promised to cure her of the false memories that woke her every night. Esme was Frantiska's mother. She died in 1932 when Frantiska was nine. Her dreams had never been cured.

Katya's inner world was a riot of memories. 'Where are you today?' Papa would sometimes ask, when Katya's eyes were closed, when her concentration slipped, when she seemed unnaturally focused on the far horizon. 'New York today? Dijon? Vienna?' Sometimes it could be all three. Sometimes, as she would tell her father, the memories weren't her own. They belonged to a third person. They played in her head like the pirouetting of dancers in a theatre. But at other times they were *her* eyes. Katya's eyes. A man in her bedroom bleeding like a stuck pig when she was Marianne Muse and the year was 1813. This memory never felt like Marianne's memory. It was her own. It was Katya's. It was a brutal, bloody, vengeful memory, sharp and clear.

She had given birth. Sylvie was her first in 1784 when she was twenty-five, and she, then Heloise Montbelliard, lady of the Chateau, bled so badly that she fell into a stupor and the priest was sent for to chant the last rites, and he put his hand on her face, and his hand stank of incense so strong, it tore her from her slumber. She gave birth in 1814, this time as Marianne Muse, to Marguerita, a bastard child, and this time there was no priest to bring her round from the pain and the weakness, only the cold winter wind of a Salzburg brothel and the crying of a hungry infant.

Birthing. Nine children she had carried. Every one a girl. Every memory ended with a birth. That was the way it worked. A mother's memory ended, and before too long, a child's memory would begin. One child had been cut from her when her life was gone. It was a missing memory. Another child, she knew, was Katya Němcova, was herself. How strange. How curious that she could remember the pain of her own birth, the desperate midwife, the wind at the door, the hot hand of her anxious husband, and then she could remember no more.

How strange.

'Your dreams are phantoms created by the unconscious mind,' her husband Bernard Dvorak used to tell her when she was Esme. 'They are apparitions. Inventions. There is no mechanism, no ether, no biological fluid, no conduit to carry memories from a mother to a child.'

And yet there was.

Once, in 1922, she, as Esme, just twenty-one years old,

travelled with Bernard on a sea voyage to Southampton and onwards by train to London, and there she showed him places she knew, locations she had visited as Sophia Lester three generations earlier, and later as Margaret, Sophia's daughter. 'Around this corner will be steps that go down to the river,' she told him, 'and a statue of a king mounted on a horse. And up that alley is an inn called The Lion, and two of the windows are false.' Yet many of her recollections had been overwritten by the passage of time. The pub wasn't there. The king had gone. And even when her memories proved accurate, Bernard was unmoved and unconvinced. 'You read this all in books,' he told her. 'You have seen the *Illustrated London News*.'

Memories. How fragile they sometimes seemed. Most came unbidden in her sleep, but not all of them. Some came suddenly in daylight, like unwelcome interlopers at a party, a flash, an image, a scene, intruding on her day. Her hand would fly to her mouth. What had she just remembered? Running down a long, dark tunnel. The *Te Deum*. The funeral of the Queen's consort when she was just six; gold coins in the hems of her skirts; Lidice. She had seen, as Esme, as a seventeen-year-old, the bodies of Austrian soldiers from the Kaiserschlacht offensive of 1918, carried back to Vienna on open wagons, heaped like soiled laundry, stinking, still dripping blood into the street. She had seen days of sunshine, and days of rain. There were wedding days she could revisit. Rosa's wedding to Miloš in Paris on a day in 1900 when the cherry blossoms were in bloom and the World Fair was in the city and everyone wore fine clothes; and along with all the wedding guests they saw the great telescope, and watched a cinéorama projection of *Salomé*, and travelled in a lift to the first level of the Eiffel Tower and walked to the Palais de l'Électrique when night fell to see the thousand multicoloured lights. Or the little, intimate wedding in the Tatry Katolícky Kostol when Frantiska married Jaroslav, when the sun shone and the guests sang old Slovak songs and drank *slivovica* into the early hours of the morning. Or the grand wedding of Heloise and Jean Sebastien with four hundred guests in wigs and lace, and Jacques-Étienne Montgolfier releasing one hundred paper balloons each with a sputtering, mutton-fat candle, when all the lords and ladies stood outside on the lawns and watched the lanterns rising, precious orbs of light, each a tiny life seeking out a destiny in the night sky before they flickered their last and were gone.

Sometimes, for a day or two at a time, Katya could keep the memories at bay. They were there, like books in a library, flaunting their seductive spines but never opened, their secrets hidden. But on other days she would retreat into the worlds she had left behind, a visitor from a curious future, looking strangely on this antique world of horses, and brave ideas, and revolutions, and killings. On these days she would try to be alone with the memories. She would linger in the milking parlour when all the cows were back at pasture, or she would find her way to a quiet place, a hillside, a forest glade, a hidden corner of the meadow, where she could become Heloise again, just for an hour.

They saw the lynx the next day. It was hunting mice in the river meadow. At first they thought it might be a domestic cat, slinking almost unseen within the long grasses, but it was way too large. It emerged into a clearing and they could see it well. It had spots like a leopard and ears tipped with black tufts of fur like misplaced decorations. They stood and watched it, Katya and Milan, hand in hand and barely breathing in case the noise might frighten it away.

'I have never seen one so close,' Milan whispered. 'Have you?'

'Just once,' she said.

Just once. But not as Katya Němcova. The memory made her heart beat faster. Her name then had been Marianne. Marianne Muse, a stick of a girl in a cream tailored dress with gold coins sewn into her petticoats. The winter had been cold. She had fled across the mountains with a soldier and a servant girl, and on a day when snow was falling a lynx had startled them high in a valley pass. It had stalked right past them, unafraid.

'Just once – here?' Milan asked.

'No. Not here.'

A bang in the distance, the firing of a motorcycle perhaps, startled the cat and it rose up, alert, inquisitive, its whiskers trembling. Across the field of yellow grass the lynx caught Katya's eye.

'*Sacrebleu!*' she whispered. The lynx was making sense of Katya's face as she was making sense of his. His eyes seemed to widen. His nose tested the air. He might have been issuing a challenge. 'Come for me,' he might have been saying. 'Come for me.' The moment was as still as a photograph. Only the hum of the meadow bees disturbed the silence. And then the lynx was gone, dissolved into the grasses and the undergrowth.

'They say, if you catch the eye of a lynx, there is going to be a death,' Milan said.

'It's a foolish superstition.'

In the long grass of the meadow they lay down, Katya and Milan, almost touching, watching the cotton-wool clouds drifting away from the mountains.

'Shall I tell you about Heloise?' Katya asked.

'You can tell me whatever you like.'

She nudged him with her elbow. 'But do you want to hear it?'

'Of course I do.' Milan returned the nudge.

There were tiny corn flies darting in and out of the grasses. Katya swept one away from her face. 'It might make you cry,' she said.

'Is it a sad story?'

'It has a sad ending.'

'Then perhaps you shouldn't tell me,' he said. 'Not if it upsets you.'

'It doesn't upset me,' Katya said. 'It makes me angry.'

36

'You're beautiful when you're angry.'

She half sat up to look at him. 'Am I?'

He closed his eyes, embarrassed now. 'I think so.'

She laughed for him, and he laughed in reply and soon they were lying back in the grass, head to head like the hands of a clock at half past five, both with shoulders shaking.

'Tell me about your Heloise then,' Milan said, when the giggles had subsided.

'She was born more than two hundred years ago,' Katya said. 'Imagine that.'

'Two hundred years?' Milan mused. 'And you remember it?'

'No!' She nudged him again. 'I don't remember her being born. She could remember the labour pains of her own birth. But I remember her childhood.' She reached out her hand and touched Milan's arm. Her fingers wound around his elbow. 'Parts of her childhood. I remember it as clearly as my own. Sometimes I remember it more clearly than my own. Are you sure you want to hear this?'

'Yes.'

'1759 was the year Heloise was born. Her father was an aristocrat – Le Comte Fouchard. He was a landowner, quite a rich one, and something of an astronomer, and it happened Heloise was born on a night when a great comet lit up the sky. It was *Le Comète d'Edmond Halley*, the one predicted by the Englishman Mr Halley and the Frenchwoman Nicole-Reine Lepaute – a famous comet. Astronomers had been waiting for it. Le Comte had been waiting for it too. He'd been one of the first in France to see the comet return. Everyone said it was an auspicious sign. The family called the baby *Heloise* because it reminded them of Helios, the god who circles the world in his chariot; and the name could be shortened to *Hélé* and that sounded similar to *Halley*, and Monsieur le Comte Fouchard liked that. He would call her '*my little comet*'. 'You came into my life like a little comet,' he would tell her. 'My little Hélé comet.'

'It was a town called Annonay, a village in Ardèche in France, on the very east of the country near the border with the Swiss Confederacy. That was Heloise. She had the same fair hair that I have. The same green eyes. She grew to be very intelligent, and very beautiful.'

'As beautiful as you?' Milan asked.

'More beautiful,' Katya said. She squeezed Milan's arm. 'Heloise travelled widely for a woman of her time. She spoke three languages. *Yeah yeah yeah.*'

'*Yeah yeah yeah*,' Milan sang, and they both laughed.

'She would do this with her hair,' Katya said. She took a coil of yellow hair from her forehead and wound it around her index finger, and then back the other way.

'You do that,' Milan said.

'I did it long before I knew about Heloise.' Katya lifted herself up onto her elbows. A butterfly settled on her bodice and the two of them watched it folding and unfolding its patterned wings. 'I sometimes wish I was a butterfly,' Katya said.

'You would only live for a day.'

'Two days, I've heard.'

'And no memories of former lives.'

'How would we know?'

The butterfly flew off. They watched its awkward flight. 'Do you want to hear any more?' Katya asked.

'Are you sure all of this is true?' Milan asked. He looked up at the clouds to avoid her expression, aware perhaps that his words hadn't been chosen well. 'Are you sure these . . .' he hesitated, 'these *memories* are real? Maybe they're stories you were told as a baby. Things you've remembered from your cot?'

Katya exhaled slowly. 'Father calls them my ghosts.'

'Well then.'

'Your grandfather was Petyr Hašek,' she said. 'He worked at the paper mill, just as you do.'

'I think I told you this.'

'He was a small man with a bad eye. I think he lost his eye in the war,' Katya touched her own right eye. 'This one,' she said. 'Your grandmother was Ludmilla Hašeka. She was a seamstress.'

'She was.'

'I have memories of Milla. They're my mother's memories. Milla was Moravian, I think. Not a Slovak. She ran a little dress shop on Richarda Bekessa just behind the train station. My mother bought a gown from her for six korunas in 1949. She only wore it once. But it was always one of her most treasured possessions.'

'Is this supposed to convince me?'

'It's supposed to help.' The summer sunshine felt warm on their faces. 'It was blue, the gown,' Katya said, 'with a fur collar.' She closed her eyes. 'Heloise was a mathematician,' she said. 'And a musician. And an astronomer, of course.'

'An educated woman?'

'Yes. She was a close friend of the Montgolfiers – a family of Ardèche paper makers.'

'I'm a paper maker,' Milan said.

'Indeed you are. Perhaps that's why I like you.' She squeezed his hand. 'They all went to the same church in Annonay, the Montgolfiers and the Fouchards; they took two long pews, one in front of the other, and after church, every Sunday, they would walk home together. They lived in the same town, just a few streets apart, and she saw them almost every day. There were sixteen Montgolfier children. It was a big family. One hot summer, Jacques-Étienne Montgolfier made Heloise a paper parasol.' Katya paused. The memory of the parasol seemed sharp in her mind. 'It was beautiful,' she whispered. 'Emerald and gold paper, with a design of songbirds all around the rim. Heloise was just thirteen and Jacques was twenty-six. She would take the parasol to church every Sunday and insist that he held it for her all the way home.'

'He was too old for her,' Milan said.

'Father says you are too old for me.'

'Were these the same Montgolfier brothers . . . ?' Milan started to ask.

'. . . who made the first balloon?' She finished his question and smiled a secret smile. 'They were. Joseph-Michel and Jacques-Étienne built the world's first hot-air balloon. Well, the first one to carry a person. Jacques-Étienne was Heloise's favourite Montgolfier. She never forgot that parasol. They were very nearly lovers despite the difference in their ages. He would sit behind her in church and whisper terrible blasphemies into her ear to try to make her laugh. One afternoon they kissed, and a short while later he proposed, but she turned him down. She was nineteen then. She wasn't ready for marriage. Not yet. Jacques-Étienne went away and married a girl who worked in the family paper mill. Heloise was fine with that. All the same, Joseph-Michel treated her like a younger sister. She would call at the Montgolfier house and Joseph would set her to task doing calculations on the balloon's construction. She was smarter than any of them. "How much will the balloon weigh?" he would ask her. "How much smoke will we need to lift it? How much wood will we need to burn? How much paper will we need? How much paint?" When she went with them to Paris to see the great balloon fly in 1784, she was twenty-five. It was the great adventure of her life. It's five hundred kilometres from Annonay to Paris – ten days of travel in a coach. She stayed in Paris for a month, living with an aunt of the Montgolfiers in Rue de Grenelle. One night she met a very rich widower, a man called Jean Sebastien Montbelliard, at a huge society party thrown to celebrate the balloon, and he wooed her with gifts of gold, and lace, and white horses. They married two months later, and a year after that they had a daughter called Sylvie, and they lived a very comfortable life in Chateau Montbelliard-les-Pins, a huge country estate near Dijon, where they grew grapes and made wines, and where nothing could disturb their easy lives.'

Katya exhaled and turned her face away to avoid his gaze, to look at the shadows on the mountains.

'I thought the story had a sad ending,' Milan said.

She sat up. 'Shall we dance?' she asked him.

'What? Here in the meadow?'

'Yes.' She was climbing to her feet. 'Right here.' She tugged at his arm. Her eyes were ablaze.

'We have no music.'

'You are so serious, Milan. It's one reason I like you. But why would we need music? We have birdsong. We have the bees. We have the cowbells.' She took his hand, and swayed. 'Da da da, da da da,' she sang. 'Pretend it's the Beatles.'

'I'm not much of a dancer,' he protested. But he fell in with the rhythm of her hips and the rolling of her shoulders. 'How is this?'

'Wonderful,' she said, and she was counting a waltz. '*One* two three, *one* two three.'

She pulled him towards her and rested her head on his chest. 'Never assume, Milan,' she whispered, 'that the course of your life is set or the comfort you know today will last forever.' She kissed him gently on his nose. 'Come,' she took his hand. 'Let's walk.'

They took the path through the pasture to a wooden bridge over the river. 'All these tracks lead up into the mountains,' she told him. 'At weekends, couples from Poprad cycle out here and walk through the forests. It's romantic. There's a waterfall if you walk far enough.'

'We should do it.' He sounded excited.

'Not today. Father will need me for the afternoon milking. But we will. One day.'

'What became of Heloise?'

'Walk me back to the farm,' Katya said. 'And I'll tell you.'

4

Heloise, 1789

July in the Bourgogne is a sleepy month. There is little to do, in the heat, apart from worrying about rain, and watching vine leaves scorch in the summer sun. Heloise and Jean Sebastien had been married five years. In the evenings, slaves already to routine, they would walk the vines, a stroll rather than a serious inspection, an amble through the rows, with just a small retinue from the estate as company – the vintner, the vintner's lad, a nursemaid, a lady's maid, a companion, a watchman, and perhaps a footman if one could be spared. Sylvie was three. Jean Sebastien carried her on his shoulders. It was a fine evening. They walked to see the western slopes. Heloise carried her parasol, the one Jacques-Étienne had given her. Her ladies in attendance walked a few steps behind. She had not a care in the world. Why would she?

There was some commotion in the distance and it caught their attention – raised voices and the thump of hooves – and then a rider on a black horse came up the carriageway at a canter, shouting something as he rode, dust rising from his tracks.

The servants were all a-fluster. Two men from the Chateau ran out and tried to apprehend the horse, but the rider would have none of it. He had caught sight of Heloise and her parasol, and of Jean Sebastien, and Sylvie, and the evening promenade among the vines. He spurred his horse up between the rows and slid down onto his feet in front of them. His horse was wet with sweat.

'*Madame!*' he said, and he dropped to one knee, pulling his hat and his wig from his head as he did so.

'Maurice?'

He was Maurice Montgolfier – one of Jacques-Étienne's younger brothers – alone, and a long way from home. He flung his arms around Jean Sebastien, and kissed Heloise's gloved hand. 'I have ridden all the way from Paris,' he said. 'I am on my way to Annonay. I have bought a new horse in every town.'

'My dear sir,' Jean Sebastien said, taking his arm, 'you must stay with us. I can give you a fresh horse in the morning.'

'You are kind, sir,' Maurice said, 'and I will take a horse if you can exchange one. But we still have three hours of daylight. I prefer to ride on. I bear news from Paris that I am taking to my father, but I can share it with you.' His hands were shaking. 'They have taken the Bastille,' he said. '*The Bastille!*'

Jean Sebastien barely frowned at this announcement. 'Who?' he demanded. 'Who has taken the Bastille?'

Maurice bent low, and dropped his voice. 'Sir, it was the mob,' he whispered. 'The mob have taken Paris.'

'The mob . . . ?'

'The people. The masses,' Maurice said. 'You must prepare. What happens in Paris can happen in Dijon.'

'My dear young man,' Jean Sebastien said. His expression suggested there was no reason to be concerned with this news. 'We should not be hasty. The people love us. We have nothing to fear from them. We should wait to see what the King does. What is La Bastille, after all? An insignificant prison six days' ride from here.'

Maurice said, 'M'sieur le Comte, I am riding to warn my father. You are free to disregard my warning, but you were not there; you were not in Paris. I was. I saw the mob. I have read the treatises circulating the city. *La France Libre*. It will reach Dijon. It will threaten you too. Believe me. It will.'

'What should we do?' Heloise asked her husband that evening. They stood in the window of the southern withdrawing room, watching the sun, fat and red, setting over the distant hills.

'We are a long way from Paris,' Jean Sebastien said.

'All the same . . . ?'

Jean Sebastien shrugged. 'What can they do?' he asked. 'In every century there are malcontents, and sometimes they win a skirmish, and sometimes even two. But this is all. Let them enjoy their little victory and let them publish their treatises. We are of no interest to them. The King will rebuild the Bastille and these men will lose their heads.'

'So we do nothing?' Heloise asked.

'We do nothing.'

They did nothing. For almost two years the Montbelliards did nothing. What could they do? The revolution was a long way away. There were vines still to be tended. There was a Chateau still to manage. In France a rich man was a rich man and a poor man was a poor man, and there was no clear way to change this truth, unless, as Jean Sebastien Montbelliard would often say, 'You would have us all be poor, and if that's the way the wind blows from Paris then I won't be there to help it blow.'

But the wind was blowing, and Jean Sebastien wasn't needed to fan the gusts. Every week news came from the capital. It was rarely good news; not for Heloise, or Jean Sebastien, not for the owners of chateaux, or vineyards, or silver, or gold.

More riots. More threats.

Yet this was Dijon. This was Burgundy. Bourgogne. They would say of Burgundians, the men of Burgundy, 'They've never seen the sea,' and this was true. It was over ten days' hard ride to Saint Nazaire on the wild Atlantic coast, and much the same south to Marseilles or north to Dieppe, and who would make that dangerous journey to drown in an unfamiliar ocean? Not the men or women of Dijon.

Jean Sebastien Montbelliard, eighth in line to his family name, had never seen the sea and never would. They were wine makers in Burgundy. They lived their lives by the cycle of the grapes. In the Montbelliard vineyards, Jean Sebastien walked his vines, every morning. His slopes faced east – ideal for the soft, red wines he made. He would run his fingers through the leaves, would touch the grapes, the first, small buds in the spring, the growing bunches as the summer came, like the barrelled fists of newborn infants, and the black, swollen fruits in September. He would pluck them and taste them, apprehensive, searching for sweetness. He would look anxiously at the skies for rainclouds. He would watch for mildews and oidium and fanleaf. He would shout orders to his vine hands and send the men out with rakes and clippers and barrows of water when the soils were too dry. One day in September, every year, he would put a fat, purple grape into his mouth and suck the flesh through his teeth, and caress the juice with his tongue, and he would turn to Guillaume, his vintner who would lead the picking teams, and he would say, 'It is time.' He would exhale slowly through his nose, testing the scent of the grape. 'It is time.'

Guillaume, too, would taste a grape. 'Maybe two more days,' he would say. 'Four days for the grapes on the high slope.'

'But will the skies be clear of rain?' Jean Sebastien would anxiously ask. He respected the knowledge of his growers.

'I believe so,' Guillaume would say.

Two days then. Two more days and there would be three hundred pickers on these hills.

They did nothing.

There was a revolution in Paris, but in the Bourgogne the grapes needed tending, the vines needed pruning, the fermentation needed watching, and even the Jacobins needed wine to drink.

More news came from Paris. 'I'm glad we're here in Dijon,' Jean Sebastien said to Heloise. 'Let them fight each other in the capital. They still want our wines.'

A day came when the Assembly in Paris abolished all titles and privileges. A notice was posted on the town hall in Dijon and a man in a tricorn hat read the proclamation from the back of a hay cart. Jean Sebastien would no longer be '*Le Comte*'. He was incensed. 'How can they take away what God has given?' he railed to Heloise. 'They will still call me Le Comte. Everyone will use those words. I am still the master of the estate. They can't take that away.'

Heloise was circumspect. 'It won't make any difference to our lives,' she said.

But it did. They lost their cushioned seats in the cathedral. 'Sit here with us,' a man called from the narrow wooden pews where the common people sat. 'Shove along. Make some room for Monsieur Montbelliard.'

Monsieur!

People spat upon them in the street. Four maids left their service with no explanation. Someone stabbed two of their horses in the market place where a hundred people must have been watching, but no one saw a thing, not even the coachman. One horse died of its wounds.

'It will turn,' Jean Sebastien said. 'It is a fashion. It will end.'

But it was a frightening time to own a Chateau in France.

In 1791 news reached the Montbelliards of an incident with the Royal Family. A friend of Jean Sebastien relayed the story. The King and his family, so the tale was told, had fled the Tuileries Palace under the cover of darkness. Some said they disguised themselves as peasants. They rode as far as Varennes, and there they were captured and sent back. Their escape lasted just four days.

'The King of France can go where he chooses,' Jean Sebastien said, when he heard the story. 'He needs ask permission of no one. This is a wicked rumour.'

But a day or so later, news of the royal humiliation reached the people of Dijon. They clearly didn't consider it a rumour. On a carriage ride through the town, Heloise and Jean Sebastien saw a crowd partying in celebration. 'They're drinking and carousing to mark the capture of our beloved King,' Jean Sebastien said in disbelief. He shook his head, as he so often did in those days. Who could understand the common man? 'If we have no King,' he said, 'then what will become of France? Our enemies will overrun us.'

Sylvie celebrated her sixth birthday. She was an awkward child with dark eyebrows and a gap in her teeth. She spoke with a lisp. She had a tutor from England named Robert, and together they would play music on the harpsichord in Jean Sebastien's library. Heloise taught her tunes by Mozart. 'When I was a girl,' Heloise told Sylvie, 'I saw Wolfgang Mozart and his sister play. He wasn't much older than you are now.'

Items of value started to disappear from the Chateau – a gold statuette from the stairway, silver knives from the silver store, jewels from Heloise's dressing room. 'My rings!' Heloise called to Jean Sebastien one evening. 'My rings have gone!'

'I took them,' he told her. 'It is nothing but a precaution.'

'And the statue on the stairs?'

'That too,' he said. 'I shall leave you sufficient rings – say one for every finger. But we must protect ourselves against the vandals.'

One day, on a visit to Dijon, a rock thrown from a window struck Sylvie on the forehead and drew blood. Men were sent into the house but no culprit was found. Jean Sebastien's tolerance was turning into fury. He rode to the city hall and returned with twenty extra guards. They were young men from the town. He was paying them well. He had breeches and buckled shoes made for them. Five guardsmen now travelled with the family everywhere they went.

And still there were grapes to harvest, and wine to be made. The sun still shone, and the fruit still ripened, and thirsty throats still needed wine. Some days Jean Sebastien would stand in his fields and pluck his grapes and turn his face to the blue skies of Burgundy. 'We are living in a dream,' he would tell Heloise. 'Nothing will change here. The people love us. They need us. They will go hungry without us.'

But there were nights in the great Chateau where the cry of a voice in the dark would awaken him and he would see the flash of torches outside his window, and he would hear the urgent footfalls of his guardsmen running down the carriageway, and those were nights when a cold fear would descend on the Montbelliard estate, and he and Heloise would lie awake and listen to every chime of the castle clock on every quarter hour until the dawn.

A year later news came to Dijon that a mob had overthrown the royal palace. The King and Queen were to be put on trial.

'We'll be next,' Heloise warned.

'My dear, you are overdramatic,' said Jean Sebastien.

But every day there were fewer treasures in the house.

The Assembly in Paris was raising an army to defend France from Austria and Prussia. There had been a decree from the National Convention, a *levée en masse*. Every able-bodied man was to be enlisted into the army. One day a committee of *sans-culottes*, representatives of the third estate, came to visit Jean Sebastien at Chateau Montbelliard-les-Pins. There were thirty or more in the *comité*, all men; they travelled on foot, and their mood was not good. They had walked through a rainstorm from Dijon and their clothing was soaked. All the same, Jean Sebastien refused to allow them through the door. They stood and spoke for an hour on the carriageway. Heloise watched from a window.

This could be the moment, she thought. *This could be our time.*

She was surprisingly calm.

There were raised voices and waved arms. At one point Heloise feared the *comité* were about to arrest her husband. The guardsmen in their breeches and blue tunics looked rattled. If it came to it, Heloise wondered, could their own guards be counted on to protect the family? Or would they side with the revolutionaries?

The moment passed, and a little while later, Heloise's question was answered. When they left, the *comité* took all but one of the Montbelliard guardsmen with them for the National

Guard. They also took groundsmen, and gardeners, and men who worked the vines, and the boys who ran errands, and every able man in the household staff from the cook to the coalman, leaving two elderly coachmen, a footman who was no more than a boy, and the vintner. The one guardsman they left was too old to be of much service. He had a crooked back.

The pressed men gathered in a loose assembly in the carriageway. It took some time for them all to be summoned. Each one carried a parcel of his own belongings. One of the maids sang a lament, and there were tearful goodbyes, but it was also clear that some of the men were struggling to contain their excitement. They were off for a great adventure. The prospect of war was a great deal more exhilarating than treading grapes.

'Half of them will be dead by Christmas,' Jean Sebastien predicted, darkly. He had rejoined Heloise in the house.

On a command from the leader of the *sans-culottes* the recruits shuffled away down the drive between the vineyards. The road was still wet from the rainstorm. They looked less like warriors than kitchen staff. One carried a pitchfork.

'We cannot run the estate without the men,' Heloise said at dinner. 'For a start, we are no longer safe. We must do something.'

'We should find somewhere secure for Sylvie until it all blows over,' Jean Sebastien said. The meeting with the committee of the third estate had rattled him. 'Somewhere she can flee and stay if they ever come for us.'

The wine cellars at Chateau Montbelliard-les-Pins were extensive. They ran for hundreds of metres underneath the Chateau and cut deep into the hillsides beneath the vines. Jean Sebastien and Heloise showed Sylvie a narrow passageway hidden behind an empty bottle rack. It led through a dark tunnel, emerging into a barrel store on the far side of the hill. 'If ever we are attacked or if men come to take us away, you must lift a lantern from the wall,' Jean Sebastien said, 'and you must run all the way down the tunnel and into the hills. Go to

Guillaume Forestiere. You know his house. Madame Forestiere will protect you. I will ensure you have money to pay her.'

They buried three heavy purses of gold coins in a box beneath one of the vines. Sylvie and Heloise watched as Jean Sebastien dug alone. 'This gold will be your security,' he told Sylvie. 'Count fifty rows of vines from the stream and dig beneath the fiftieth vine in that row. Fifty and fifty.'

'Fifty rows from the stream,' Sylvie echoed, 'and fifty vines from the path.'

'We should hide our household treasures,' Jean Sebastien said. 'All of them.' There was a darkness in his eyes now. There had been news that several great houses in Paris had been ransacked, all their gold and silver taken, their paintings and tapestries destroyed.

'When?' Heloise asked.

The cloud over the western hills was as heavy as Jean Sebastien's mood. 'We should do it soon. Tonight.'

Jean Sebastien gave each servant a coin. 'Your menfolk have gone,' he told them. 'Go into town and be merry. Drink to their safe return.'

With the servants away, the great house was empty. Only Jean Sebastien, Heloise, Sylvie, the two ageing coachmen, and the hunchbacked guardsman remained. Heloise's wooden heels clacked on the terracotta floors and echoed into all the rooms.

Later that evening Heloise walked to the coach houses to summon the coachmen. On Jean Sebastien's instruction, two open landau carriages had been prepared, each with six horses. The coachmen and the old retainer helped to lift twelve heavy oak cases into the carriages – six into each.

It was almost nine o'clock. There was moonlight, but thin cloud too.

There were servants at the gates as the carriages drove away. A party was taking place in the gatehouse. They closed the gates as the family departed. The Montbelliards had left the Chateau. They were taking all their treasures. They would not be back. No one needed to say the words. But everyone knew it to be true.

There was no room to sit inside either carriage. The leather seats were laden with the oak chests. Jean Sebastien sat in the front of the first coach on the bench with the coachman, facing forwards. Heloise and Sylvie did the same in the second. The old guardsman stood on the gun-rail holding tight to the carriage.

As they turned onto the road in the direction of Beaune, a crowd outside a tavern started to jeer at them. A young man shouted an obscenity. A goblet of wine was thrown. It struck the flank of one of the horses, and the horse reared up with the shock. Two men from the tavern gave chase, on foot, but failed to catch the carriages.

Moments later, three more men came after them on horses. As they swung around a corner onto a woodland track, pursuers and pursued, one of the heavy wooden boxes broke free of its ropes, slid off the rearmost seat of the landau, and smashed open on the trackway. A stretch of rope still held one end of the box to the carriage so the chest was dragged, bouncing and crashing, spilling its contents as the horses galloped on. The three pursuers stopped and leapt from their mounts to gather what they could. There were riches unimaginable scattered for a hundred *pieds* along the lane: a dozen bags of gold coins, silver plates, promissory bonds from the national treasury, a gold statuette, two rolls of Lyonnaise silk, candlesticks, silver knives, copper dishes, an oil painting of a dog, a silver bust of the King, silk gowns, an ivory snuff box, lace, and a necklace that snapped and rained pearls all along the lane and into the ditch. The two men chasing on foot arrived upon the scene and it became a frantic scramble for treasures.

The Montbelliard family rode on. They had a single lantern burning on each carriage and eleven unplundered chests.

A few kilometres out of town Jean Sebastien called for the horses to stop. He jumped down and pressed one purse of gold coins into the hands of each coachman and another for the old guardsman, and dismissed them. The family rode on alone, Jean Sebastien at the reins of one carriage, and Heloise the other. The last sight anyone had of the carriages or the oak cases was at Les Baraques on the trackway leading to Chamboeuf. After that the Montbelliards vanished, and the treasures vanished with them.

5

Katya, 1968

They made their way back to the farmhouse. There was work to be done.

'Shall I see you tomorrow?' Milan asked. 'When I finish at the paper mill?'

'If you want,' Katya replied. She was teasing him.

'Is there more to the story?'

'Some.'

In the farmyard a motor car was parked awkwardly alongside the cattle byre. Two men with humourless faces were climbing in. A chauffeur in a grey cap gave Katya a wave. Jaroslav was watching.

'What did they want, Papa?' Katya asked as the car rolled away towards the lane.

'Pah!' Jaroslav mimed wiping a taste from his mouth with his hand. 'They want what they always want. They want the farm.'

'Our farm?'

'"Small farms are not sustainable." That's what they say. We have to join one of the collectives and take our orders from them.' Katya's father shook his head with an expression of disbelief upon his face. 'We will find ourselves working for Ivan Makovec and his dreadful committee. All the farmers in this valley were permitted to keep our farms so long as they were under fifty hectares, but that was twenty years ago, and now, they say the law has changed. All private ownership is illegal now. We must be part of some thousand-hectare collective if we want to stay in our house and look after our own livestock.'

Jaroslav turned his face away, but not before Katya caught

the unmistakable impression of a tear in his eye.

'We shall resist them, Papa,' Katya cried. She snatched a rake and held it aloft in a gesture of defiance. 'We shall refuse to join their stupid cooperatives.'

'Oh, Katyusha,' Jaroslav sighed. He put a hand on her shoulder. 'We can't resist. They'll send us to jail.'

'They can't send every farmer in Czechoslovakia to jail.'

'Oh, I expect they can if they want to. But they won't have to. Most of the farmers will go along with the new rules. Me too, I expect.'

'Oh, Father!' Katya put down the rake, and now she could feel a tear in her own eye. 'This has been a Němcov farm as long as anyone can remember.'

'I know.'

'So then we must leave,' Katya said. The fire had returned to her voice.

'But where should we go?'

'To the West.'

'And what would we live on?'

'You're an experienced dairyman. You could find work in West Germany. We could go in search of Heloise's treasure.'

Katya's father gave a sigh. 'These are the sort of things your mother would say.'

Into the yard, leading the cows from the pasture, came Jordy, the stockman with the crooked teeth.

'We should stop this conversation now,' Jaroslav said.

As the cows lumbered into the yard, steaming and stinking of muck, the farmer thrust his hands deep into his pockets and stood, immobile, a figure of stone, staring upwards towards the hills.

'And was there a lot?' Milan asked. 'A lot . . . of treasure?'

They lay again in the long grass of the river meadow. Katya smiled. 'Lots,' she said.

'Lots?'

'And lots. Sometimes I think it's the curse of my family. Jean Sebastien collected gold. It was his passion. He had gold artefacts from all over the world. Gold goblets, candlesticks, plates, statues. Gold and diamonds from India. Gold from the Americas. A case of gold coins. Can you believe that? A whole case of coins. Silver too. And all manner of artwork. Bronzes. Statuettes. Paintings. Telescopes. He was a very rich man even by the standards of the time.'

Milan was quiet. After a while he said, 'Is the treasure still hidden?'

'So far as I know, it still is,' Katya said.

'Do you know where to find it?'

Katya looked away. 'In 1794,' she said, 'when she was thirty-six years old, Heloise was beheaded.'

'Beheaded?' Milan let the shock show in his voice.

'By guillotine. Jean Sebastien and Heloise were apprehended in Beaune living in a town house under assumed names. They had been there for three years. They were taken back to Dijon and charged with being enemies of the revolution. Heloise's trial lasted about five minutes. The crowd jeered so loudly she barely heard a word.' Katya released a long, slow breath. 'In prison,' she said, 'Heloise was abused.'

'Abused?' Milan had heard the tremble in Katya's voice.

'These things are past,' Katya said. 'These things are past.' She wound a tress of hair around her finger. 'Heloise was tortured,' she said. She dropped her voice to almost a whisper. 'She was raped.'

Milan reached for Katya's hand and squeezed it. In the summer sunshine the word *raped* seemed uncomfortably violent, an interloper of a word, a word that shouldn't belong among the wildflowers and long grasses. It hung heavily over the meadow. Milan tried to mouth the word back, to echo it to Katya as he did with so many of her words, but this whisper wouldn't come.

'A man called Roderique Églefin,' Katya said, and she closed her eyes. She spat his name as if the sound of the syllables hurt her mouth. 'His name is a fish,' she said. 'You would never find an *églefin* in Dijon or in Nová Vyšný – we are both too far from the sea. *Skvrnitá treska* we would say in Slovak, a haddock. These things are past.' She reopened her eyes and looked at Milan. 'Do you want to hear this?'

High above the meadow a hawk was circling, around and around on warm air currents from the valley. Down below, half buried in the grasses, Katya and Milan might have been its prey.

'What if this isn't a memory?' Milan said. His voice sounded small.

'It *is* a memory.'

'But what if it isn't?'

'Do you think I'm making it up?'

'No.'

'Then what?'

They lay together to reflect on this.

'Heloise survived Églefin's captivity for more than thirty weeks,' Katya said, after a while. 'He kept her alive for his own entertainment. For his own profane use. He kept her to torture and to abuse.' The word Katya used here was *súložiť*. It wasn't a word she had used before with Milan. *Na súložiť* – to *fuck*. 'He kept Heloise to torture and to fuck,' she said.

'You don't have to tell me, if you don't want to,' Milan whispered.

'But I think I do,' she said.

6

Heloise, 1794

By cruel coincidence, the place where Heloise was taken after her arrest was the Chateau Montbelliard-les-Pins. Her own home. She was held there as a prisoner. The Jacobins had commandeered the conveniently empty castle as their headquarters in Dijon, and their young leader was Roderique Églefin, the man who had captured her. Églefin, the haddock. He smelled to Heloise like an *églefin*. He was cold like an *églefin*.

He was her abuser. He was also her jailer. Her private jailer. Only he had the keys to her cell. It amused him to have her in a cellar of her former home. He would mock her. 'Would you have a fine bath?' he would ask. 'Shall I command the servants to light a fire and draw scented water for you to bathe in?' And he would fling the pot of her own piss over her. 'Bathe in that,' he would spit. 'Bathe in your own stink.' He chained her onto the wall of her cell, her wrists and ankles broken, and he stuffed linen into her mouth to spare the castle from her screams. Later, months later, he would cut out her tongue to ensure her silence. She lay on hard, cold stone, barely conscious, unable to stand. He denied her food or water. It pleased him for her to suffer. He would drip into her cell, a poisonous presence, and she would smell his *églefin* stink and the stench of his tobacco breath, and there, in the puddle of her own excrement, he raped her.

The tower clock would chime out the passing of the hours. *Dong. Dong.* A tuneless call. A hammer strike. Iron on iron. *Dong. Dong.* In Heloise's dark cell the faint tolling of the bell was a thread that held together the fragile parcels of her life. Cold nights. Hungry days. The visits of Églefin. Pain.

He came to see her. The malodorous commander and his victim, close to death. He dragged a chair behind him so that he might sit, and he hung a lantern from the wall. 'My Lady Montbelliard,' he taunted her. 'Baronne Heloise the Condemned. Do you have some pretty poetry for me? Can you show me the stars?'

'I will be avenged,' she whispered. She still had her tongue. 'That's my poem for you.'

'Avenged? Ah, well, we all deserve a little vengeance,' he said, as if here he was, an urbane, reasonable man, and this was a discussion on philosophy in a drawing room in Paris. He rocked his chair back and forward on its hind legs. 'The peasants who slaved in your household – do they deserve vengeance? I think perhaps they do. The men who toiled in your vineyards? The pitiful poor in Paris who died in gutters for want of bread while you, Madame la Baronne, dined on sweetbreads from Vienna and honeyed wines from Padua? Should they be avenged too?'

'And how do you dine, Monsieur Poisson?' she asked him. 'Does your plate hold stale bread? How did you feast while the poor in Paris starved? Last night I smelled oysters. And yet we are so far from the sea! Perhaps it was you I smelled.'

She earned a beating for this offence. But what was a beating anymore?

Dong. The clapping-out of time. After a while your nose will overlook a reeking stench, your body will bear a beating, you will turn your face away from the abuser and the abuse.

'Give me names,' Églefin would demand. 'Tell me the names of your accomplices – those who plotted with you.'

Dong.

'There are no names.'

Her tormentor would light himself a long clay pipe and suck smoke through it. 'I saw your husband face the blade,' he told her. He had told her this before. 'I saw him weeping. He wept like a girl.'

'He went bravely to his death,' Heloise countered. 'I have heard this.'

'Bravely?' Églefin laughed. 'No one goes bravely. Everyone pisses on the scaffold. Even the King. You will too.'

Away from the Chateau, the reign of terror was limping towards its end. Not that Heloise would have known. But there are only so many necks you can sever. The public was turning against mass executions. The lust for blood was abating. Églefin had the certificate of judgement of the court. Heloise's only release from imprisonment could be the swift justice of the guillotine. She was alive on the pretext, and the pretence, that she could provide information to help uncover more enemies of the revolution. She never did. In the end, Églefin sent Heloise to her death, not because she had failed to betray any other offenders, but because he couldn't risk her being spared. He sliced out her tongue with a butcher's knife. 'She bit it off,' he would tell her guards. Two soldiers in leather aprons came to her cell to carry her away. They washed her and dressed her in a fine yellow dress from her own wardrobe so all the world could see at once she was a lady, could understand her crimes.

A maid from the barracks, a girl with a club foot, barely into her teens, pinned up Heloise's hair. 'Make her look like a courtesan,' the maid was told. But the condemned woman's hair was so matted with blood and filth, there was very little the servant girl could do.

Mute, and mutilated, Heloise nonetheless conveyed a message to the maid. She ran her broken hands across her belly, and her eyes told her story. 'I will do it,' the servant girl promised, with the faintest of whispers into Heloise's ear. 'I will tell.'

A few hours later Heloise was tied and carried in a tumbril to the guillotine at Place du Morimont, happy, truly happy, to have escaped her persecutor at long last. She had prayed for this release. She was executed for betraying the revolution, for the crime of being rich, for royalism, for Fayettism, and for being of no further interest to Églefin who had, perhaps, found another plaything. A respectable crowd was there to watch. Her name was printed at the top of the bill of fare, her death was to be the star attraction. In exchange for this honour she was executed last.

A health official, in a tricolour waistcoat and black shag trousers with a sabre strapped to his waist, was invited to inspect her. Églefin himself was present to deal with the formalities. 'She cannot speak,' he told the official. 'She has bitten off her tongue.'

'They will often do this,' the official nodded, as if he had encountered this obstructionism a thousand times. He chewed on his moustache. 'It is to prevent themselves from giving away the names of their co-conspirators.'

'Alas, I believe so,' Églefin said. 'Also she cannot stand. She has broken ankles.'

'And did she break them herself?'

'She did.'

Along the wall of the city hall was painted, in red and blue, 'REPUBLIC ONE AND INDIVISIBLE; LIBERTY, EQUALITY, FRATERNITY, OR DEATH.' A bell was tolling in the steeple. The square reeked like an abattoir.

Heloise lay in a hand barrow, arms and legs tied, while one by one, a dozen victims were guillotined before her. A marshal would call out a name, and the crowd would hush. A prisoner, sometimes wailing, sometimes silent, sometimes belligerent, sometimes repentant, would be dragged towards the dreadful device. 'Last words!' a voice would cry, and some in the crowd would take up the chant. A reporter with a quill pen would lean in to scribe the fateful words, and moments later the apparatus would shake and the blade would fall, the crowd would scream, and the executioner would hold aloft a bloody head. Crash! Cheer! Cry! Crash! The terrible machinery of ritual murder.

She didn't have too long to wait. Four *gendarmes* lifted her and carried her, head first, like a basket of grapes, towards the guillotine. A cheer rose from the crowd.

'Heloise Maria Montbelliard,' the marshal shouted, reading from his roster. 'Enemy of the Republic.'

On the scaffold, Heloise turned her head and watched the blade fall.

The yellow dress she wore to her death might once have fitted, in the days when she was the mistress of the Chateau, when balls were held in the great hall, when musicians would play, and rich people would dance. On the day of her execution she had barely eaten for months. The dress hung on her body like a shapeless sack. It concealed from the health officer the one thing he should have checked.

Heloise was nearly eight months pregnant.

7

Katya, 1968

'The woman who slid the carcass from the bascule knew,' Katya said. 'She was told by the servant girl, the girl with the club foot, the girl who did Heloise's hair. A holy sister slit Heloise's belly open with a knife and pulled out the baby, and miraculously, the child survived. It was a girl. They sent her to a nunnery in Quetigny. That was where she grew up. The name they gave her was Marianne Muse.'

'Marianne Muse.' The French name sounded unfamiliar and foreign in Milan's mouth. 'And she was the first to . . . inherit the memories of her mother?'

'Or perhaps the second.' Katya slid her arm around Milan's waist. 'Don't forget Sylvie. Sylvie Montbelliard was nine years old when Heloise was executed. She wasn't arrested with Heloise and Jean Sebastien, so maybe she fled from Beaune and found Madame Forestiere. There were safe houses in Beaune she knew about. Maybe she went to one of them. I don't know what became of her. I can't find any clues in Heloise's memories. I think perhaps Jean Sebastien made all the arrangements and spared Heloise the details to protect her from torture. So I don't know. I think about Sylvie a great deal. I know she survived the revolution. But I don't know if she inherited Heloise's memories. I only know I'm descended from Marianne Muse, the girl who was pulled alive from a headless corpse. I have Marianne's memories too. Although they are not ones I choose to think about very often.'

High above them, the hawk decided the lovers in the hayfield were no longer of interest. It emitted a call, circled away and flew off to roost in a tree.

'One day,' Milan said, 'we shall find a way to go to France.'

He sounded oddly confident. 'When they open the borders, we could look for Sylvie's family.'

'I'd like that,' Katya said. Her voice had shrunk to a whisper.

'Perhaps she has a descendant like you. I can picture her. She's lying in a field in France, right now, looking up at the sky, wondering about you.'

'Is she pretty?'

'She's adorable.'

'Does she have a boyfriend?'

'Not one who's good looking.'

'Or modest,' Katya said. She squeezed him. Funny how comfortable she felt in his presence. 'We can never go to France,' she said.

'One day. One day we will. Maybe Mr Dubček will open the borders.'

'I don't think he has the keys.'

Milan smiled at this. 'My brother says the West makes it difficult for citizens of Soviet republics to travel because they're frightened of spies.'

'Do you think that's true?'

'Of course.' But Milan had turned his face away.

'Yet nobody believes it, do they?' Katya whispered, after a short time had passed. 'Not even your brother.'

'Do you believe it?'

The summer sunshine felt too restful for this conversation. Katya closed her eyes. 'I've had a thought, Milan. Just now. I've had a thought and it may not be a happy one.'

'What thought?' He didn't understand. He raised himself up on his elbows.

'If you grow too close to me,' Katya said in a small voice, 'I might be dangerous for you.'

'Dangerous? How?'

There was a sharpness in her eyes. 'I don't know. But perhaps I think too much. My grandfather says they shoot you if you ask too many questions.'

63

'Then don't ask questions,' Milan said.

How serious his face looked. His spectacles were smudged. How could he see?

'I know too many things,' Katya said. She said it so quietly he could barely hear her.

'What things?'

She sighed. 'Too many things.' Things a fifteen-year-old shouldn't know. 'I know how it feels to dance on the stage in New York and to hear the cheers of the crowd. I've seen Paris from the great tower. I've ridden through London in a carriage pulled by six horses. I've dined with the King of France and I've curtseyed to the Queen of England. I once signed a petition that went to the House of Lords in London, calling for women to be granted suffrage.'

'And did they?' Milan asked. 'Did they grant women suffrage?'

'Not then. But it was the beginning of something. I've stood on the prow of a great ship as it crossed the Atlantic. I have spoken with Dr Freud in Vienna, and I've met Harriet Taylor Mill the reformist, and I've listened to Mr Darwin speak about worms, and I saw the first great balloon floating over the rooftops of Paris.'

She reached out and took the spectacles from his face, unwinding them gently from his ears. She started to clean the lenses on the hem of her frock. 'I've seen freedom, Milan. Do you know what that means? Freedom can be a dangerous idea in Czechoslovakia.' Softly she pushed the glasses back onto his nose. 'Is that better?'

'Yes, thanks.'

'It isn't just my dreams that are dangerous, Milan. It's me. Sometimes I want to run into the street and shout, "*Down with Khrushchev, Down with Russia, Down with the Party.*"'

'That could be a little dangerous,' Milan admitted.

'You can run away from me now, if you wish. You can run, and run, and never look back. I wouldn't blame you if you did.'

A soft breeze was making the meadow sway.

'I will never leave you,' Milan said.

'You shouldn't say *never*.'

'I will never leave you,' he said again. 'If you run into the street shouting, then so will I. If you go to jail, then I'll go to jail.'

Katya nodded. 'And what if it's a bullet?'

'They will have to shoot me too.'

As fast as it had come, the wind dropped. The meadow subsided.

'I won't shout *Down with Khrushchev*,' Katya said.

'Well, I might,' said Milan.

They lay and listened to the noises of summer.

'Can we go home?' Katya asked.

In August 1968, all anyone talked about was politics.

'In the West they're calling it the *Prague Spring*,' Hana Anya, Otillie's mother, told them. She was becoming impatient for reforms.

'Why just *Prague*?' Jaroslav grumbled. 'Why not the *Prague and Bratislava and Poprad Spring*? They always forget the Slovaks. They forget the farmers in the Tatras.'

Milan had become more engaged in politics. Some of Katya's fire was starting to burn him too. He would bring copies of *Literární listy*, the party newspaper, and wave articles for them to read. 'They're starting to tell us the truth,' he said one morning. 'Look here.' One full-page article was an unveiled criticism of Joseph Stalin, highlighting his impact on Czechoslovakia, and not altogether in a good light.

'Whoever wrote that won't live long,' Krystof snorted when he saw the piece. 'You shouldn't keep it. Burn it. One day they'll take you away just for possessing it.'

'Stalin is dead, grandfather,' Katya said. 'Why would he care?'

'Stalin is never dead,' Krystof said. He sucked in a lungful of smoke. 'There is always a Stalin.'

Jaroslav made plans to keep geese on the river meadow without consulting the collective. He built fences and a goose shed. 'What do they know about our farm anyway?' he would say. 'We're free men now under Dubček. No one can tell us what to do anymore.'

Krystof was more cautious. He was *always* more cautious. 'We're not free yet,' he would say, ominously, stabbing the air with his cigarette. 'If Dubček wants to make us free, why wait so long? If I was chairman of the party I would do it in my first hour. I would go onto the radio and make a decree.'

Milan started writing articles for a student newspaper in Poprad, the *Voice of Youth*. It was a party paper but its tone had become markedly revolutionary in recent months. 'People are questioning the whole system,' he would say to Katya. He would show her his articles. 'You can't have freedom without economic freedom. That's what my teachers at the academy say. No man is free unless he can control his own economic destiny.'

'Just be careful what you write,' Krystof warned. 'It will only take one bullet for Dubček to be history.'

'But ten million bullets to silence all of Czechoslovakia,' Milan said.

'I'm sure Mr Khrushchev won't miss ten million bullets if he wants to use them.'

'Mr Dubček says socialism isn't just about liberating us from class exploitation,' Milan said. 'This is what I'm writing about. Socialism must provide better lives for all men than a bourgeois democracy does. Otherwise, what is the point of it?'

'And what about women? When will our lives be better?'

On the morning of 21st August, Katya rose early for the dawn milking and slipped rubber boots onto her bare feet. She was the first to rise. Upstairs she could hear Jaroslav pulling on his overalls. Clouds were rolling down the mountainsides like laundry steam. In an hour, or maybe two, the mists would evaporate for another fine day. From the byre she could hear the garrulous groans of cows heavy with milk, waiting at the gate to be let in. Where was Marat? He should have been here on his bicycle by now. Katya, wearing only the boots, a long T-shirt of her father's, white cotton knickers, and a ribbon in her hair, strode out into the farmyard, Zora the dog and one of the puppies making circles at her heels.

With a squeal of rubber, Marat, on his bike, flew through the gate. His eyes were red and he was shouting something, but his words were unclear.

'What are you trying to say, Marat?' Katya said. 'Slow down and take a deep breath.' She rested a hand on the boy's bony shoulder. 'Try again.'

'They shot the lynx!' Marat said. 'The bastards shot it. I saw them shoot it.'

'Who shot it?' Katya asked.

'I saw them in a truck,' the boy said. 'One of them got out with a gun and shot it.'

'Who were they, Marat? Did you know them?'

'Soldiers,' he said. His shoulders were shaking with emotion. 'Russian soldiers.'

'Russians?'

Jaroslav appeared at the kitchen door. He wore an expression of alarm. 'What's that?' he asked.

'What's what?'

The farmer held up a finger for silence. 'That,' he said.

Drifting through the dawn air from the village sounded the monotonous but insistent ring of the town hall bell.

'There are tanks already in Prešov,' Hana Anya told them. 'I've heard there are a thousand tanks.'

The family was gathered in the farmhouse kitchen to digest the news.

'I knew it would happen,' Krystof rumbled. 'I knew it.'

Otillie was red around the eyes. 'It isn't fair,' she said. She

67

stood in bare feet on the cold stone floor of the kitchen, her toes curled up.

'We're not giving up without a fight,' Otillie's mother said, brandishing her invisible banner. 'The women of Tatras will march to Prešov. We shall stand in front of the tanks.'

'It's eighty kilometres to Prešov,' Jaroslav said. 'How will you get there? On the bus?'

'The women of the Tatras need to stay in the Tatras,' Krystof said. 'What good will it do to get shot? Eh? Tell me that.'

'They won't shoot us,' Hana Anya said. 'They won't shoot defenceless women.'

'Hana Anya, I'm as fond of you as my son is of your daughter, but you do talk nonsense,' Krystof said. He gave a long smoker's cough. 'First, if you are truly defenceless then you don't stand any chance of stopping a column of tanks. Second, if they didn't intend to shoot anyone, why have they come in tanks and not in Trabants?'

This intervention silenced the room for a while.

'All the same,' Milan said, 'I think the men should go to Prešov and see what is going on. If there is to be any fighting, it should be men fighting men.'

'Very nobly put,' Jaroslav said. 'But I don't think your argument will go down well with Hana Anya.'

'Nor me,' Katya said. 'I have a better idea. We don't need to go all the way to Prešov. The tanks will be on their way to Prague. We should rouse all the women we can to barricade the road near Švábovce where the track is too narrow for anything to drive around. There's a stretch where the ditches drop sharply three or four metres on either side of the track. If anything tries to drive us off the road there, we can jump down into the ditches. They can't follow us down. We can take the dray cart. We'll deliver the milk to the dairy and load up with women and children on the way back. It will be a peaceful barricade. No weapons. We won't be violent. We'll just ask to talk to them and try to persuade them to turn around. Even if we hold them up for a few hours it could give Mr Dubček a chance to do something.'

'To do what?' Krystof asked.

'I don't know. Something. Anything.'

Jaroslav snorted. 'No one is going anywhere until the cows have been milked,' he said.

'Of course.'

For an hour or two it might have been a picnic. A baker from Poprad brought a tray of loaves, and Jaroslav supplied a wheel of soft cheese. People were arriving in groups of a dozen or more, many with provisions of their own. A clutch of women from the collectives wearing dungarees and carrying pitchforks made the protest look like something from a Soviet poster.

'What's our plan?' people would ask. They sat on the narrow strip of yellow grass of the verge, happy to have found a protest location not too far from home.

'In a short time the tanks will come up this road on the way to Prague,' Katya said. 'We will be a peaceful demonstration. This is the power of communism. We act together. We will ask them very politely to turn back.'

The men eyed Katya suspiciously. Why was the plan being explained by a teenager with curls in her hair?

'You're headstrong, just like your mother,' a pig farmer from Poprad said. 'You always have been, and so was she. Frantiska always spoke about brewing up rebellion.'

'This isn't a rebellion,' said Katya, defensively. 'This is a respectful request.'

'You don't make respectful requests to a tank,' the pig farmer said.

'What if they don't want to turn back?' someone asked.

Hana Anya stepped in, raising a fist skyward. 'Then we stand in their way,' she cried. 'They can't go around us without falling off the edge.' She pointed to the steep escarpment on either side of the narrow track. 'If we stand still they can't go through. They must not pass.'

'They must not pass,' the crowd echoed.

It was a hot day to be outdoors. The steamy weather injected a sense of stupor into the crowd. The righteous energy that had infected the group in the morning was dissipating into the clear sky.

There was very little traffic on the road; when there was, it was local. Drivers would wind down their windows to discover what was going on, and to wish them well.

Around midday a fleet of around twenty Zil motorcars – black, four-door sedans – sped towards them from the direction of Prešov, throwing up a cloud of dust from the poorly made road. A group of protesters gathered uncertainly in the road, but when it became clear that the cars had no intention of stopping, or even of slowing down, they jumped to the edge of the road and the motorcade flew past.

'NKVD,' Krystof said, knowingly. 'The Russian secret police. You can always recognise them.'

'It will be easier when the tanks come,' Hana Anya declared.

'It will be the same, but slower,' Krystof said.

At two o'clock, it was necessary to send a delegation back to the farm for the afternoon milking. Katya, Marta and Marat took the dray cart. Jaroslav and Krystof stayed with the crowd at the roadside, along with Otillie and her mother.

'I hope you don't miss all the fun,' Hana Anya said, kissing Katya on both her cheeks.

'I hope not.' But Katya could feel foreboding in her blood. 'You will take care?'

'Of course.'

Cows are awkward creatures, Katya thought, not for the first time. They won't wait for anyone.

At four o'clock, when the last impatient beasts had pushed through the gate from the milking parlour on the Němcov farm, back towards the meadows, Katya unroped the dray horse. 'Come on,' she said. 'We're going back.'

Seven kilometres away on the Prešov road, there was at last some sign of activity. A column of Soviet tanks had appeared on the skyline. The dust cloud was visible long before the tanks themselves. It hung like a ribbon of smoke, following the dips and bends of the road like a ghostly aerial shadow.

'Oh shit,' one of the men in the protest said. He was passing round a set of old army binoculars. There were considerably more tanks than anyone had imagined. In the distance the rumble of engines was already audible.

'How many?' a voice asked.

'Too many to count,' the man with the binoculars shrugged. 'Two hundred? Four?'

Four hundred tanks?

'The men should drop back,' Otillie said, speaking to the crowd. 'This should be a women's protest.'

'I'm staying,' Jaroslav said.

'No!' Hana Anya stood with her legs apart like a gymnastics teacher. 'Men will be a provocation. We don't want any shooting.'

'Where is the Czechoslovak army?' Krystof asked. 'Why aren't they protecting us?'

'Confined to barracks,' a young woman told them.

'Really?'

Over the village of Švábovce a dense cloud of smoke and dust hung in the sky like the memory of a fire. It seemed to linger there for an age.

'Perhaps this is as far as they plan to travel today,' someone said.

There was a murmur of approval. Standing up to four hundred tanks no longer seemed the bright idea it had been at midday.

But in the distance the grumble of engines and the maelstrom of dust was growing.

'Look!'

The first of the tanks emerged from behind a low stand of trees, and turned the corner onto the narrow strip of road, just half a kilometre from the crowd. It was a squat metal beast, a giant insect of olive green, a T55 tank, all grinding gears and churning tracks, its gun barrel extended menacingly ahead like a monstrous phallus. With a groan from its motors, it started down the road towards them. Behind it another tank appeared, and another.

'I don't like the look of this,' Jaroslav said. A tone of fear had entered his voice.

'Then drop back,' someone cried.

'They can't mean to stop Mr Dubček like this,' Jaroslav said, incredulously. 'You can't stop a popular movement with tanks.'

'I think they mean to try,' Otillie said. She linked her arm with Jaroslav. 'Forward the revolution!' she shouted.

'Forward the revolution!'

On the Prešov road the column of tanks was building up speed. In the cupola of the first tank, two young soldiers in Soviet army uniforms stood, their heads and shoulders clear. A glance passed between them as they came to terms with the crowd of people ahead on the road. There was a grinding of machinery and an awful noise.

'They're slowing,' Hana Anya said.

And so they appeared to be. The lead tank seemed to check its speed, but it was now out of control. A cloud of dirt was ascending skyward. The tank was skewing across the road.

'Hold the line,' shouted Hana Anya. 'Forward the revolution!'

One by one, farmhands and tractor drivers, postmen, nurses, teachers and shopkeepers, the cluster of Slovaks on the road, began to link arms. An old woman with a thin scarf over her head thrust her face forward and closed her eyes. 'Death before freedom!' she shouted.

'Death before freedom,' echoed the crowd.

'That makes no sense,' Jaroslav said. 'Death *or* freedom. That makes better sense. Freedom or death. That's even better.

72

Freedom or death. Freedom or death.'

'Freedom or death,' came back the crowd.

'Freedom or death,' Jaroslav cried. 'Freedom or death.'

Behind the melee, Katya, Marat and Marta had arrived on the dray cart. The old horse, unused to the extra exertions in its day, had dropped his head and was snorting wearily. The dust cloud was starting to envelop them all.

'Hold the line!'

Ahead of them all, the column of tanks was getting closer. The moment of decision would be upon them soon. One of the young soldiers in the cupola of the lead tank was shouting something in Russian. There was a crunch of gears and the tank swerved, taking it clear of the narrow road, and sending it sliding down the rough scree of the bank. A cheer rose from the crowd.

'*Sacrebleu!*,' said Katya on the dray cart. 'They've crashed a tank.'

The T55 had lost its grip on the steep bank. The tracks roared, but to no avail. Like a useless dead weight, the tank slid downwards. Behind it, the whole military retinue was shuddering to a stop.

'Turn back,' Hana Anya cried. The crowd picked up her chant. 'Turn back. Turn back.'

Down the steep ditch, the lead tank had lost its battle with gravity. It rolled like a dying monster, toppling over and landing on its turret. From the tank behind, someone was shouting commands. A soldier leapt from a tank further down the column and ran forward. Time stopped.

In the dray cart, Katya's sense of foreboding had returned. 'I hope no one was hurt in that tank,' she whispered.

And then came the explosion. A dreadful thud, like a cracking in the Earth. The falling tank, upside down on its turret, had burst into flames. A second explosion followed, more terrifying than the first.

The crowd was shocked into silence. Could their peaceful

protest have claimed its first lives? A soldier emerged from the second tank waving a handgun. He was shrieking something at the crowd in Russian.

'We only want to talk,' Hana Anya called, but Krystof took her arm.

'I don't think he wants to talk,' he said.

The first soldier was joined by a second, also armed, also shouting in Russian.

'We should move,' Krystof said.

'Death or freedom, remember,' Hana Anya said.

'Freedom or death.'

'Freedom or death,' called the crowd.

The Russian soldier with the handgun paused his harangue. He straightened his arm and pointed the barrel of the gun directly at the crowd. '*Pyhat*,' he shouted. He waved the gun slowly from side to side. '*Chihteereh, tree . . .*'

'He's counting down,' Krystof said. 'Quick. We must leave.' He snatched at Hana Anya's arm and started to pull her away. 'Quick.'

'*Dvah*,' called the soldier. His hand-waving was coming to a stop. At the front of the crowd Krystof was breaking into a run.

'*Ahdeen*,' said the soldier. His eyes were cold. A fearful bang echoed in the space between the tanks and the civilians. The crowd was in retreat. Linked arms had been unlinked. Like a fluid, the mass of people was flowing away from the scene, down the sides of the road, some of them sliding down the scree. More soldiers had joined the man with the gun. More guns were being waved, warnings being shouted. But the Slovaks had got the message; they were in full flight.

Standing on the dray cart a short way back, Katya watched events unfold with increasing terror. A coil of black smoke was rising from the fallen tank. The dust from the Russian column was swirling like a fog. Caught on the road, like actors on a stage frozen in a tableau, were a cluster of soldiers with gun-arms outstretched. The protesters had vanished. Only one figure remained. Collapsed like a broken doll in the road lay the body of a man wearing the one-piece boiler suit of a farmer, a pool of dark blood around what was left of his head.

8

Katya, 1978

Frantiska, 1942

'I can scarcely believe I've found you,' the woman said. She sounded ecstatic. 'Frantiska's daughter! Here in Poprad. And I've found you. After all these years.'

They embraced warmly, and the woman kissed Katya on each cheek. 'You look so much like your mother!'

'I do,' Katya said. 'Everyone tells me so.'

They sat together across the table of a pavement café on Námestie Svätého Egídia – St Egid's square – the central public space in Poprad city. They ordered dark *turecká káva*, Turkish coffees, made the Czechoslovak way by slowly stewing the beans until the coffee emerged like soup, and when the waiter appeared with the cups they stirred in heaps of sugar.

'My name is Romula Sherevna,' the woman told Katya. 'It is so good of you to see me.'

'Believe me,' Katya said, 'the pleasure is all mine.' She was beaming as she spoke.

'My mother was Edile Mikulka,' Romula said, her inflection rising as if Katya might remember the name. 'She was from Lidice. She died in the massacre.' She paused at the word *massacre* as if the word itself deserved a solemn silence. 'I was nine years old.'

'I know the story,' Katya whispered.

Romula Sherevna was dressed in black, from her collar to her boots. She wore a hand-stitched frock of strong Hungarian cotton with heavy breast pockets that could carry a handful of spanners, should the occasion ever demand it. Her head was covered with a black linen scarf with flecks of red. It concealed her hair and framed her square face like a picture, lending her the doughty appearance of a middle-aged revolutionary.

Katya, now twenty-five, still dressed like a farm girl in dungarees that bore the memories of countless agricultural stains, and a man's shirt with sleeves rolled untidily up to the elbows. Her hair was still a swatch of untamed flax, random, uncoordinated curls escaping from an inadequate woollen hat. She still had childhood freckles on her cheeks, and her skin glowed the way a farmer's skin will always glow from the heat and cold of the seasons.

'I was a friend of your mother, Frantiska Dvorak,' Romula Sherevna said. 'A long time ago. She knew our family.'

'I know,' Katya said. She nodded gently.

'Then you have her gift?' Romula raised an eyebrow.

'My mother was nineteen when Obergruppenführer Heydrich was killed,' Katya said, avoiding the direct question. There was another long pause. Katya dropped her gaze for a moment, but then raised her face and looked Romula directly in the eye. She allowed the faintest of smiles to cross her lips.

'Dear God – you *do* have her gift.'

Into the square a retinue of Slovak child-soldiers, cadets in blue uniforms, wooden imitation rifles across their shoulders, came marching to the pressing rhythm of a snare drum. *P'tum, p'tum, prrrrrr'tum tum.* The two women paused their conversation while the parade passed by, rewarding the marchers with a soft ripple of applause, and then turning away as if they had never been there.

'I have some of my mother's memories,' Katya said. 'Not all of them.'

'But you remember Lidice?'

'Memory is the only thing anyone can ever have of Lidice,' Katya said. She stirred her coffee slowly, watching the swirls. 'Frantiska wasn't from Lidice,' she said. 'She was just a visitor. She had a boyfriend there. For a while.'

'Josef?'

'Yes.'

'He was a miner.'

Katya nodded.

'He was my brother.'

'He was.' Katya sipped her dark coffee. Memories were organising themselves in her head; she could sense them, as if each one had a physical presence in her mind, like the child-cadets who had marched through the square they were shuffling themselves into line, jostling for position, marching forward into bright daylight to the steady heartbeat of a drum. *P'tum. P'tum.* She knew this feeling. There were memories emerging from the dark ravines of her mind that she, Katya, had never accessed. They were images from her dreams – some sharp and clear like a painted landscape where every feature has its precise outline, and others insubstantial and vaporous – reminiscences that belonged to someone else, yet strangely too, belonged to her. For the thousandth time she asked herself if the dreams were real, and for the thousandth time the memories coalesced to confound her doubts. Colours began to flow into the images. Details moved into focus. Sounds drifted in – soft at first, but growing in volume until, BANG, she was there.

Lidice.

Lidice.

She could see it. Just as Frantiska, her mother, remembered it. Just as it appeared in her dreams. She could see it with Frantiska's eyes. A village, almost lost in the green rolling pastureland of Bohemia. A scattering of low, half-timbered, houses with whitewashed walls and red-tiled roofs. She could see the fields, small and square, designed and scaled for farming with horses and for harvesting with human energy and muscle. She could see the dirt lanes topped with limestone, overhung with beeches and twisted oaks. She could see the people. Poor folk. Farmers mainly. Miners. Women in cheap grey coats and scarves. Men in soft wide caps. Horses. Mules. Black bicycles that wobbled down the pot-holed tracks. 'I do have memories of Lidice,' she almost whispered to Romula. 'I remember Edile Mikulka, your mother. I remember you as well.'

'Your mother was in Lidice when the SS came.'

'Yes.' A tear had appeared in the corner of Katya's eye. 'She had said goodnight to Josef . . .'

'Yes . . .'

'She had tied her headscarf. It was late. She had a bicycle. She was ready to cycle back to Makotřasy to stay overnight with an aunt of Josef's.'

'Aunt Marissa,' Romula said.

'Why don't you tell me the story,' Katya whispered.

'She cycled a few metres, and her tyre burst,' Romula said.

She could remember it. The moonless June night. The dim lights from the little row of houses. The smell of hay. The silence. And far away where the hay fields met the sky, the faint glow of headlights appearing and disappearing behind trees.

Then the door of the Milkula house flew open and Edile was there in her nightdress and clutching her hand was the nine-year-old Romula. 'I'm worried,' Edile said. 'I don't like the lights.'

'It's all right,' Frantiska said. 'It'll be a military exercise.' Nazis playing war games, she had thought to herself.

'Take Romula,' Edile said. She pushed the girl's hand into Frantiska's hand. 'Take her with you to Aunt Marissa. Just for tonight.'

'My bicycle . . .' Frantiska protested.

'Leave it.' Edile was insistent. A note of pain had sounded in her voice. 'Just go. Please go. Now.'

'Are you sure?'

'Run.'

They could hear the motors now – a low and unfamiliar rumble. The sky was getting brighter. There was a bang. Perhaps a vehicle backfiring, but it made them all jump.

'Run!'

And so there was nothing for it. Frantiska squeezed Romula's hand and they ran.

'I had bare feet,' Romula said. 'But I knew the way. That was what saved us. Late at night we ran through a ploughed field. We ran faster than I had ever run. Probably faster than Frantsya had ever run. There were bright lights behind us. Shouts. Gunshots. But I knew the paths. Every path. Every step. Even in the dark. I knew where to cross the stream. I knew the only gate in the barley field. I never let go of Frantiska's hand.'

'I have the memory,' Katya half said, and now the tears were making her shake. 'I have it.'

Romula was weeping too. She leaned forward and wound her arm around Katya.

'You saved my mother's life,' Katya said.

'And she saved mine. Do you remember the soldier?'

Katya dropped her head. She was searching her memories. Frantiska's memories. 'The soldier?' Her tongue wet her lips. 'Yes.' The memory was back. 'Yes I do.'

'The Nazis had placed a lookout on every path out of town to catch people fleeing,' Romula said. 'We jumped a ditch and there he was. A German solider with a bright torch and a rifle.'

'He shouted something . . .'

'*Halt!* He shouted for us to stop. I was so scared I thought we were going to die there and then.'

'He was an old man,' Katya remembered. 'He had lines on his face.' She thought for a moment. The memory was still coming back. 'He looked more like someone's grandfather than a young stormtrooper. His chin was trembling. His hands were shaking. He whispered something . . .'

'*Run, you silly fools.* That's what he said. We ran past him and he touched my head – just a touch – and I thought it was a trick. I thought he was about to shoot us in the back. But we ran anyway.'

'Yes,' Katya said. Frantiska had seen the soldier's eyes in the light of his torch. He had been as frightened as they were.

'We stopped running after six or seven fields,' Romula said, 'and Frantsya gave me her shoes. They were way too big for me, but my feet were bleeding badly; I couldn't stand. When we got to Makotřasy I hid in the woodshed outside Aunt Marissa's apartment and I gave back the shoes. Your mother kissed me. *Be careful*, she said. And she pulled the shoes back on and disappeared into the night. I never saw her again.'

'Frantiska went back to Prague. She was working there, in a feed mill.' Katya could see the pictures in her head. 'She walked all night. She heard about the massacre on the radio a day or so later, the same way everyone else did. The Gestapo made a big thing of it. Dear God, they were proud to have massacred a village and razed it to the ground. Can you believe that? They wanted everyone to know what they'd done. They thought Lidice had helped the government-in-exile to assassinate Heydrich. God knows what gave them that idea. They rounded up all the men and shot them. One hundred and seventy-three men. Josef was among them.'

'My father too.'

'I'm sorry.' Katya leaned forward and rested her hand on Romula's forearm. 'And you know what happened to the children?'

'I do.' They were gassed.

'It was an awful time. Awful. Frantiska stayed in Prague for a year. She wasn't able to go back to Lidice. She didn't know what had happened to Josef, but she suspected. In the summer of 1943, when the Nazis were too busy on other fronts to worry too much about Czechoslovakia, she walked there from Prague. There were no buses. It took two days, walking in boots that were too tight for her feet. She couldn't walk on the main roads. It was too dangerous. She trekked across fields and hid behind hedges. She slept overnight in woods near Středokluky. And when she got to Lidice, well, you know this; it wasn't there. The village had gone.'

'I went to see it on my thirteenth birthday,' Romula said,

'after the war had ended. They had burned and flattened every building; they had taken away every brick and every stone. They even dug bodies out of the cemetery and cleared it. They diverted the river, moved the road. No trace remained. All the paths I knew as a child were gone. Every tree had been uprooted. I couldn't be sure where the village had been.'

'I suppose that was the point.' Katya looked away. St Egid's square was one of the prettiest places in Poprad. The shadow of the old baroque church was edging around towards them. A church bell was gently tolling the hour. 'How did you stay hidden?'

'It was too dangerous to stay with my aunt. A widow in a village five kilometres away took me in and looked after me. She had lost two sons and a husband in the war. I slept underneath her bed for three years alongside her commode, smelling her pee, and listening to her sob. She schooled me in her bedroom. I barely went outside except under cover of darkness. She was terrified of the consequences if we were caught.'

Katya rested her cup gently on the table. 'At least you survived.' She exhaled slowly. 'Why did you seek me out?'

'Two reasons,' Romula said. 'After the war I learned Frantiska had travelled east. She was one of the only people alive who had known me as a child, who had known my family. I went to the central office of registration in Prague in 1953 and discovered she had died in 1952.'

'She died having me.'

'But my mother had spoken to me of her gift. *Her memories last forever*, my mother said. I swore one day I would track down her daughter. When she was old enough. To see if she had memories of that time. And now here we are.'

'Your mother was a good woman,' Katya said. 'She treated Frantiska kindly. I don't have much to tell you about her. My mother didn't know her all that well. She made *kolaches* with apricots and cheese from her goats. Quite the most delicious *kolaches* Frantiska ever tasted, and I can taste them too, from

82

my mother's memories. She had a kindly smile.'

'I remember the *kolaches*,' Romula said.

'Your brother was a kind boy. Josef. A clever boy. He was younger than my mother, but he had a good heart. That's what Frantiska would say.'

A tear appeared in the older woman's eye. She dabbed at it with a napkin. 'Thank you.'

'After Frantiska discovered Lidice had vanished, she didn't stop walking. She didn't turn back to Prague. She wanted to travel west, but it was too dangerous. West would have taken her into Nazi Germany, south would have led to Austria, and north to Poland. None of them was safe. She was looking for a place war had forgotten. So she headed east, to Brno, and then to Poprad. She walked for seven weeks, sleeping in ditches, in barns, in old churches. Finally she reached the mountains and found work on a farm, milking cows, and she ended up marrying the farmer's son. And here I am to prove it.' Katya held her hands out with palms facing upwards. 'And I'm a farmer too. No longer on the same farm, sadly; but I'm a dairy manager. I work for a collective near Gerlachov. Not far from here.'

'Is your father still alive?'

'He was shot by a Russian solider in 1968 for standing in the way of a tank.'

The two women sat for a while in silence. 'Shall I order us a pastry?' Romula asked.

'Why not?'

The evening shadows were growing.

'What was your second reason for coming to see me?' Katya asked. 'You said there were two.'

'I thought perhaps I might do you a favour,' Romula said. 'Your mother was kind to me when I was a child. And I owe her something for saving my life. I can repay her, perhaps, by doing something for you.'

Katya dropped her eyes. 'What do you have in mind?'

'I work for the party now. I work for the Ministry of Labour in Bratislava,' Romula said. 'It's a steady job. A little dull, but what job isn't?' She leaned forward and let her voice drop. 'I can find work for you and your husband near Bratislava.'

'It's a very kind thought,' Katya said. 'But I don't know if I want to move. Our little village is perfectly lovely. Bratislava is three hundred and fifty kilometres away. All our friends and family are here in the Tatras.'

'Yes,' Romula said. Her dark eyes seemed to blaze. She nodded slowly. 'I understand that. However, you also live three hundred and fifty kilometres from our only border with the West. Think about that. From my office window in Bratislava I can see Austria. From my window I can see freedom. Just a thought.' She drew a piece of paper from her bag and pushed it into Katya's hand. 'Here is my address. When you're ready, give me a call.'

9

Katya, 1979

The small town of Záhorská Ves lies in a winding crook of the Morava River, a thumb-shaped pinch of land that pokes the great river out of the way as if it were an unruly hosepipe. In a thousand years' time, if left to its own devices, the river will surely discover the shortcut and will snip off the bend, creating an ox-bow where the waters used to flow. When that happens, Záhorská Ves will find itself transplanted from one country into another, from Slovakia into Austria, for the border is a fluid line drawn down the centre of the river. To the west of Záhorská Ves (and to the north, and to the south too, given the curious geography) lies the Austrian market town of Angern an der March. To the east lies Slovakia, and Romania, and Ukraine, and Russia, and in 1979, when this chapter unfolds, these lands were the USSR and the nations of the Warsaw Pact, timid subjects of a regime run from Moscow, whose influence and tanks kept any rumblings of dissent in check.

Katya and Milan stood on a small rise and considered the view, looking across the Morava River to the rooftops and undulating landscapes of a different world. An Austrian man was fishing from the far bank, resting on a low stool underneath a willow, a straw hat pulled close over his eyes.

'How narrow the river is here,' Katya said, her voice sounding strange this close to the border.

'Thirty metres,' said Milan. 'No more.' His voice was changed too. He was watching the Austrian fisherman, transfixed by his patient demeanour.

Thirty metres. You could throw a pebble from the East

into the West. Somewhere on its trajectory, it would cross the hidden line. It would be a Slovak stone, and in an instant it would become an Austrian one. A sparrow could peck seeds from one side of the river, and then fly to catch a worm on the other side. No paperwork would be required. No bullets would fly. Thirty metres. But not an easy thirty metres for a person. A patrol track ran the length of the river, faithfully following the curve of the bank. Between the track and the river the view was interrupted by an unruly construction of barbed wire and posts. There were loose barbed wire strands and tight strands, some horizontal and some diagonal, maybe thirty or more, stretched out between T-shaped wooden posts, three metres high. Behind this forbidding barrier lay a short stretch of wilderness, tall grasses and weeds, and behind this, another barbed wire edifice, an echo of the one before. The whole structure looked hastily made, like a fortress built by a tramp. It looked as if it might have been constructed by idle schoolboys, not by the fearsome border force, the Pohraniční Stráž. There was still tree bark on some of the posts, and the posts themselves were irregular in size. Many leaned this way or that. But the oddly shambolic construction didn't make the fence any less fearsome. No one, you would conclude, could climb this barrier without injury. As if to underline this point, a sign with two red bolts of lightning read, POZOR! ELEC-TRICKÝ OHRADNÍK. And not far away a lookout guard in a high command post watched idly as if willing Katya and Milan to tackle the fence, and maybe to give him some target practice.

'You would need to be a pole-vaulter,' Milan said.

'You could vault the first fence, but how would you manage the second?'

They stood and contemplated the challenge.

'This is the closest I've ever been to the West,' Milan said. He was still watching the angler.

On the far bank the fisherman had a bite. He tugged on his line and started to spin the spool. 'An Austrian fish,' Milan whispered with a hint of reverence. 'A free fish.'

'A dead fish,' Katya echoed. 'Or it will be soon. More than four hundred people have died trying to cross the Morava River. A girl in town told me. Shot, drowned, or electrocuted.'

They watched the Austrian man unhook the fish and slip it into a bucket. He never glanced their way.

'I wonder how many of those dead people were crossing from the West to the East,' Milan asked. He shrugged. 'This is what they tell us. This is what it's for, all this security, all this wire; to stop Western spies.'

'Perhaps they're less stupid than we are,' Katya said. 'Maybe they don't risk their lives.' Katya was thinking of her father, and the pool of blood that swelled around his head on the Prešov-to-Poprad road. 'Maybe our lives are cheap.'

'Maybe they are.'

They linked arms and picked their way back down the path towards the town. 'They say you only need to see the border once,' Milan said, a tone of bitterness creeping into his voice. 'Now I understand why. See it once and abandon any dream of swimming across.'

The farmhouse was a kilometre from the river. It was a rectangular concrete block of four small apartments, homes for the farm manager and his family, for the ploughman, for the principal farm technician, and for the beef and dairy operations manager – Katya Hašeka. Compared to the Němcov farmstead, it was an austere home. Inside, the walls were still rough cement. 'If you want to paint it,' the manager of the collective had told Katya, 'you can pay for it yourself.'

They could have enjoyed the more luxurious apartment in the town of Suchohrad that came with Milan's position as production technician at the paper mill, but the distance was too far for Katya to consider. 'I need to be close to the cows,' she had said. But she had given Milan a look. *We need to be close to the border*, was what she meant.

'I can walk to the river every day,' she told Milan. 'I can

watch the guard patrols, work out their routines.'

'Maybe there is somewhere we could tunnel,' Milan offered. 'Somewhere out of sight of a guard tower. We only need to wriggle through to the riverbank and after that we can swim.' But he sounded unconvinced, even by his own suggestion.

Why had they done it? Why had they moved? It was a question Katya asked herself almost every day, and so often had she turned the reasons over in her head, that as the weeks passed, she lost track of the answers she had given herself. 'What brought you here?' her colleagues in the collective would ask. 'It was good for my career,' she would reply. 'What is there in Poprad?' And they would nod knowingly at this. What, indeed, was there in Poprad?

'Mountains,' one colleague suggested.

'What can you do with mountains? Here you have the city. The lights. The shops. The bars.'

But the bus ride to Bratislava was an uncomfortable trip, and they had no money to spend in the shops or the bars.

'I know why you came,' said a sour-faced man with cigarette-breath, from the Bratislava cheese factory. 'You came to be close to the West.'

'The West?' Katya contrived to look surprised.

'One day, you hope, the Pohraniční Stráž will take their eyes off the border for an hour, and in that hour you'll be on the road to Vienna. Tell me if I'm lying.'

'You don't like my idea?' Milan said.

'Which idea?'

'For a tunnel? A tunnel under the wire?'

She took his hand. 'I don't like your idea,' she answered him. 'But that's OK.' She kissed him lightly on the tip of his nose. 'I don't like tunnels. Take me shopping. I have a better suggestion.'

In the old town of Bratislava, down a narrow bricked street that had miraculously escaped the wrecking ball of the communist town planners, they found themselves in front of a shop selling Hungarian bric-a-brac and Russian antiques. 'Look at that,' Katya said. 'You can buy me that.' She pointed in the window to a gold-and-red paper lampshade – an almost perfect sphere decorated with Chinese characters and supported inside by a series of regularly placed wire hoops.

'It's a Chinese lampshade? You want that?'

'I do.'

Inside the shop the assistant detached the lampshade from the bulb, and with a gentle press of her hand she flattened it so the paper skin folded and every wire ring collapsed; it became no more than a hoop – a wire-and-paper disc less than a centimetre high. The assistant slid the flat object into a bag.

'Are you sure you like it?' Milan asked. 'We have no money to spare for luxuries.'

'I love it,' Katya said. 'And so will you soon.' She gave him an enigmatic smile and whispered the rest into his ear. 'This lampshade,' she whispered, 'is not a luxury. It is our escape route to the West.'

In Záhorská Ves there were cows to milk, and a small apartment to furnish. The collective made Katya and Milan a gift of a bed, and they built a table from a loading pallet, and bought chairs with their first month's wages. Milan worked the night shift from seven at night to four in the morning, and when he came home at five o'clock, Katya would already be out delivering milk churns to the cheese factory. At eight o'clock he would find her back in the byre raking up the soiled straw.

'How was paper making?' she would ask him.

'Fine. How was milk making?'

They shared half an hour for breakfast. It was almost the only time they had together. He would go back to the apartment to sleep. She would do paperwork, and prepare cattle feed, and get ready for the afternoon milking. When she got back to the apartment at lunchtime, he would be asleep.

'This isn't the life I imagined,' he would tell her.

'It won't be forever.'

At weekends Katya worked a half-shift and help came in from the village for milking. The paper mill closed.

In the loft of the hay barn, on a platform of hay bales, they started their project.

'It must be two thousand cubic metres,' Katya told Milan. She sat on a bale in the hayloft writing numbers onto a sheet of paper, while Milan paced out the dimensions of the barn.

'Two thousand!' he exclaimed. 'That's impossible.'

'I've done this before, remember. I may be a milkmaid in Záhorská Ves but Heloise was a mathematician in Annonay. Jacques-Étienne would send up balloons of different sizes, with weights attached to see how much each balloon could carry, and Heloise would do the calculations. Depending upon how much the balloon itself weighs, we shall need about two thousand cubic metres of hot air. Very much less, and it won't carry us. The Montgolfier balloon was seventeen hundred cubic metres.'

'And it carried two people and a heavy basket,' Milan said.

'It didn't have a basket. It had a gondola.'

'And a brazier, and fuel. We are, neither of us, especially heavy. We won't need a basket or a gondola, we won't carry anything more than we're wearing, and we won't need a brazier or fuel. If we have a fire blazing in the sky it's going to attract every border guard for twenty kilometres. We must get the balloon as hot as we can before we cut free and it has to carry us over the border with no more heat. We can allow, perhaps, a small tin bucket of hot coals to keep the air from cooling too fast. That's all. We have the advantage of being close to the river. We won't need to stay airborne for long. So we need to pick a night with a strong steady breeze, and no moon. We'll hang on a rope underneath. We'll wear black so they won't see us.'

'Fifteen hundred then,' Katya said. She was scribbling out numbers with a pencil.

'How big does that make it?' Milan asked.

'Give me a moment.' She was adding a column of figures. 'Fourteen metres,' she said. 'Just over.'

'Fourteen metres? In diameter?'

'Just over.'

Milan stopped pacing. 'That's enormous.'

'Balloons are big.' Katya made a shrug.

'Well here's our problem,' he said. 'This barn is ten metres wide. We can't build a fourteen-metre Chinese lantern in a ten-metre barn. And the door is four metres wide. Even if we could build it, we couldn't get it out of the door without folding it.'

'Then we have to be able to fold it,' Katya said. 'Perhaps we can elongate it. The Montgolfier balloon wasn't a sphere. It was a cylinder with a rounded top and bottom. Maybe we could build a ten-metre cylinder tapered off at the top.'

'How do we get it out of the door?'

'It'll be made of paper. With thin wire hoops. We can roll it up.'

Milan looked thoughtful. 'The paper comes in ninety-centimetre rolls,' he said.

'How heavy is it?'

'We should go for the brown parcel paper. It's heavy but it's strong. It weighs 200 grammes per square metre. But there's 250 metres in a roll.'

'Good.' Katya was doing more sums, but she looked worried. 'A ten-metre cylindrical balloon will need to be over sixty metres tall,' she said. 'That's way too tall. The top will cool too fast.' Her pencil was scribbling numbers. 'Also,' she said, 'it would need around two thousand square metres of paper, not allowing for any overlapping. We'd need at least ten rolls.'

Milan sat down heavily beside her. 'Katya, my sweet,' he laid an arm over her shoulder. 'This idea is crazy. I can't possibly steal ten rolls of paper.'

'Besides,' she said, 'the paper alone would weigh four hundred kilogrammes, and there would be extra weight for the wire hoops and the glue, and the ropes, and the bucket of hot coals, and us. That's over half a tonne. It's way too heavy.'

'This plan isn't going to work,' Milan said. 'We should think again about a tunnel.'

'This plan will work,' Katya gave him a look. 'We need lighter paper. And we need a more spherical balloon. What is the lightest paper you make?'

'We do a very light paper for air mail – sixty grammes per square metre. But it really isn't very strong.'

'It will have to do.' Already Katya was crossing out numbers. 'And forget the cylinder idea – it's too inefficient. We need to build a spherical balloon, as round as possible, fourteen metres wide. That only needs 615 square metres of paper – so only three rolls to steal – and it will weigh . . .' she ran her pencil down the calculation, '. . . under forty kilos. One tenth as heavy. That would work.'

'Easy for you to say; it isn't you that has to steal the paper,' Milan said with a groan.

'When can you get the first roll?'

10

Katya, 1980

G unter Dross was the manager of the paper mill at Such-ohrad. He was an East German. In his twenties, Dross had driven a Panzer VI Tiger tank with the 101st Schwere Panzer-Abteilung in Northern France, and in battle at Villers-Bocage, he had been part of the tank unit that destroyed an entire column of the British 7th Armoured Division. In the scrabble of fighting that took place after the British unit had been defeated, when there were still combatants loose in the field, he flung out his hand to catch a grenade thrown by an enemy soldier, and as his arm flexed to send it back, the grenade exploded, but only partially. He took shrapnel in his forearm, elbow and shoulder, leaving his right arm useless, and he lost one eye. Now he wore a patch over the eye, and the dead hand he would tuck into the pocket of his overalls as if it was simply resting.

Disability had made Dross bitter. At the age of sixty he managed the mill by never sitting down. He was a prowler. He would stalk the corridors and the plant like a villain from a spy film, his right hand tucked awkwardly away, his left hand waving, his face furious, his eyebrows trembling. At any moment, on any floor, Dross could be (and probably was) just around the corner, his antennae drawing him unerringly to malfunctioning machinery, or to subversive conversations.

'Hašek!' Dross would bark, if ever Milan relaxed for just a moment. (Dross mistrusted all Slovaks. They were insufficient-ly communist, he felt. Slovaks had held up the liberation of the country in 1968 when the fool Dubček almost handed the country to the Americans. And Slovaks, he was sure, had been less than enthusiastic in their support for the Reich.) 'Hasek!'

'Yes, Comrade.'

'Why is our production failing on plant three? Why is there oil on the factory floor? Why are the rollers jamming?'

'The irons are too hot, Comrade. The oil filters don't work at that temperature. The oil leaks. The rollers jam. And production falls.'

Dross glowered. He never liked clear responses to his questions. 'Then cool the irons, Comrade.'

'We are cooling them.'

'So get on with it.'

The paper mill at Suchohrad was not a glowing example of communist modernity. Much of the machinery was a hundred years old. There were brass wheels, steel cogs and iron gears that dated from the time of the Austro-Hungarian dual monarchy, and very few parts of the plant had been updated in the twentieth century. In the timber yard the cords of timber were delivered by trucks, where once they had floated down the Morava River. The drum that stripped the bark from the logs was an ancient contraption that still ran on steam power. There was a machine to convert the logs into chips; this machine had come from Germany in 1931. It burned so much oil, the air around the plant was black with diesel smoke. The woodchips were shovelled into the digester using bulldozers from China, but only because the purpose-made mechanical shovellers no longer worked and no one was left who understood how to repair them. The bulldozers were messy, and slow, and wood was wasted, but what else could they do? The rollers, where wet pulp would be rolled into paper, had once been machined to a level of smoothness that would ensure perfect, consistent rolls; but now there were tiny pits in the surface, and the wheels were fractionally misaligned, so the paper that coiled onto the dryers at Suchohrad was of the poorest quality Milan had ever seen. Some papers would never sell. They had a warehouse full to the rafters with rolls of newsprint that no printer wanted because (the newspapers said) it tore so often, it would damage their machines. Offices wanted rolls of computer paper, punched and perforated for their new Japanese printers, but this was outside the capability of the Suchohrad machines. Instead, they manufactured the kinds of industrial paper used for wrapping, for toilet paper, and for routine office paperwork.

'I want to check our paper stocks, Comrade Dross,' Milan told the manager one morning. 'I am anxious that the central committee might carry out a quality inspection and I don't want us to fail.'

'We check our stock every week,' Dross grumbled. 'Stock isn't the problem. Our production is. If we don't improve, then the party will close us down.'

'We only check recent production. We have rolls that have been stored for months. Some for years. We should check their quality. If they have any damage we should destroy them and clear some warehouse space.' Milan let his eyebrows drop to suggest warning. 'If an official inspection finds damaged rolls on our shelves, it would be worse than finding low stock levels.'

The plant foreman looked doubtful. 'And what would we do with the damaged rolls?'

'We would destroy them.'

Dross's features were quivering. There was some logic in what the young man was suggesting. 'I will assist you.'

Was he being helpful or suspicious? Milan couldn't tell. They started in a long, cold warehouse with wooden walls through which the wind leaked. A girl of around fourteen, freshly out of school, was assigned to write things down. She stood nervously with a pencil poised over a pad of paper. A quality inspector was called for. Two arrived. They were women in their fifties (both of them), each with a stern and unforgiving gaze. They started with the newsprint. Milan would pull a roll from the shelf, examine it, and pass it to the quality inspectors, who would tut and sniff and tear pieces off to hold up to the light.

95

'Damp,' Milan said. 'This roll is damp.' He pushed the paper towards them. The women conducted their review. 'Damp,' they both concurred.

'All the rolls on this shelf. Damp.'

Three men were called up from the loading bay to carry away the damaged rolls. A stock manager and an accountant were summoned to make corrections to the ledgers. Two accountants arrived. Each wrote numbers in a separate book and glanced at the other with suspicion every time a change was made. A manager from the shop floor arrived with an assistant, and the party convener. The deputy in charge of storage and paper control, a Russian suspected of being NKVD, appeared, his moustache bristling.

'God's bones, it shouldn't take a hundred people to throw away a roll of wet paper,' Dross barked. He waved his good arm. 'If you must stay, stand well back.'

Forty-eight rolls of newsprint paper were discarded. They were carried away and stacked neatly onto a pallet. A committee was convened to decide what to do with them. 'Can they be recycled into new paper?' someone asked.

'I'm afraid not,' Milan said. 'They will make the paper too soft.'

'What then?'

'We can't allow customers to have them,' Milan said. 'It would damage our reputation. We should either put them into the furnace for the steam boiler . . .' he paused to look at the anxious expressions on the faces of the committee, '. . . or we give our valued workers the opportunity to take a roll home. For domestic purposes only.'

This was clearly a popular alternative. A free gift is a free gift, and even twenty-five kilogrammes of damp paper on a roll had some value – however marginal – especially to people whose pay was extremely low. 'We should put the decision to the management committee,' someone said.

'I think, under the circumstances, given that the paper is

damaged and of negligible value, Comrade Dross should make the decision,' Milan said.

Dross liked this. He stabbed the air with his good hand. 'We will give the workers on the plant floor the opportunity to take one roll each,' he announced. 'And each person on this committee may have two rolls.'

It was a popular decision. The quality check began again with renewed enthusiasm. By the end of the afternoon, over four hundred rolls of paper had been removed from the shelves. The rolls were heavy. Every worker, it appeared, was struggling home with at least one when the shift ended.

'Two rolls of sixty-gramme paper,' Milan announced when he arrived back at the farmhouse on his bicycle that night. He carried them into the hall and leaned them carefully against a wall.

Katya was impressed. 'You stole two rolls?' She kissed him firmly on the lips.

'No stealing was involved,' Milan said. There was pride in his voice. 'They are a gift from the mill.'

'We need one more roll.'

'I already bought one from a colleague.' Milan gave Katya a squeeze and almost danced into the room. 'We're on our way!'

'Three o'clock in the morning is our best time,' Katya said. 'When everyone is asleep. On a cloudy night with no moon and a light, steady wind from the east.'

'A week on Wednesday,' Milan said. 'Weather permitting.'

A week on Wednesday it rained. They sat in the barn and listened to the clatter of rain on the tin roof. The following day was dry, and the wind was in the right direction, but it was too strong. It felt almost like a gale. By Friday the skies were clear and there was a sliver of moon.

'I'm not too worried about the moon,' Milan said. 'So long as there's cloud. But it's way too clear. They will spot us in the searchlights.'

They waited for a month. The spirit gum that glued the sheets of paper began to relax its hold. Milan stayed up late for several nights making repairs. 'I think we should paint the balloon black,' he said.

'Won't it mean more weight?'

'Not much. And it will make it harder to spot us in a dark sky.'

'We should make a fishnet too,' Katya said. 'The Montgolfier balloons were contained within a net of string to stop them overfilling and tearing.'

'We can make one ourselves out of fishing twine,' Milan said. 'I like the idea. It will be negligible weight.'

They spent the month knotting twine in their bedroom until their fingers bled from the effort. 'Thank goodness we had these extra weeks,' Milan said. 'This will give the balloon so much more strength.'

The finished fishnet slid over the body of the balloon like a string vest. 'We can tie our ropes to it,' Katya said, 'one each side for balance. We can hang onto the ropes like acrobats.'

When the first moonless night came there was barely a breath of wind. Katya was getting anxious. 'We can't take any risks,' Milan would say. 'Everything has to be perfect. The wind. The moon. The cloud. We need an easterly wind or we'll go up and come down in Záhorská Ves.'

They waited a second month. It was May. 'Soon the skies won't be dark enough,' Milan grumbled. They strengthened the netting. Every day was hot. Every morning the sun rose into a clear sky and clear skies were unhelpful. Katya awoke on the morning planned for their escape, and from the window she could see clouds. 'The weather's changed,' she told Milan.

Her heart was fluttering through the day. She milked the cows, and shovelled slurry, and took the milk to the dairy. Milan was on an early shift. He would be home by eight at night. They would lie together on the hay bales waiting for perfect darkness, measuring the wind.

But beware of your plans, Katya would often think. Plans can liberate you but they can also be a trap.

At half past seven, alone in the apartment, she pulled on her black overalls and walked the kilometre from the farmhouse to the hay barn, and right away all was not well. The barn door was ajar. There were soft noises within. 'Who's there?' She swung a torch.

From the hayloft there came a soft groan. A scrabble.

'Who is it?'

A young man's face appeared above the hay. He had bare shoulders.

'Franz?' Katya said. Her heart was rattling in her chest.

'Comrade Haseka,' Franz replied.

He was a farm hand from the Záhorská Ves collective – no older than sixteen. Maybe younger. He had been digging ditches all through the spring, out in the sunshine with the land crew. Katya knew him. She had treated the blisters on his hands when digging had worn away his skin. 'What are you doing here?'

And then a second face. Of course. A girl from the town, her hands protecting her naked breasts.

'I'm sorry if I interrupted you,' Katya said. 'Would you like to finish whatever you were doing, and leave me to lock up the barn?' Her voice sounded sterner and more disapproving than she intended. 'Please,' she added.

'Please don't tell my father,' the girl said.

Katya tried to think who the girl's father was, but couldn't find a face. 'I wouldn't dream of it.'

They were scrambling now to get dressed. They had been lying, in the semi-darkness, on the thin covering of hay that Milan had scattered to conceal the balloon. Had they seen it? Perhaps not. Perhaps they only had eyes for each other.

The girl was pulling on shoes. Franz was already on the ladder. Katya made the mistake of swinging the torch up to light his way. 'Thank you,' he said, and then his hands were on the balloon, on the circumference of wire and the netting, and the black paper, and string, that had become exposed by their actions in the hay. 'What's this?' he asked. There was suspicion in his voice.

'It is summershading for the youngstock,' Katya said. But the answer had taken too long. She swung the torch away.

'Give me some light. What is this, Eva?'

The girl was descending a second ladder. 'Paper from my father's mill,' she said.

'Your father's mill?' And now Katya knew her. 'You're Eva Dross? Gunter Dross's daughter?'

'Your husband works for my father,' the girl said. 'If you say a word about this I'll make sure he loses his job.'

'I don't intend to say anything to anyone.' Katya's heartbeat was so fierce she thought they might hear it. 'Here,' she threw the girl a heavy key. 'If you two want to fuck, you can fuck in my house.'

Eva picked up the key. 'Perhaps we will.' She smirked.

Franz was still on his ladder. 'Wait,' he said. He swept at the hay with his arm. 'I want to see what this is.'

'It's none of your business,' Katya said.

Another mistake. The boy's curiosity was aroused still further. The light in the barn was thin, but there was enough illumination to make out some of the detail. He brushed away more hay. 'It's big,' he said.

'Cows are big.'

'Not this big. Shit!' He turned to face Katya. 'I know what it is.'

'What is it?' Eva asked.

'You two fuckers are planning an escape.'

'That's nonsense,' Katya blurted.

'You are! You're planning to fly away in this, aren't you?'

'What is it?' Eva demanded again.

'Look,' Katya said, the stress appearing in her voice, 'you keep quiet about this and I'll keep quiet about you and Eva.'

100

Franz waved this concession away. 'Oh, I don't think so,' he said. 'There are good rewards for finding traitors. And who will believe your stories anyway? Who believes a spy?' He dropped from the ladder to the floor. 'Besides, Eva may not want her father to know, but what do I care? Girls like a boy with a reputation.' He pushed past Katya, grabbing Eva's hand as he went. 'Come,' he said.

'We still have this,' Eva said in a small voice, holding up Katya's key.

Franz regarded it and cast a look back at Katya. 'I do so hate to be interrupted, don't you? You may have bought yourself an hour. If I was you, I'd run as far from Záhorská Ves as you can.' He threw his arm around Eva and steered her out of the barn.

Milan was there ten minutes later.

'We have to go tonight,' Katya urged. She told him about Franz and his threats. 'We can't risk them telling the border guards.'

'Or her father,' Milan said. 'We may not have much time.'

'So what do we do?'

'We fly.'

It was dusk. With only the distant lights of the Austrian town lighting up the sky, they carried the balloon outside and unfolded it onto a shoulder-high wooden frame supported on hay bales. Both wore black. They had soot smeared on their faces. Milan lit a charcoal brazier underneath the belly of the balloon, and worked a leather bellows. 'We have enough charcoal to roast an ox,' he said.

'We'll need it.'

It didn't take long to light the blaze. With both of them pumping air into the fire, the flames rose high. They propped up the roof of the balloon with light wooden battens, to let the warm air in.

'Nothing's happening!'

'It will.'

And as they spoke, something *was* happening. The great Chinese lantern was starting to swell. The top of the balloon was lifting and the sides were rocking.

The excitement was almost terrifying. 'Pump harder!' With a set of bellows each, they bent to pump. The charcoal was roaring. Katya shovelled on more fuel.

'Don't let the balloon catch light,' Milan warned. They had a tin frame around the mouth of the balloon, and Milan had a water spray ready for this eventuality, and he used it to cool the rim. A great energy had filled the construction, and like a wakening beast it was lifting itself. Katya could feel air rushing past her into the belly of the balloon. 'More heat. More heat!'

It was fearsome. They pulled harnesses over their shoulders and clipped themselves onto the ropes as the huge, wobbling edifice began to lift itself clear of the hay bales on which it had rested. 'It's going to work,' Katya almost cried, trying to control the volume of her voice.

Somewhere they could hear a dog barking.

'Try not to wake the neighbours,' Milan said. It had happened more quickly than either of them had expected. The balloon, already, was wholly afloat, pulling at the anchor ropes. He picked up his bellows. 'We'll give it one more minute and then we go.'

Katya strained to manage a final effort on her bellows. It was like feeding a dragon. The fire was so fierce she could no longer stand close enough.

'Leave it. We're going.'

From somewhere they could hear a bang – like a door slamming.

A tin feed bucket hung on thin metal chains beneath the gaping, hungry mouth of the balloon. With a shovel, Milan scooped out a load of red charcoals from the brazier and dropped them into the bucket. It should, they hoped, be hot enough to keep them climbing.

They could hear the sound of a car engine – rather too close for comfort. Who would have a car on a dairy farm at this time of night? Was this the Pohraniční Stráž?

'It may just be Mr Lukaczs,' Katya said. Lukaczs was a mechanic who lived with a family on the farm. 'He has a motorcycle.'

'That doesn't sound like a motorcycle.'

For a moment they froze – listening to the sound. The reflection of headlights showed on the side of the barn.

'Hold tight.' Milan pulled the guy ropes free of the anchors, and with a lurch they were suddenly airborne, each swinging from a rope harness, one each side of the balloon. It was a curious sensation. A year of fear and anticipation distilled into an enormous wave of emotion as the huge lantern above their heads rose higher, pulling upwards like a giant bird escaping from a cage, dragging them up into the dark void. Katya grasped her rope tightly. 'Are you OK?' she called.

'Yes! You?'

She was twisting slowly, facing the wrong way. She could barely see Milan. Was there enough wind? They hadn't checked. She had felt the breeze pulling on the balloon, but now they were aloft there was no sense of movement. She felt suspended in a dark vacuum. A quiet dark vacuum. Beneath them, small, occasional lights. The dim street lights of Záhorská Ves. But the silence was all enveloping. And they were climbing. Climbing. There seemed little doubt of that.

Somewhere she could hear a voice shouting. Was it Milan? She strained to twist herself around. Far below a small light had appeared. Someone was waving a torch.

'Hush . . .' She could just make out Milan's whisper. 'Stay quiet.'

The voice again. A man's voice. A car was speeding down the farm track. They could see the headlights.

And suddenly the lights were fading. And so too was the torchlight, and the street lights of Záhorská Ves, and the subversive lights of Angern an der March. 'What's happening?' She barely dared to mouth the words.

Another shout came from below, but it sounded a very long way off.

'The cloud,' she heard Milan say.

The cloud. The cloud would save them. It was all around them like the fog in a graveyard.

And now what could they do? They hung on ropes. Living pendulums in the dark and the mist. It was like this, Katya thought, for Jacques-Étienne Montgolfier, the first man to rise into the sky beneath a balloon. Or for Pilâtre de Rozier and François Laurent le Vieux Marquis d'Arlandes who made the first untethered flight, watched by the King, and by a crowd of thousands, and in that crowd a young woman called Heloise.

She had always wanted to do this. Katya understood this as the cold mist folded around her legs and arms. She had always envied Jacques-Étienne. She had always wanted to fly.

From somewhere far below there was a cracking noise, like a log snapping in a fire.

'I think they're shooting at us,' Milan called.

There was another bang. And then another. Katya was strangely unafraid. 'They can't see us,' she shouted.

It was too peaceful, dangling from the balloon, to be afraid. Were they heading the right way?

They were puppets, suspended in a slow tableau, swaying with the motion of the great Chinese lantern above their heads. There were no lights. There was no north, no south, nor east, nor west, nor up, nor down. There was only mist and darkness. If she closed her eyes Katya could feel like a child on a swing rope, swaying slowly this way and that. '*Dobrú noc má milá,*' she found herself singing, the words of an old Slovak lullaby. '*Nech sa ti snivajù o mne sny,*' 'Goodnight my darling, good-night my love, I hope I'm in your dreams.'

Were they moving? Was the wind blowing? The noises from

below had stopped. The silence wrapped around them like a blanket.

'I think we're dropping,' Milan said, after a while.

A bright light appeared some way away. A searchlight. It was combing the sky.

'They're looking for us.'

A black balloon in a black sky. Let them look.

And then there came a barrage of shots. '*Sacrebleu!*' The whistle of a bullet flew close past Katya's head.

'Are you all right?'

'Yes.'

Ba ba babababababa ba ba – the urgent, uncompromising call of a machine gun. *Bababbabbabba.* Was it firing at them? Perhaps it was. But it was firing this way and that. High and low. It was scattering the sky with shot.

And still Katya was unafraid. She could fall hundreds of feet to her death. She could be torn apart by gunshots. She could spend her life in a Russian gulag. But the sky takes away your fear. She had known one death – she had memories of the death of Heloise. But one death is enough. It had robbed her of her curiosity, and strangely, it seemed, of her fear.

'We've been hit,' Milan shouted. 'The balloon has been hit.'

They were falling. Air was rushing upwards into the balloon.

'Unclip yourself and hold tight. We may need to drop and run.'

Katya fumbled for her clip. The balloon seemed to wobble. A long strip of paper had come loose, and was uncoiling like a snakeskin. She could see naked wire hoops, and these were bending. Their fishnet was pulling apart. They were falling faster.

Maybe this was it. Maybe this was death. Maybe her long memories had run their span. If that was so, then it was so. She had seen a lot of death. She was thinking of Jaroslav on the Prešov-to-Poprad road.

'Hold tight. I love you,' called Milan.

'I love you too.'

They were spinning. The whole balloon was turning, toppling. Somewhere, a long way away, there was still the *babbaba* of the guns. Time to let go, she thought. This wasn't like a child's swing anymore. The wind was whipping past her.

Time to let go.

Her fingers relaxed and she fell.

PART TWO

The Fifth Commandment

Own only what you can carry with you; know language, know countries, know people. Let your memory be your travel bag.

Alexander Solzhenitsyn

1

The Matrilineal Line of Katya Hasek

How *does it work?* Katya would wonder. How did these memories flutter so obstinately down the generations? She would wake before dawn, and there would be Milan, asleep alongside her, his mouth half open, his eyes not yet ready for the day; and if she were to wake him and ask about his dreams, they would be strange, unreal affairs. His dreams were fragments of imagination, like the scattered glass from a broken mirror, reflecting tiny images of his world and compounding them with fiction. 'And what of your dreams?' he would always ask. 'Where did you go while I slept?'

She could feel her lives like the ribbon of a road that led away across distant hills, disappearing, and reappearing, swinging past familiar landmarks, plunging into long, dark tunnels and emerging again into sunlight. At first, she had struggled to see a shape within the memories, to connect the women in her dreams, one to the other, to fathom the order, the sequence of events, the causes and effects, the births and the deaths; but piece by piece the road had assembled in her mind. She lived, and relived, a day here, a week there, a year somewhere else. She learned the names, and the places, and the histories. She called them, from time to time, her *ghosts*, these women who populated her dreams; but they never really felt like ghosts. In truth, she understood, *she* was the ghost. She, Katya Hasek, was the spirit; she was the invisible voyeur eavesdropping on the lives of Heloise and Marianne and Marguerita and Sophia and all the rest. She was the secret audience to their dramas, knowing in most cases how their stories would end, how things would unfold.

How had they gone for so many generations without troubling Heloise's hidden gold? It had been a very long wait. Events, somehow, had conspired in each successive generation to keep them away. Marianne Muse, the first to carry the memories of the treasures, had fled too far east to go in search of the hoard. She had run all the way to Salzburg, on foot across the mountains, in flight from Roderique Églefin and the armies of Napoleon, with no opportunity of finding her way back home. Marguerita Muse, Marianne's daughter, had been too young to travel back to France. She died in Vienna when she was just nineteen. The treasure remained untouched.

She, Katya, had dreamed just that night of Marguerita, a dream of Salzburg in 1831. It was winter. Marguerita's coat was too thin for the north wind that stole through a dozen cracks into the dark attic room she called home. She lined the coat with oil papers that once wrapped candles, and when she moved she crackled. She was a street rat, Marguerita, born, they would tell her, to a half-starved French *flüchtling* in a brothel on Stauffenstrasse, her infant cries lost amidst the rhythmic sounds of creaking beds and groaning whores, the shrieks of girls, and the grunts of old men, and the stinks of sweat, and semen, cheap white wines, and sour perfumes. She had grown up in the city, barefoot, thin, unwashed, and always cold, and somehow, through the inscrutable process that haunted all of those in Heloise Fouchard's line, her knowledge of every narrow alley, stinking ditch, and dank stairway had found its way down the generations into the memories and dreams of Katya Hasek. 'Keep your legs crossed,' Frau Muller would tell Marguerita. Frau Muller was the *bordellbesitzer*, the brothel owner who sat guard, fat and squat, on the Stauffenstrasse doorstep with a broomstick, a heavy purse, and an attitude. 'If any man asks for you he will feel my stick. We shall find you rich bankers from Vienna or Zurich. They will pay handsomely for your virginity, my dear. Soon enough.' She would grasp Marguerita's wrist and gasp the words into her ear like a threat. 'Soon enough.'

Virginity. They could sell it a dozen times or more in *der puff,* the whorehouse, if the girl was convincing. 'The first time is for real. The second time we plant you with blood from a bleeding girl,' Frau Muller would tell her. 'We put it in you with a spoon. Just a spot. Like fish sauce on a sausage. No man will know it isn't yours.'

Marguerita Muse. Too young to be whored, but not for much longer. *Soon enough.* It felt as if a clock was ticking. 'Tell me when your bleeding starts,' the *bordellbesitzer* would breeze into her ear. 'I have your first banker waiting.'

Marguerita wore boots in the brothel to serve drinks and to clear tables, but outside in the streets, she was barefoot. 'If I let you have boots,' Frau Muller would say, 'you would walk away in them and never come back.' She was right. One cold autumn day, Marguerita was sitting on a wall by the Salzach River, her bare feet swinging, doing nothing more than watching the boats, when a young man in a black coat with a high collar turned up against the wind, came to sit beside her.

'Will you walk with me?' he asked her.

She recognised him from the brothel. She had seen him just once. She had served him with ale. He had taken her hand and given her a coin. He was the kind of young man who would slip through the *bordell*-house door, all shy and awkward, red in the cheeks, embarrassed to be seen, unsure of the protocols, uneasy with his money, and taking forever with his beer, building up courage for what had to be done, and then rushing for the street after just a few minutes with one of Frau Muller's girls.

'I have no shoes,' she said.

He nodded at her and tipped his hat. 'If you had shoes,' he asked her, 'would you come home with me?'

'Where do you live, sir?' she asked him.

'I am from Vienna,' he said.

'Ten days' walk,' she said. 'Would you have me walk ten days?'

'I would rather say fifteen days for young legs to walk from here to Vienna, with a break for Sundays,' the young man said. 'A lot of walking and a great many hills. But I don't need you to walk that far. I have a horse to take us to Linz and from there we can take a boat. The Danube is busy with boats. You only need walk as far as my horse, and my horse is in a stable in Strubergasse.'

'Then it's a pity I don't have shoes,' she said.

'But I do.' With an extravagant gesture the young man bent and unlaced his boots.

'Are you a banker, sir?' she asked. 'Are you offering to buy my virginity?'

The man looked unsettled by this question. 'I'm an innkeeper,' he replied. 'I am not looking to buy or steal your virginity, I assure you. You are too young anyway. I thought perhaps I might take you away from that place. That's all. You don't belong there. You could work in my inn.'

The sun was bright on the Salzach that day.

'In that case, sir,' Marguerita said, 'I *will* walk with you. I have sworn never to entertain a banker, but an innkeeper sounds to me like a fine profession.'

'Shall we go back to Stauffenstrasse to collect up your things?' he asked.

She pulled one of his boots onto her foot and wiggled her toes. 'Let's just go straight for the horse,' she said.

And that very night, in a room in an inn south of Linz, the first night she had ever been outside the city of Salzburg, she dreamed of a fabulous gala, with lords and ladies, and a balloon of gold. And when she awoke, her eyes were wide open and her thighs were wet with blood.

Sophia, Marguerita's daughter, was just two years old when her mother died. These were brutal times. Sophia grew up with no warning of the dreams, just as Marianne had done, and Marguerita too. She was raised in Vienna by her father who kept an inn near the *fleischmarkt*. When the dreams began, her father sat beside her, and told her, for the first time, how Marguerita had suffered with the visions. 'I never believed they would afflict you too,' he told her.

Life for an innkeeper's daughter in Vienna was comfortable, but never idle. Sophia worked long hours in the tavern. In 1853, at the age of eighteen, she met and married John Lester, an Englishman ten years her elder. John was making a grand tour of Europe. He fell for her *Germanische* looks and wooed her with English poetry and promises of travel. They married in St Michael's Church near the Vienna coal market, and Lester swept her off on a bumpy coach ride to Graz, and Trieste, and Venice, and Rome, a whirlwind journey of six months during which time she never told him about her gift – never once mentioned Heloise's memories, nor her gold. Englishmen don't take well to information like this. Sophia could sense it. She, like Marguerita, suffered her ghosts in silence. After Rome they took a barque to Marseilles and boarded the newly opened *Chemin de fer de Lyon à la Méditerranée* – the railway to Lyons, the first time Sophia had been aboard a train. From Lyons, a week later, a second train took them to Dijon. They stayed in a hotel in the Place du Morimont, the very square where Heloise had been beheaded, and from the window of their room Sophia could see the city hall where once had hung the sign: 'REPUBLIC ONE AND INDIVISIBLE; LIBERTY, EQUALITY, FRATERNITY, OR DEATH.' Death. There had been no liberty, equality, or fraternity for Heloise. Only death. But still Sophia kept her silence. She could look from her window and picture the braying crowd, could almost smell the butchery, and yet she blinked and smiled when John Lester showed her the view and she softly pulled the shutters closed. They were thirty minutes' ride from the place where Jean Sebastien had hidden his gold. She could have told him then. She could have slipped away alone in the night and gone in search of the hoard. How would he, an Englishman in a foreign town, ever find her again? He didn't even suspect that she might speak French. Yet these opportunities never troubled Sophia. She didn't hanker for riches. She had found her fortune in John Lester, a man she truly loved. She loved the kindness in his eyes, the tenderness of his embrace, his gallantry, his musty smell, his woven jackets; she loved the way he looked at her, the way he listened to her, the way he smiled at her stories. She loved the way his face had been blackened with soot on the railway journey as he leaned outside to watch the engine. She loved the precise way he held a knife and a fork, the attention he paid to the shining of his boots; the way he laughed with a hand to his mouth. He was a handsome man. A gentle man. How could she reveal to him the secrets of her past lives? He wouldn't understand. He would be jealous of long-dead lovers. He would think her possessed. How could she go with him to England with her past lifetimes like heavy luggage to be carried, to be dragged onto every carriage, and stacked away in every hotel room? From time to time she would still wake screaming, for this was a consequence of her dreams; but John never suspected anything more than an overactive imagination and a tendency towards nightmares. She didn't speak many words of English then, but John had learned German as a captain in the Royal Horse Guards and an aide to Prince Albert of Saxe-Coburg and Gotha, the husband of the English Queen. And language, in the early days of love, is less important than you might imagine.

'This place upsets me,' she told John Lester. 'Perhaps it is the air. Can we travel on to Paris?'

Sophia was three months pregnant when she and John arrived in London and set up home in a fine new town house in St Mary-le-Bow, a little way east of the City. Sophia became a figure of Continental fascination in the drawing rooms of the capital, admired for her Teutonic beauty and cultivated for her disarming wit. Her daughter, Margaret Lester, was born at home, attended by a doctor from the nearby St Bartholomew's Hospital. There were no complications. Soon afterwards, John inherited his father's home in Stafford and they travelled there together, the three of them with a lady's maid and a nursemaid, on the London and Northwestern Railway.

Sophia was different from me, Katya would think; and she was right. They were, each and every one of them, distinct, the women in her matrilineal line. Where Marianne had been hot-headed, spirited, and fiercely independent, Sophia had been reserved, courteous, often deferential. Where Heloise had been studious, she, Katya, had little appetite for books. Where Marguerita had been stoic, patient, tolerant, Frantiska had been impulsive, often volatile. Yet, in some measure, these shades of personality could seem like varieties of seasoning on the same dish. They were, Katya would often feel, the same sitter portrayed by different artists. There were more common features than there were disparities. Every woman in her memory, Katya understood, had a thread of passion, and of self-belief; every one possessed a mental map of virtues and vices and a recognition of injustice, and a sense of direction in human affairs that allowed little time for pomposity, or any real drive for self-enrichment. They were honest. They were true. They were down-to-earth people. They never looked too far ahead. Perhaps this was why, Katya would feel, there had never been an irresistible impulse among any of her ancestors to track down her fortune. Perhaps this was why it had taken so long.

John Lester died in 1858 when Margaret was three years old. He fell from his horse and broke a bone in his arm, and when the wound became infected, the surgeon took his arm off at the shoulder, but this wound too became infected, and within five days John was dead. How did Sophia react to this? Katya would never know. Her memories of Sophia ended on the day Margaret was born. From that moment, she would remember Sophia, not as the protagonist of her story, but as a mother, Margaret's mother. She would have no memory of John Lester's death, no memory of Margaret's infant years. She would remember childhood with the absence of a father. She would remember

115

the empty, echoing house in Stafford. She would remember her mother preparing her for what was to come. 'You will have a gift,' Sophia would tell her. 'You will wake one morning with my memories, just as I once woke with my mother's.'

Margaret sailed to the New World with her German beau, Otto Schmidt, when she was twenty and he was twenty-one. Only when they had made a home in New York and Otto was working on his great statue did she tell him about the dreams. He professed to believe her stories, but he clearly suspected they were fantasies. Margaret came to understand this. The gold at Montbelliard-les-Pins remained safe.

Rosa Schmidt was Margaret's daughter. She was slight, and nimble, and she danced the ballet. She became, for a short while, a sensation on the stage in New York when she was just seventeen, dancing as an understudy in *The Pharaoh's Daughter* when the prima ballerina fell ill. In 1898 she joined a ballet troupe setting out for a tour of Europe; the young Rosa had every intention of breaking away once all the dancing had ended and of making her way to Dijon in search of the Montbelliard fortune. Her plans were interrupted by Miloš Seifert, an Austrian businessman she met on the sea crossing. Miloš was a rich man. He had made his money importing American whiskeys into Europe and his singular vice was a passion for his own products. Miloš had no need of extra money and neither, once they were married, did Rosa. They made their home in Paris. The treasure would wait.

Rosa's daughter, Esme, was born in 1901. She was a sickly child for the first two years of her life, a sufferer from a succession of childhood afflictions, any one of which might have killed her. Four times Miloš and Rosa came to terms with losing their daughter as she lay on her various sickbeds, and four times they saw her revived. 'She's a survivor,' Rosa told her husband. But Miloš's emotions had been washed away with too many tears and too much whiskey. He hired a nursemaid and a governess and did his best to avoid spending time with his

116

daughter, anxious, perhaps, that the next ailment would take her from him, determined not to shed more tears.

Rosa died in childbirth in 1910, at the Pitié-Salpêtrière Hospital in Paris. The child, her second, was stillborn. 1910 was the year of the comet; its passage by the Earth was close that year. For six hours on 19th May, the Earth swept through the comet's long tail, and the night sky gleamed with flecks of fire; for those same six hours, Rosa was in labour. 'Call Esme for me,' she begged Miloš and the nurses, 'there are things I need to tell her.'

'This is no place for a child,' she was told.

Rosa was insistent. 'Please, please!' She tugged at her husband's hand and wept. 'There are things I must tell her,' she implored. 'Things she can only hear from me.'

'You can tell them to me,' Miloš said. 'Or you can tell them to Esme yourself when your baby is born.'

But the baby was never born, and Rosa never told Esme about her dreams. The infant, a girl, was cut from Rosa's body and they were buried together in the Père Lachaise Cemetery on the Boulevard de Ménilmontant. Esme, at nine years old, was considered too young to attend the funeral.

Within a year the widowed Miloš married a vaudeville singer from Bohars, near Brest, and they set up a new home in a suburb of Paris, not far, as it happened, from the Chateau de la Muette where the first Montgolfier balloon had flown. Esme knew nothing of that, of course. She found herself a faintly unwanted presence in the family home, the constant and unwelcome reminder of a former wife. She was an isolated child, a solitary creature who learned to live in shadows, unseen by the disapproving family, a girl wholly unprepared for the dreams when they came; and when the dreams came, they came as demons, as intrusions from another world, with their visions of death and deprivation. 'What are they?' she wailed to her father. 'I want them to stop.'

Had she waited, Esme would have discovered that most of

her dreams would, in time, become familiar friends; but she was fifteen and motherless, and scared. Miloš took her by train to Vienna to consult with Dr Sigmund Freud, a world expert on matters of the mind, but despite arriving unannounced on Freud's doorstep and despite the offer of a considerable fee, the psychoanalyst refused the consultation. Freud was suffering from a cancer of the mouth, caused, it was later assumed, by his fondness for cigars. He was losing his ability to speak. He referred Esme to an eager young analyst called Bernard Dvorak who worked at the Vienna Ambulatorium. Dvorak was a specialist in dreams. He would go on to write *Über Träume und ihre Vorzeichen* (*On Dreams and Their Portents*), a bestseller of a sort, at least among those who aimed to interpret dreams for money. Esme was a godsend to Dvorak. Her dreams were like nothing he had encountered before. He told Miloš that Esme should stay in Vienna. Her course of treatments would require at least a year. This advice could scarcely have been better tailored to Miloš's preferences. He rented an apartment for Esme on Stubenbastei square, employed for her a housekeeper and a companion, and there he left her, departing, drunk, on the train back to Paris.

The house in Vienna was where the young Parisienne lived out the remainder of her teens, visiting Bernard Dvorak three times a week to lie on his couch and provide him with details of her most recent dreams.

In 1920 Esme and Bernard were married. You cannot lie for six hours a week on a young man's couch discussing sex without giving him ideas. They travelled widely to promote *On Dreams and Their Portents*, but Bernard never allowed himself to believe that what Esme was experiencing were memories, and perhaps not dreams at all. 'I know this phenomenon well,' a colleague of Miloš told them both during a visit to the colleague's home in the Vienna woods. 'This is reincarnation. It is widely recognised in Eastern medicine.'

'The man speaks nonsense,' Bernard told her, once the visit

was over. 'It might be reincarnation if every mother in your dreams died in childbirth, but several, in your imagination, did not.'

'Sometimes it feels to me like reincarnation,' Esme told him. 'Sometimes I feel the lives of these other women were *my lives*. That I lived them, as surely as I'm living my life now.'

But Dvorak was stubborn and could never be convinced. They moved north, from Vienna to Prague, and the Montbelliard treasure was undisturbed.

Frantiska was born in Prague – Frantiska who was Katya's mother, who fled from Lidice, who tried to walk away from a war that was shaking the whole world, who met and married a farmer's son in a remote village in a remote corner of a remote country. Frantiska dreamed of the gold. But the Iron Curtain had fallen across Europe, and there it stayed, an impenetrable barrier to all within its bounds. There was no way back for Frantiska.

The treasure would have to wait.

2

Marianne, 1812

How familiar the road was from Dijon to Chateau Montbelliard-les-Pins. The vineyards still wound up the hillsides in neat mathematical rows, the army of vines parading like obedient soldiers in columns. The pines still grew from Chateau les Tiles to the bridge at Pont Angles. The river Ouche still swept beneath the bridge as if not a thing had changed. The same birds were in the sky. The same sun. The same clouds.

Nothing had changed.

But everything had changed. This was the first time she, Marianne Muse, had ever visited Dijon. It should have been a strange place for a girl who had lived her whole life cloistered in a damp convent in Quetigny. Yet it wasn't. The sight of the road with its recognisable landmarks was the most precious thing Marianne could imagine after doubting her memories for so long. The familiarity was not mundane. It was extraordinary. It was a long-lost creature awakening from a slumber. It was an avalanche of images and smells and sounds, so sharp, and so precise, she could hardly bear to see them, to hear them, to smell them.

If these vines are here . . . she thought, and the logic of this was unfolding in her mind like a linen bedcloth, if that cottage on the hillside is there. If the bridge is made of white stone. If the church has twelve marble steps. If the tannery still stinks. If the road was to come to a fork, and left was to go to Urcy, then right would go to the Chateau, and her dreams would not be dreams.

They would be true.

And if these dreams were true, these mundane dreams, these

dreams of places and things, of churches and vines and road-ways . . . if these were true . . . then could everything be true?

She was possessed of a devil. They told her this in the Abbaye Sainte Médrine, the sisterhood where she, Marianne, the bas-tard child of an executed criminal, had been brought as an infant. *Couvent Pleuvoir*, they called it in Quetigny, the home of the congregation of the rains, les Chanoinesses de Saint-Médrine de la Pluie, the dark, rancid, backstreet home of a score of nuns, an institution that stank of piss from the *pissoir* wall where the town boys relieved themselves in full view of the abbey. 'They will go to hell,' the holy sister Mother Marie de Sainte Médrine de la Pluie would promise them, 'and so will you, Sister Marianne, if you make a home for these devils you call your memories.'

She was a home for devils. Her soul was a nest of devils. Everyone in the convent knew this. Devils invaded her dreams. Fearsome devils. She would awake screaming. Screams so loud they would rouse the whole sisterhood and half the town. 'My dear, my dear, my dear,' Sister Agata would say. Sister Agata, with her big face and her smoky eyes, was Marianne's closest confidante; she would wipe Marianne's brow with a cloth soaked in holy water. Together they would chant the *Te Deum*, and the *Agnus Dei*, '*Agnus Dei, qui tolis peccata mundi, miserere nobis*,' and Sister Agata would whisper, in French, '*Tu est saint, trois fois saint. Dieu tout puissant. Louange à l'agneau.*' Worthy is the lamb.

The *Agnus Dei* would settle her.

Worthy is the lamb.

The priest who came to hear Marianne's confession at the Convent of the Rains was a young man called Father Philippe Emmanuel du Chambrais, little more than a boy, barely older than she. Every priest who had once ministered to the Sisters of Saint-Médrine had been guillotined during the revolution, but the fashion for executing priests had passed as the supply of necks diminished. New priests had been permitted as part of Robespierre's Cult of the Supreme Being, and some of these had drifted carefully back to the Church as the revolution gave way to the Empire. Father Philippe was one of these, a cautious, halting, boy-child of a cleric, with eyes that focused onto the tip of his nose, red spots around his mouth, a stink of sweat from his armpits and the habit of absently rubbing his groin with the back of his hand. All nuns made him nervous, especially the vestals in the Abbaye de Saint Médrine, and even more especially, Sister Marianne, the girl who had been plucked as an infant from the teeth of the devil himself. 'What do you want to confess?' he would ask her.

'I have nothing to confess, Father,' Marianne would say. She would pull a strand of hair loose from beneath her black headscarf, and she would coil it absently around her finger. 'I have committed no sin,' she would tell him.

But it was hard to be in the presence of Sister Marianne and not be reminded of sin. The devil who had so nearly claimed her on the scaffold still sought her as one of his own. Even the affected way she played with her hair hinted at sinfulness. And despite her denials, her protestations of virtue, and her nun's habit, she possessed an aroma of sexuality, a warm infusion of human excretions and musk that made her evil in the eyes of Father Philippe, and she filled her habit with a sensuous construction of curves that was impossible to look upon without sinful thoughts, and this, for the young priest, simply compounded the evil.

Father Philippe rubbed his groin and tried to look elsewhere. 'Mother Marie tells me you hear voices.'

'Mother Marie has no right to tell you anything about me. The only voices I hear in this place are the voices of my sisters. And . . .' she added, sweetly, 'your voice, Father Philippe.'

Her flesh was too new and too soft for Father Philippe. 'The girl is possessed,' he told the Mother Superior after Marianne's confession. 'I have no doubt about it. She is possessed.'

'Can she be cured?' Mother Marie asked him.

The Abbess Marie was, in this life at least, the closest person Marianne knew to a parent. She was the holy sister who had taken responsibility for the infant on the day she, Marianne, had been brought to the sisterhood, the day of her birth – if *birth* is the right word for the butchery that brought her into the world. Sister Marie (then just a humble novice), had recruited the wet nurses, had hand-stitched the swaddles, had fed and washed the tiny child, had slept with her in her own narrow bed, in her own dark cell, and had she not been a bride of Christ and a servant of Sainte Médrine, she would surely have thought of the girl as her own. But the calling of God can be a cruel thing. '*You are too close to the child*,' she was told, more than once, by Reverend Mothers and by priests, and this was surely a sin in the eyes of the sisterhood, to love a child when one's life and devotion had been offered to God; and so sometimes the care of the child was passed to other sisters, and sometimes it was equally shared among all, and Mother Marie, as she eventually became, had grown, or had been nudged, by degrees, apart from Marianne, even as her own heart ached for her the more. It is a curious thing when the gospel of love demands the withholding of love. It requires a discipline and a sense of duty, and an unquestioning belief in authority. So Mother Marie of the Rains, the Abbess, the Prioress, the Holy Mother of the sisterhood, was a woman hollowed out by duty. The strings that should operate her heart did so invisibly behind a curtain of denial.

'She wants to kill a man,' Father Philippe told the Abbess. 'She said she dreams of finding this man and killing him.'

The reverend mother crossed herself three times. 'Did she say this in the privacy of the confessional?'

'She may have done.'

'Then it cannot be repeated.' She offered the young priest a stern look to underwrite his silence. 'I have heard her confess this too, but it seems to me a harmless, childish delusion.'

'I believe it is a devil.'

'A devil? I see.' They walked together through the gloomy cloisters. 'Then it can surely be expelled?'

'Not by me.' The priest toyed anxiously with his beads. 'Father Sauvigne might have had the skills . . . but . . .' he left the sentence incomplete, and allowed his head to drop. Father Sauvigne, they both knew, had wept like a baby on the scaffold, had renounced all his worldly wealth, had pissed himself and shat in his breeches, had confessed to sodomy, had offered himself as a priest in the Cult of Reason – but all to no avail. A falling steel blade is no respecter of contrition.

'The devil may rather be an angel sent to test her,' Mother Marie said. 'He visits her by night in dreams. Is that not more the behaviour of an angel?'

'It is the devil's vengeance upon her for escaping the guillotine,' the priest replied.

'Who is the man?' Mother Marie asked Marianne later as they stood waiting for vespers.

'Which man, Holy Mother?'

'This man you want to kill? You confessed it to Father Philippe.'

'He may not be a real man, Holy Mother,' Marianne said. 'He may be a demon placed in my mind. A man of my imagination.'

'You must be careful what you say to Father Philippe,' the Abbess said. 'He has a rather active imagination. Have you ever seen this man?'

An easy question. 'No, Holy Mother. I have never seen him.'

'Do you know where to find him?'

'No, Holy Mother.'

'Then you should pray to Sainte Médrine and Saint Jude.' The Mother Superior took Marianne's face in her hands and kissed her temples. 'You are a good, kind child. I know you. These thoughts are not yours.'

'They are not,' Marianne said.

'Do you know the name of this demon? The one you must kill?'

Églefin. His name was Roderique Églefin. He had a narrow face and eyebrows that crossed, and no top teeth. He had eyes that instilled hatred and fear. He had a duelling scar on his cheek, black hairs on his body, a wart on his chin. He had a stinking phallus that he pulled from his striped breeches at every opportunity, that he slapped in Heloise's face as if it was a weapon. She could see him. Hear him. Smell him. Feel his oily sweat and his sticky excretions. But even as his name rose in Marianne's throat, she choked upon it. 'No, Holy Mother. I do not know his name.'

She could taste the lie in her mouth. Églefin. His name was Roderique Églefin.

'Would you know his face?'

'No, Holy Mother.' She could see his narrow eyes, the curl of his lip, the gap of his teeth. 'No.'

The older woman released her hold on Marianne's face. 'Then you are no danger to anyone,' she said.

'May I go, Holy Mother?'

The Abbess released a sigh so soft and so deep that Marianne failed to observe it. 'It is your time, child. You may go. You may do whatever you please.' The Holy Mother blew out the single candle flame that had lit their conversation. Tallow was a precious thing. No one needed light to speak. 'Perhaps you would like to go further than the chapel?' she said, and the darkness seemed to amplify the words.

'Further?'

Mother Maria touched Marianne on her shoulder. A faint glow of moonlight through the convent window brushed her face. 'You didn't choose this life, my dear. You came here as an infant. We cannot keep you if you wish to go.'

'If I wish to go?'

'Don't decide yet. Ask Sainte Médrine.'

Ask Sainte Médrine. If there was one thing Marianne had

learned in the Convent of the Rains, it was the certain knowledge that Sainte Médrine would never reply. She knew it, and so did the Holy Mother. A supplicant who took her problems to Sainte Médrine could impute any answer of her own choosing. *Ask Sainte Médrine.* It was a way of saying, ask your conscience. What would *you* like to do?

What *would* she like to do?

And now, here she was among the vines of the Montbelliard estate with the sun fat and heavy over the southern hills. The grapes were still young. If Jean Sebastien had still been here, the man she knew only from her dreams, he'd be caressing the leaves with his big hands, sucking the fruit between his teeth. Up that track, she knew, were the drying sheds where the grapes would be taken in the mule wagons. She had never seen them. But they were there in her memories, and she was beginning to believe her memories might be real. A little further down the same lane would be the presses where the townsfolk would tread the grapes. Heloise used to pull up her skirts and join them. Marianne could remember that. There was always a great deal of laughter. Two of the gypsy boys who appeared at harvest to pick grapes would play a dancing tune on a fiddle and a pipe, and treading the fruit would become a dance. People would throw arms across each other's shoulders, men and women together, children too, rich and poor, all red with the juice, all stamping in time with the music. As the day grew long, some of the boys would play-fight in the grape press, and Guillaume would bark at them, but Jean Sebastien would say, 'Leave them be. It will all go to flavour the wine.'

How did she have these memories? Where had they come from? Were they shadows of a past that really happened? Should she walk the track to see the presses? Just to be completely sure? If they were there, as her dreams had told her, then there would be no doubt.

But already there was no doubt.

126

And if there was no doubt about the vineyards, and the Chateau, and the chapel, then there was no doubt about Roderique Églefin, the man she would have to kill; no doubt either about a hoard of great riches hidden so close by, it made her heart quicken to think about it.

She was on foot. She wore the only dress she had ever possessed – a gift from the Holy Mother – a stiff, flaxen shift with no dye, with wooden buttons, stitched in turn by every one of the sisterhood and kissed on the hem by Father Philippe. She wore boots that had been cut from a dead woman in La Place du Morimont. She wore a rosewood cross from the convent chapel, and a headscarf of wool that someone had given to the convent in penance.

And that was all. These were her possessions. All of them.

Except for her memories.

What a curious thing is a memory, she thought. Where does it belong? In the head? In the heart? Where does it go when it isn't used? How do you find it? How do you know it's there? How can you tell a true memory from a false one? Even her own memories, she knew, even the memories of Marianne Muse and the Convent in Quetigny – even these memories could fool her sometimes. How could she trust memories from a woman she never knew?

Standing on the roadside, looking out over the Montbelliard vineyards, Marianne Muse felt older than her eighteen years. She felt taller than her modest height. She felt more beautiful than a looking glass would allow. She felt more confident than any other girl, ejected by the Sisterhood of the Rains, would have a right to feel. 'Worthy is the lamb,' she whispered to herself. *Dignus est agnus.* Worthy is the lamb. She knew the secret meaning of that line. She was the lamb. She was worthy.

There was something she had to do.

Fifty rows of vines from the stream. She counted each one. She made a mark in the earth and counted them again. Fifty rows.

Fifty vines along the fiftieth row.

She paced them out.

It was dusk. The sky was mauve and yellow. Her shadow was long. One. Two. Three.

Fifty vines.

She could hear voices some way off. She dropped down and waited for them to pass. High voices. Girls from the farms.

When they were gone, she began to dig. She dug with her hands. The soil was rocky and hard on the fingers. Silly. She should have brought a tool. Something to dig with. She cast her eyes around, but nothing came to mind. She tried snapping a short branch from a vine, but it was little help. Never mind. She wasn't short of time. She lay in the gap between the rows and dug slowly. It would be a long way down. She knew that.

The sky grew dark. Yellows turned ochre and the ochres turned vermillion. These were God's colours. That was what Sister Agata with the smoky eyes would say. God was painting the sky.

She rested for a while. There were more voices. The *clop clop* of a weary horse. The sound of geese finding their way home. A dog.

She felt hungry. The grapes were too young to eat, but she tried some anyway, and spat them out. Inedible. Jean Sebastien would have done the same.

She dug some more. Her fingers were sore. There were so many roots to dig past. She contemplated giving up, and coming back in the morning with a good sharp stone, but instead she dug on. Small handfuls.

The hole was getting deeper. What would Mother Marie say if she knew Sister Marianne was out in the dark, her arms buried deep in soil? The thought spurred her on. Another handful. And another.

Her hand closed on something hard. She felt around it. It was too dark to see what it was. Her nails were bleeding. She swapped hands and tried to dig with her left.

It was a box. She was sure of it. A brass box.

It took twenty minutes to dig it free.

Three bags of coins, Jean Sebastien had said. The man in her memory. The man she had only seen in dreams.

Excitement was growing in her chest. She pulled the box up and peered at it in the dim light. There was something inside. She shook the box. Something heavy.

There was a catch. It took a few moments to figure it out, and she prised the lid open. Two small leather bags, one tied with a thong, its contents packed tightly, the second smaller, and looser. She untied the smaller bag.

Gold coins! Even in the half-light she could see them glow. One hundred coins or more. This much gold could make a person rich. Very rich.

And in the second bag . . .

. . . more coins. Twice as many.

She counted the gold pieces carefully. The large bag held two hundred and twenty coins, the small one, exactly half that number.

One and a half bags. *Someone had been here before her.* She could see that now. Three bags, Jean Sebastien had said. Three bags he had shown to Heloise.

Someone had taken half the gold.

On an impulse, she counted thirty coins into her hand, refilled the bags, and pushed them back into the box. Someone had left coins for her to find. She would do the same. Thirty coins was more than she needed. It could be a risk to carry many more. She scooped the soil back, and when the hole was full, she stamped it down. In the darkness she pushed coins into the hem of her dress, and into the cuffs. She pressed coins into her boots underneath the arches of her feet and around her toes. She had a long swathe of flax tied around her breasts. The gold that remained she secreted there.

One coin left. She squeezed it tightly in her hand.

She couldn't sleep here among the vines. They would

discover her in the morning. But the night would be dry and there were woods nearby with a thousand places to hide. She threw back her hair, and something inside her was issuing a shout of utmost joy.

'Worthy is the lamb,' she said, out loud. No one was there to hear her, but her voice filled the valley. 'Worthy, worthy, worthy . . . is the lamb.'

The money changer in Rue Ducat wore a soft, wide beret which almost covered his eyes. He surveyed Marianne thinly over his ledgers. He had a set of scales onto which he placed her coin. 'What is your name, child?'

'Marianne Muse.'

He wrote the name into his ledger in slow, flowing script and blotted it with a cloth. 'You are fortunate,' he said. His voice was a soft drone. 'These coins are valuable. It is a *franc à cheval*. Napoleon will give you an *assignat* for this, a promissory bond, to help pay for his armies in Russia.' He surveyed her and his head rocked back and forward. 'But I dare say you want something you can spend today.'

'If you please.' Marianne gave a narrow smile.

'How did a peasant girl come upon a *franc d'or*?'

'My father left it to me.' The answer felt truthful.

The money changer dipped his quill into an ink pot and laboriously wrote the details down. 'Twelve francs,' he said. 'That's all I can give you.'

'Fifteen francs,' suggested Marianne.

'Twelve francs and I'll ask no more questions,' the money changer said. He was already counting the coins.

For five centimes, she bought bread and olives. She sat on the cobbles and devoured a whole loaf.

She found a dressmaker down a narrow alley near Rue des Forges. He measured her using strands of wool that he clipped onto a frame. 'I have a pale-brown dye, or a green dye,' he told her. 'The more you pay, the more I use.'

'Do you have blue?' she asked. Heloise had worn bright-blue dresses. 'Or red?'

'Do you want to be mistaken for a lady?' he asked. 'Pay too much and they'll have your head.'

'Use the brown dye,' she said. 'Not too much.'

From a hat maker she bought a modest bonnet with ribbons that would tie beneath her chin. She would keep the boots she had, but she visited a cobbler who made repairs and sewed on a decorative buckle.

'Be careful flashing about that purse,' the cobbler told her. 'A girl with a handful of francs can attract the wrong kind of attention.'

She slept in the forests again. She drank from a stream. Her dress would take four days to make. She needed a bed. She could go back to Quetigny, to the sisterhood, but they might want evidence that her demons had been vanquished. She could try to find a room in a tavern, but the risks for a young woman on her own would be too high to contemplate. Down in the valley she could see a trail of smoke from the vintners' cottages, little smallholdings where the vineyard workers lived. Perhaps one of them would offer her shelter in a barn in exchange for a few centimes. She tied her swathe tightly around her chest and made her way down the hill.

'Are you a courtesan?' demanded the vintner's wife of Marianne when the young woman presented herself at the door, looking for shelter.

'A courtesan?'

'A whore.'

'I am a virgin,' Marianne said. 'Until last week I was a ward of the Sisterhood of Sainte Médrine of the Rains in Quetigny.'

The vintner's wife regarded the young woman with suspicion. 'If you fuck my husband I shall cut out your silken purse with a butter knife.'

They settled on a sou – five centimes – as a fair price to share a stall with the mules. There was no fresh straw. The stable had not been cleaned for weeks. Marianne pulled up armfuls of dry grasses from outside, and laid them on the wet straw to afford herself some protection from the shit and the damp.

'It won't work,' her landlady warned.

'Why not?'

'The mules will eat it.'

And so they did.

'For one sou more you can have sacking.'

'And a knife, please.'

'I can sell you a picker's knife for ten. What do you want it for?'

'To protect my silken purse.'

She slept between two mules, with the heat of their breath on her shoulders. The jack mule let her use his flank to rest her head. She was visited on the first night by the vintner, fresh from a tavern, his moustaches stinking of wine.

'Ha,' he cried when he leaned over the door and saw her. 'They told me I had a whore in the stable but I didn't believe them.' He started untying the rope that held up his breeches.

'And they told me a eunuch might visit me in the night,' Marianne said.

The man snorted. 'I'm no eunuch,' he boasted.

'Not yet,' Marianne said. She showed him the knife. 'But come any nearer and I will cut off one *pelote* and your wife can cut the other.'

She made a friend of the vintner's wife. After two nights in the stable, she, the vintner's wife, gave Marianne a mat on the kitchen floor and a chamber pot to piss in.

'Do you know who lives in the Chateau?' Marianne asked her. 'I've seen soldiers there.'

'They use it for the *Armée*,' she was told. 'Lucien Napoleon, the Emperor's brother, stayed there once. Then, for a few years, they kept it for the commander of forces in Dijon. A Jacobin.

Now it's a barracks of some sort. They've given licences to local vintners to manage the grapes and make the wine.'

'The commander of forces in Dijon?' Marianne echoed. 'Who is he?'

'Roderique Églefin,' the vintner's wife spat. 'He's a hero of the revolution.'

'I should very much like to meet him. A hero, you say?'

'He brought over three hundred enemies of the people to justice.' The vintner's wife may once have been round and merry, but poverty and illness had left her drawn and thin. She bore her misfortunes with a heavy expression of melancholy and not a little helping of spite. 'Including,' she said, 'the Montbelliard family who used to bleed the poor in this valley.' She spat on the ground and watched her spittle disappear into the dirt. 'Églefin kept the city true to the ideals of the National Convention. Not like those spineless fish in Lyons.' She spat a third time.

'How can I meet him?'

'Églefin? Who knows? He went back to Paris several years ago. He never enjoyed Dijon, so they say. Good wine made his liver ache. And he guillotined so many people, he lived in fear of a revenge attack. A thousand people in Bourgogne want him dead, they say.' The woman laughed and showed the gaps in her teeth. 'Maybe he lost his head too.'

'Maybe.'

In daylight Marianne helped on the smallholding, digging up roots for the pig, and carrying muck to the pile. When she returned to Dijon, down the dark alley to the dressmaker, she stank like a shit heap.

'Shall I sell this dress?' the tailor asked, turning up his nose at Marianne's modest flaxen shift. Marianne had emptied the hems of any gold.

'Wash it and send it to the Convent of the Rains in Quetigny.' She gave him one franc for his trouble. 'It belongs to them. How do I look?'

133

The new dress was a fine fit. First there was the *corset et jupon* – a grey petticoat without hoops – which laced up the front from the waist to the bosom, and fell, heavy and full, to just below the knee. Over this came the dress. It fastened with beads at the back and the sleeves, and ties at the front, and it pulled tight with a drawstring around the waist. It wasn't the colour of soil, it was a soft cream, like buttermilk, with almost a hint of red. There were two modest beads on the cuffs, and four more beads on the neck. The dressmaker had found cloth for a blue waistband that tied about her middle and dropped behind her like a tail. It was a fine blue – a shade Heloise would have liked. Marianne dressed herself and tied the waistband. With her bonnet pulled low, she looked, not like a respectable lady, but more like a champion of the revolution.

'You could be Josephine,' the dressmaker said, flatteringly.

For four francs she paid to sit on the back of a wagon taking wine barrels to Paris. She could sit up against the backboard, her legs dangling over the end. It was a nine-day journey. ('Eight days if the sun shines, ten days if it rains,' the coachman told her. 'Longer if we get held up by soldiery.') The price didn't include food or lodgings. She slept underneath the wagon. She ate berries, and made every loaf of bread last for two days.

She made friends of the two coachmen. After a day she moved from the back of the wagon to the front, and they sat together for the long hours of daylight, Marianne in the middle with a coachman on either side, feeling the warm press of their shoulders on her own, watching the steady pull of the two horses, telling each other stories.

The older of the two coachmen had known Jean Sebastien Montbelliard.

'I think my mother may have known him,' Marianne reported, vaguely.

'He was a good man,' the coachman told Marianne. 'A kind man. But an enemy of the revolution, which cannot be

134

forgiven. And his wife Heloise was the most beautiful woman in Dijon. Maybe in all of France. She looked a little like you. The same hair. I saw her in the market many times.'

Marianne could remember Heloise's trip to Paris. She, Heloise, had visited only once. But the magic was there in the memories, and those memories, for Marianne, were as sharp as pins. The fine carriages. So many horses. Footmen in red and blue uniforms, ladies in outfits of every colour, bursting with fabrics, with hemps and woollens from London, and mohairs from Constantinople, and silks from Lyons. The church bells rang like music. They drank fine wines in goblets of silver. They ate smoked fish and apricots and they sipped dark cognacs and danced to music from a Breton fiddle band. They watched the gilded balloon and the brave fliers rise silently from the gardens at Chateau de la Muette as if they and the whole crowd were possessed by invisible magic. 'It is no demon,' she, Heloise, had told a woman who threatened to faint at the sight of the balloon. 'It is nothing but the smoke. The smoke makes it fly. It is no different from the embers that fly up your chimney.' Pilâtre de Rozier, one of the two aeronauts in the gondola of the balloon, caught her eye and waved, and his eyes were like those very embers. Jacques-Étienne Montgolfier slid an arm around her shoulder, and they and the press of people cheered until they were hoarse.

Paris. The centre of the universe. Heloise had met the King at the party and had curtsied so low, she almost fell on her face.

Paris.

It wasn't the same for Marianne, arriving on the wine wagon from Burgundy along the busy Route Charenton, south of the great river. It had rained in the capital every day for a week and the roads were mud. The wine cart was heavy, and the wheels stuck so often in the ruts, the coachmen took to walking in front, throwing sticks beneath the tracks, and helping the horses by pushing from behind. Marianne could smell the stink of the city before they reached the Charenton Gate. Ahead of them in the queue of carts and carriages, an ossuary wagon carried the half-rotted bones of a hundred or more people, on its way from a distant city to the catacombs of the capital.

The reek of human decay was foul enough to make Marianne choke on her bread. A slow drive of twenty thin and lame Aubrac cattle trudged ahead of the ossuary cart, and ahead of these were a dozen casualties from Napoleon's ventures in Spain who had individually paid to be brought back from the campaign on two-wheeled traps drawn by mules and donkeys, and ahead of them were six grain carts because the city had run out of bread, and ahead of them was a priest in a curtained carriage who never showed his face, and a mail wagon with coach lamps and a coachman and two guards in wigs, and somewhere in the traffic, a seller of horses taking lame mares to Paris for slaughter because, lame as they might be, they would be edible enough in the city if they walked there by themselves, and a Berlin carriage bearing someone of importance drawn by six thin horses that looked to have been whipped so soundly throughout the journey that now there were more wounds than healthy flesh. Maybe those horses, too, would soon be stew. There were dogs that had followed most of the way from Dijon, and others who had arrived since, weaving in and out of the carriage wheels in search of scraps. There were dozens of walkers, some alone, and others in groups, who had joined the convoy at various stages of the journey and were now at an advantage as the caravan of vehicles creaked slowly onwards through the mud. Together, they were a long, tedious column of weary commerce. Roadside merchants, taking advantage of the leisurely progress of the caravan, had set up stalls with fruit and bread and snails. Marianne bought a brioche and shared it with the coachmen. It was gritty and stale. 'They bake it with dust,' the coachmen told her. 'Dust and horse dung.' She spat her mouthful into the mud.

The ditches that ran each side of the roadway had been dug to drain rainwater away from the tracks, but so heavy had been the rain, they now performed the opposite function, channelling water and stink and excrement and mud in rivers down from the city and onto the trackway. Walking would be faster. A battalion of soldiers, on foot, came past them, on the way home from the Peninsula, and so much filth was caked on their uniforms, it was impossible to see if they were red or if they were blue. They could be Spaniards, for all we can tell, Marianne thought. Most of the men looked so exhausted they could barely stand. One of them directed a lewd comment at her. 'Give us a suck, love,' he said. But even he looked so drawn of energy that Marianne wondered if he wouldn't prefer a good lie down.

They drove into the city through the Barrière de Charenton, and were met by volunteers from the Comité de Sûreté wearing lookalike tunics and black bicorn hats. They sported gold braids sewn onto their shoulders to indicate their importance.

It was starting to rain. Marianne, on the wagon, sitting on a barrel of Burgundy wine, sheltered beneath the rush mat that during the night-times had been her mattress, wondering if it might have been better to have spent her money on a coat than a dress.

'What brings you to Paris?' asked a young man no older than she was, the possessor of a face pitted by pox scars.

'I help with the horses,' Marianne said. This was the agreed story. She showed the man a letter of introduction from the Sisterhood of the Rains. 'But I'm here to join the revolution.'

'The revolution has been over for a good many years,' the young man said. 'This is the Empire now. Does news never reach your part of the world?'

'Well, I've come to help the Empire,' said Marianne.

'Then you've come to the right place, Sister,' the young man said and he grasped her forearm. 'We are Jacobins but we are devoted to the Emperor. I can help you. The Empire needs youth. It needs energy.'

'I have energy,' Marianne said. But in truth she didn't. She was hungry and fatigued, and sick from the stinks, and exhausted from sleepless nights under the wagon, clutching her knife, fearful of losing her money or her silken purse, or both.

'My name is Antoine,' the young man said. He wore an olive-coloured neckerchief – an *écharpe* – that seemed, by the casual way it was tied, to suggest a rakish personality. 'Is the wine good?' He nodded towards the barrels.

'I haven't tasted it.'

The boy barked an order and half a dozen volunteers made their way towards him. He was a person of authority then, despite his young age. Perhaps the neckerchief was a symbol of rank. 'Shall we check this wine?' he asked. 'We don't want the provinces sending bad wine to the city.'

The coachmen agreed (they had little choice); the cork was hammered from one of the barrels and a long-handled sommelier's ladle was found.

'Good,' the young revolutionary pronounced, as he tasted the first cup.

'Good,' echoed each of his charges in turn as they too tried the wine. Marianne and the coachmen were offered a drink and the welcoming party had a second. Someone brought wooden goblets and more wine was drawn.

'Come with me,' Antoine the pox-faced boy said, when everyone had drunk their fill. His scarred cheeks were glowing, partly from the wine, and partly, Marianne realised, with the germ of an infatuation. 'I shall show you our city and I will find you work with the Comité.'

They set off into Paris on foot. This was the Corsican's city now, Marianne was told. 'Who is the Corsican?' she naively asked, but she knew the answer as soon as Antoine's eyebrows rose. 'Ah. You mean Napoleon?'

'Is there another Corsican?'

'Not one that I know.'

'They're rebuilding the city to welcome the *Grande Armée* from our victories in Moscow,' the boy explained.

In the centre of the city a huge arch was under construction. Covered with wooden scaffolds, it was as large as a cathedral. They went to stand beneath it. 'They are pulling down the slums to make great boulevards,' Antoine said. 'North to England,' he pointed, 'South to Marseilles and to Spain and Africa, East to Moscow, West to the lands of the Americas. All the world will meet here. Here!' he pointed proudly at their feet. 'You and I, Marianne Muse, we stand at the centre of the world.' His face was flushed.

She could never love him, Marianne thought. But she could bear his company for a while. That might be enough. 'Where do you live?' she asked him.

'With my mother, in Rue de Sèvres.'

'Could she find room for me?'

The boy regarded her with a mixture of apprehension and ecstasy. 'Can I tell her we are contemplating courtship?'

'You can tell her you have recruited me into the Comité, and I am to be your protégé,' Marianne said. She liked truthful explanations.

3

Katya, 1980

'Your coin weighs three point eight grammes,' the dealer said. He punched numbers into a calculator the size of a typewriter, and wrote a figure onto a piece of paper. 'I can give you sixty-five US dollars and forty cents. Commission will be two dollars. If you want, I can give you two hundred and sixty new francs and twenty centimes.'

Two hundred and sixty francs. From a single coin!

'We'll take the francs,' Katya said.

They had stayed overnight just outside Dijon at an Auberge de la Jeunesse – a hostel with dormitories for each sex. 'We're married,' Katya had told the woman who checked them in. 'It makes no difference,' she was told.

In the dark of the night, Katya had been to the vineyard, alone, and had counted the vines, just as Marianne once had done. Fifty rows and fifty vines. She returned with thirty gold coins.

'*Sakra!*' Milan had said. 'Wow!' He fondled the coins as if they were alive. 'Are they really gold?'

'They're really gold.'

'Where did you get them?'

'I can't tell you. You have to trust me.'

Now here they were on the streets of Dijon with two hundred and sixty francs in their pockets and twenty-nine coins in an untouched purse.

'This is the most money I have ever held in my life,' Milan said.

They were Austrian citizens now. Six weeks had passed since their dramatic escape from the East. They had fallen from their

Chinese lantern and landed in the Morava River. Katya had dropped like a stone into the cold water, and the shock of the fall felt very much like death. But there had been boys on the riverbank, teenagers drinking beer out of bottles, who had heard the splash and seen the careering carcass of the balloon. They came rushing to her rescue, their high, excited voices carrying clearly through the cold air.

The next splash was Milan.

From the East, the guns stopped firing. They had crossed the invisible line that separated life from death. On one side they could be torn to pieces with bullets, and on the other they could be rescued, and photographed, and become celebrities on the television news, and be given passports, and be set free into a bigger but no less frightening world.

'What if Heloise's gold isn't there?' Milan asked her.

'It will be.'

'But if it isn't?'

Katya shrugged. 'Will it matter? In Záhorská Ves I couldn't afford a new pair of shoes. You had so many patches sewn on your jacket, there was more patch than jacket.'

He laughed at this. 'So what will you buy? Apart from new shoes?'

'A new jacket.' She touched his face. 'Maybe I'd buy a dairy farm in the Dolomites. Somewhere with a view of mountains. Somewhere we could raise a family.'

'I'd like that.'

'Good.'

'Are there more coins?' Milan asked.

'A few,' Katya said. She kissed him to stop his questions. 'We have to leave them where they are.'

'Why?'

'We just do.'

They found a little restaurant selling pizzas, and they sat across a tiny table in the window like tourists. Katya could feel a glow spreading from somewhere deep inside, as if all the fragments of her being were being reassembled into something true and perfect and worthy. One hundred and sixty-two years ago Marianne Muse, the girl who was ripped from a corpse on the scaffold, had left three hundred gold francs underneath the fiftieth vine. Today Katya had discovered two hundred and seventy coins.

Someone else knew about the money.

But whoever it was, it was somebody, like herself, who took what they needed and nothing more. Someone without the greed to take it all. Or with the good sense to keep some hidden.

Now, after her visit, two hundred and forty coins remained. She and the mystery person had settled for taking just thirty coins a time.

'Where now?'

It had been a long wait. 'Now,' Katya said, and she could hear her words like fluttering doves, 'we go to find the treasure.'

The driveway to Chateau Montbelliard was topped with white limestone. It wound through a shallow valley and emerged onto the plain, flanked on both sides by lime trees, and like a clever vanishing trick, like a *trompe-l'œil*, it swept for a kilometre, or maybe more, past eternal plantations of vines, winding precisely up the valley sides, before cresting a summit and revealing the Chateau ahead, commanding all the lands it surveyed.

'Wow,' Milan said.

This wasn't a family home. This was a castle. Its cream facade seemed to stretch unfeasibly from east to west, as big as a whole block of city homes, its limits defined by four conical towers at its corners. The slated roofs looked almost too steep to obey gravity. They carved upwards like blades, with windows of their own.

On the pinnacle of one of the towers flew the tricolour.

Milan parked their car in an area marked for guests.

The man who came out to meet them was silver haired. He wore suit trousers, a waistcoat, and a straw summer hat, but he spared himself the jacket or a tie. 'You must be the mysterious Katya Hasek,' he said to them in English. 'Forgive my very poor French.'

'You're an Englishman?' Katya said.

'An Australian. I can do French if you insist, but unless you barely speak English, then your English is probably better than my French.'

'I can do English,' Katya said. 'My husband will have to wait until later for a translation.'

They sat in the great courtyard on cast-iron seats. The Chateau had been built as a square, with a tower at each corner and a huge central courtyard. The courtyard was a formal garden, laid out with a symmetrical pattern of pathways, flower beds, and ornamental shrubberies. A water sprinkler went *thuss thuss*, sending mist over one of the lawns. In the centre of the garden, where the paths all met, was a circular pool of polished marble, and rising arrogantly from its waters was a huge stone statue of a classical god, Neptune perhaps, with a beard and a trident, several times larger than life.

'So Mrs Hasek,' the Australian said, talking slowly, and leaning back in his seat, 'your letter was intriguing. By the way, I'm Christopher. Call me Chris.'

'And I'm Katya.'

'Does he own this place?' Milan asked, in Czech. Katya relayed the question.

'Dear God, no. I'm the manager. The Chateau is owned by Vins d'Apollo, they're a big conglomerate from Marseilles. And Vins d'Apollo are owned by Richmonde Marcel Constance, RMC, big boys in the wine business, and heaven knows who owns them, but I don't let it worry me.' He gave a huge Australian grin. 'Would you like a splash of wine – now that you're here?'

They tried the most recent vintage. To Katya the flavour was hauntingly familiar. She closed her eyes and let it bring back memories.

'So,' Christopher said, after a while. 'Exciting to meet a couple of celebrities. I read about your escape. A balloon, eh! That must have taken some balls.'

'Some balls?' Katya asked.

'Some courage.'

Katya nodded. 'I suppose it did.'

'Your letter was curious. You're either as mad as a bucket of snakes. Or you're lucky as shit. Either way, I like those kinds of people.' He laughed out loud at this. 'We have ten minutes and then I have to get back to work. Why don't you tell me your story?'

Katya grinned and swallowed some wine. 'It's much as I said in my letter, Mr Leadbetter. I am a descendant of the Montbelliard family . . .'

'. . . who no longer have anything to do with this place,' the Australian said.

'I know. I'm descended from Heloise Fouchard, who married Jean Sebastien and died on the scaffold in 1794 . . .'

'. . . after leaving all her family jewels buried somewhere in the woods on the road to Beaune.' Christopher laughed again. 'I know the story. Everyone in Dijon knows the story. You're about the one thousandth person to come here with a theory about the treasure. But nobody has ever found it. It's long gone, my dear. The forests are big out there. Wherever they stashed it, it has either been discovered and spent, or it's buried there for eternity. Sad news either way. But there it is.' He dinged his wine glass with a fingernail as if this would have to be the final word on the matter.

'Except . . . I know where it is.' Katya found herself looking into his eyes.

'Ah yes.' The man's eyes twinkled but his expression suggested he had a long way to go to become convinced.

'Heloise left a letter among her personal effects. It has only just come to light.' Katya stumbled over the words. 'I'm sorry. English isn't my first language.'

'You're doing very well. Now why don't we cut to the deal? Can I see this letter?'

'No. Why should I show you the letter? Then you would know where to look, and I would walk away without a sou.'

The Chateau manager seemed to find this amusing. 'You're getting one thing wrong, sweetheart,' he said. He shook his head in mock sorrow and wagged his finger in reproof. 'I'm not a bastard.' He held out his open palms. 'Truly, I'm not. I'm one of the good guys. But hey!' He shrugged. 'I guess you're right to be careful. I take it you think Jean Sebastien's treasure is still somewhere on estate land – otherwise you wouldn't be here talking to me.'

'I know it is,' Katya said.

'According to the legends, the Montbelliard family were seen by a hundred people taking it all away in ten laden carriages,' Christopher said.

'Two laden carriages,' Katya said, 'and the carriages were a decoy.'

'A decoy? Some decoy. One chest fell off and was raided for a ton of gold.'

'Not a ton,' Katya said. 'But it was a clever decoy. Jean Sebastien was smart. There was a lot of valuable property in that box. It had to look real. People had to believe the family had ridden away with all their gold. Can't you see? One box falls off by accident just as they are being pursued. It's a sleight of hand. It proves to the world that the treasure is real. It also seems to prove that all the Montbelliard wealth was on those carriages.' She blinked. 'But it wasn't.'

'So all the time the gold was here,' Christopher said. He gave a long laugh. 'You guys are sweet but you're dumb and you're crazy. I would so love this to be true. Such a pity it isn't.'

'But it is,' Katya said. 'I swear it.'

'Miss Hasek, you are beautiful and endlessly charming, and I would love to wave a wand and make you a millionairess. But do you have any idea how hard people have searched for the

Montbelliard hoard? They roam the forests with their metal detectors. They come here. They search the wine cellars. No one has ever found a brass beermat. Not in however many hundred years they've been looking.'

Katya looked at him and nodded thoughtfully. Then she reached into her purse and drew out a handful of coins.

'Hey!' Christopher said, 'you collect gold francs?'

'These were part of Heloise's legacy.' Katya counted out ten coins. 'These are worth two hundred and sixty new francs each,' she said. 'These ten are yours if you let us look for the treasure on Chateau land. They are yours whether we find anything or not. We need a few hours. That's all.' She pushed the coins across the table to the Australian who picked one up to examine it.

'I'm a wine maker,' he said. 'Not an expert in old coins.'

'If we find the Montbelliard gold, you can have ten per cent.'

'Fifty.'

'Ten.'

'And what do we tell Vins d'Apollo?' The Australian raised his eyebrow. 'Any treasure on their land belongs to them. That's the way the law works, so far as I know.'

'Why tell them anything? The treasure has been missing for a hundred and ninety years. They don't need to know it's been found.'

This amused the Australian. He took off his straw hat to fan himself, and beneath the hat, he had very little hair. 'You forget, I'm not a bastard,' he said. 'I'll take my ten per cent, I'll pay the company twenty per cent, and you guys can keep the balance, always assuming there is any treasure to find, and I'm not at all sure there is. Besides being fair and equitable, there are forty people who work on this estate; most of them are here in the Chateau right now, or out on the farms. They know why you're here. We don't have secrets. They'll be watching from every window to see which way you go. I don't know where you want to dig but you can bet, wherever it is, someone will see you.' He held out his hand. 'That's my deal. Take it or leave it. Do you want it in writing?'

Katya glanced at Milan. She muttered to him in Czech. They spoke in low voices. Milan looked uncertain.

'He says he trusts you,' Katya told Christopher. 'But he warns you not to cheat us.'

'Or what? Is he a gangster?' Christopher seemed to be looking at Milan's wire spectacles.

Katya shrugged. 'Not exactly.'

'Then do we have a deal?'

'Half of the treasure must go into a trust,' Katya said.

Both men raised their eyebrows. Katya translated for Milan. 'Heloise had two daughters,' she explained. 'If a descendant of Sylvie, her first daughter, should ever turn up here looking, they should have their half.'

'So long, presumably, as he or she can prove it,' Christopher said.

'I will know,' Katya said.

'Ahhh,' Christopher nodded. 'Well, it'll never happen. But just to avoid any doubt, we'll take all our percentages up front, and what you do with your seventy per cent is up to you. I don't care how you divide it.'

Hands were shaken all round.

'Now where is this secret stash?'

Katya placed her hands on the table. It was a hot day. She could feel the sun burning her face. In her memory there was a time when she was Heloise Maria Montbelliard, and she would sit here with a dozen ladies in silks from China and cottons from the Americas, and the men would pull off their wigs and play boules and the women would play cards. The courtyard had barely changed. The central figure-piece of the garden, the great marble fountains and the stone figure of Neptune surging upwards out of the wake, were exactly the way they were in her memory. The paths were neater now. The courtyard wasn't full of horses and dogs anymore. There were no servants. No children playing. No one raking up horse muck. But Heloise would still feel at home here, Katya thought. Jean Sebastien too.

'When the castle was built, in 1650, there was a well,' she said.

'There still is a well,' said Christopher. 'By the western orchard. There is no treasure down the well. God knows, people have looked.'

'That's a new well. The original well ran dry when Jean Sebastien's grandfather was a boy. The family covered it over.' A faint smile crossed Katya's lips. She turned away to look across the great courtyard, along the precise pathways and watered lawns towards the centrepiece – the huge marble fountain bowl and the looming statue of Neptune at its centre. 'How heavy do you imagine that statue is?' she asked, enjoying the look that fell over Christopher's face.

'Bloody hell – ten tons at least. It's granite. Twenty tons, maybe. Thirty?'

'Let's see.' Katya rose to her feet and walked across to the pool. At each corner of the stone basin a fountain shot a steady stream of water into the ornamental pond. Neptune rose up from the centre, his beards and hair wild in the winds and the waves, one arm holding his trident, and the other gesturing towards the heavens. 'Milan,' she called, in Czech, 'would you give me a hand.'

Already she was in the water, up to her knees and beyond, her skirts becoming soaked.

'Do you know what you're doing?' Milan said. He sounded anxious.

'He looks solid, doesn't he?' Katya said. 'But he's hollow.'

'He's colossal.'

'We don't have to lift him. Only his head.' She took hold of Neptune's right arm and pulled herself up as if she was climbing a tree, finding footholds for her feet, and throwing a leg across his shoulder.

'You be careful with my statue,' Christopher called. But he made no move to stop her.

Katya sat astride one of the statue's shoulders. 'Climb the other one,' she instructed Milan.

He clambered up.

'Now,' Katya commanded. She fed her arms around the giant neck and Milan did the same.

'Lift,' she called.

Between them they strained on the statue's head. Nothing happened.

'Try again.'

Again they struggled. Again no movement.

'I think that's enough,' Christopher said. 'The head doesn't move. It's all one piece of stone. There is no join.'

'Try again. Harder.'

Together they threw themselves against the stone head of Neptune, using all their weight, straining every sinew.

'Strewth,' the estate manager said. 'The bloody thing moved.'

And now, between Katya and Milan, the great head of Neptune was lifting.

'Don't drop it!'

'It's OK. It's on a hinge.'

With a dreadful creak of ancient ironwork and with a shake that seemed to make the whole of Burgundy vibrate, the statue's head levered forward on a heavy metal pivot.

'I told you so!' Katya was triumphant. 'You can't see the join. It's hidden under the beard and his hair. It's a trick.'

'It's a bloody clever trick.' The manager had joined them on the statue, his clothes, now, as wet as theirs. He clambered up, and together the three of them stared downwards into the hollow neck of the God of the Sea. A dark, forbidding cavity appeared to go endlessly down. Fastened onto the wall of the pit were the rusty rungs of a ladder.

4

Marianne, 1813

For several weeks Marianne Muse slept with Madame Cachemaille, Antoine's mother, in the tiny two-room attic apartment the family rented in Rue de Sèvres, squashed together with her, on the same small horse-hair mattress, fighting for the same scrap of blanket. Antoine's father was absent. He had joined the *Grande Armée* and was somewhere in Spain, pursuing Napoleon's Peninsular campaign. 'Better than being in Russia,' Madame Cachemaille would say, but she didn't give any impression to Marianne that Monsieur Cachemaille was missed.

There were four in the apartment. Antoine's older brother, Nicolas, was the fourth. He was a narrow-faced young man with heavy eyebrows and a soft smile. He had played a part in the Russian offensive, driving a heavy wagon in supply lines from Smolensk to Moscow, taking grain, haricot beans, and salted meats to very hungry men. It was a posting that mercifully kept him away from most of the fighting, but on the journey home he had lost the toes of both feet to the cold. His unit slaughtered and ate their only surviving horse, so Nicolas and his comrades in arms were forced to abandon their wagon and became obliged to hobble the long route home on damaged heels. Nicolas had arrived back in Paris in the spring, three months after most of the surviving troops. He rarely walked at all after the ordeal. He lay on a couch in the small apartment with the window shutters open, watching the queues for bread on the Rue des Sèvres. 'The *Armée* will pay me a pension,' he would say, but he wasn't an officer and the army had no money. It didn't seem likely.

There were only two beds in the attic apartment. Marianne and Madame Cachemaille shared one, Antoine and Nicolas the other. Madame Cachemaille smelled of more unpleasant things than Marianne had ever before imagined or encountered at the convent in Quetigny. Her teeth were bad and her breath stank of chewing tobacco, cheap liquor, and rancid meat. Her hair smelled of her wig, and her wig had an odour of dust and rotting tallow. Her nightclothes smelled of night soil, and all of this before accounting for her feet and her boots whose stench resembled a long-abandoned cheese. Bedtime, Marianne would feel, was an invitation to slow suffocation. Sleeping in the shit pile with the mules in Dijon might have been preferable. 'Can we open a window?' she would appeal; but Madame Cachemaille had an aversion to open windows. Who knew who might climb in?

She was wasting time in Paris. 'Antoine,' she demanded, 'I want you to use your friendship with Jacques Renault and the Comité de Sûreté to do me a service.'

Her courtship with Antoine had not progressed in the way she had planned, or Antoine, perhaps, had imagined. He was as eager as ever, but she had rather lost interest. Perhaps it was his less-than-inviting home, or his suffocating mother – it was hard to say. Perhaps it was because Nicolas, the war hero brother, despite his damaged feet, was altogether more entertaining company. Perhaps it was *her*. Maybe she wasn't ready yet. 'Please remember, I am from the sisterhood,' she would caution Antoine if his advances looked in danger of going too far. She would cup her hands over the front of his culottes and fondle whatever lay beneath, until he seemed ready to choke, and then she would draw her hands away. 'This is as much as I can do,' she would tell him. 'I'm not ready for marriage or motherhood.'

She had a role to play in the service of the Empire, a position Antoine had arranged on her behalf. She, like Antoine, was posted at one of the city gates to check the comings and goings of traders. The guidelines were loose. She was to help Antoine and the assortment of Comité volunteers, like herself, to identify enemies of the Republic. 'There are so many wagons coming into the city every day,' a Comité man explained to her, 'we need all the help we can get.' 'How will I recognise an enemy?' she had asked. 'You will smell them,' she was told. Spaniards would invariably be spies. Englishmen were always suspect. Russians could be shot on sight if they carried no official letters of introduction. Anyone travelling with more weapons than might be expected for personal protection, anyone who looked shifty, anyone who cursed the Emperor, or who muttered unheard oaths beneath their breath, or had ambiguous reasons for being in the city, or who looked unreasonably rich – all of these people should be questioned carefully. The role was essentially unpaid, but there were spoils to be earned. Searching wagons could take time, and most merchants would openly offer a voluntary donation to the Comité, in exchange for which they might hope for an easy passage through the gates. These donations would be pocketed by the Comité commander, with a promise that the money would find its way into city coffers. With a flourish of a pen he would write a *reçu* and numbers would be written into a ledger. The numbers, Antoine pointed out softly to Marianne, were rarely as high as the sum donated. But that was all right. The commander deserved recognition. His diligence was keeping the city safe.

Some merchants would prefer to make a more discreet contribution; they would press a coin, furtively, into the palm of the Comité volunteer who checked their wagon. No words would be spoken, but an eyebrow might be raised, and the trader would be waved through. 'Isn't this extortion?' Marianne asked Antoine. She had noticed the difficulty travellers could have if no money was offered. But the young man scoffed at her piety. 'They choose to reward our skill at recognising honest merchants,' he said. 'And without some generosity we would have no volunteers, and with no volunteers we would have a city full of spies. Is that what you'd like to see?'

The Comité de Sûreté Générale, Marianne learned, were ever on the lookout for spies and enemies of the Empire. Marianne became, herself, a sort of spy. 'Listen out for subversive conversations,' she was told, 'and report them to the Comité.' This was an unsettling commission. Standing in the bread queue, every eavesdropping could be interpreted badly if she chose to do so. Marianne wasn't ready to initiate a persecution of hungry innocents. Instead she invented fictitious miscreants and reported these. A man with a blue suit and a plaited wig had cursed the Emperor. A woman called Mathilde with no teeth or hair had blamed her misfortune on the fall of the Consulate and on the coronation of Napoleon. Marianne's fictions were inventive, and she filed a dozen or more, but she had the good fortune to be telling them at a time when the Comité was too stretched to pursue any but the clearest-cut cases. Besides, the steam of revolutionary fervour had dissipated since the great heydays of the terror, and the shortage of food in the capital was a more pressing problem for even the servants of the Empire. A clerk with no wig would write her information down in a ledger. 'Mathilde,' he would echo, slowly, 'did you get a second name?'

'No. Sorry. But she wore a blanket shawl of black wool.'

He would nod at her and record this fact. 'Black wool. Don't worry if this information isn't acted on immediately. This is all useful to the Empire.'

'I do my best,' she would say.

'That is all any of us can do.'

'Have you spoken to Jacques?' she demanded of Antoine, one evening when her powers of invention were wearing thin.

'Remind me what service you would like from him?' Antoine asked. Perhaps he too was tiring of the charade.

'I need to find a man who served with the Jacobins in Dijon. He was in charge of security in Bourgogne during the revolution and he became commander of forces. I believe he is somewhere in Paris. His name is Roderique Églefin. I need to know where to find him, and I need a letter of introduction from the Directory. Maybe from Talleyrand himself, if possible.'

Antoine looked at her as if her suggestion was utmost folly. 'Why would you want such a thing?'

'Because I wish to serve the Empire. And because I have unfinished matters to settle with Monsieur Églefin,' she said. 'The enquiries must be discreet. I don't want to arouse suspicion.'

His eyes narrowed. 'Were you lovers?'

She spat. 'He is an old man,' she said. 'And I am a virgin, and likely to stay that way until I can find him.'

'Is it revenge?'

'It is a settling of accounts.'

Antoine looked uncertain. 'What about us?' He meant, *What about our courtship?*

'The Empire is more important than us,' she riposted. This would be a difficult argument to counter. 'I cannot allow myself to think about us, until my business with Églefin is completed.'

Antoine drew himself up and succeeded in looking offended. 'Very well,' he said. 'I will try. But I have other duties. I cannot spend all my days making enquiries about a man I don't even know.'

Whatever enquiries Antoine made, they didn't bear much fruit. 'No one I have spoken to has heard of him,' he said airily the next time Marianne asked. 'I have mentioned his name, but no one knows of an Églefin.'

'There will be records.' This intervention came from Nicolas, the elder brother, at his window. 'The *Armée* keeps records of all serving officers. Have you asked at the General Headquarters?'

'I can't go marching into Army General Headquarters demanding to know where a senior officer is,' Antoine protested. 'For a start, Marianne wants discretion.'

Marianne may indeed have wanted discretion, but her patience was running short. 'Then I will go myself,' she said. 'I had hoped you might have connections; people who could help you. But if all it needs is for someone to enquire at the Army office, I can do that.'

'No need.' Antoine sounded offended by this proposition. 'I shall find him. Tomorrow I shall find him.'

'Good,' Marianne said, and she exhaled slowly, a whistle between her teeth. Perhaps I shall not need to sleep with this family for many more days, she thought.

'I have found him,' Antoine declared the next evening, casting a dismissive glance towards his brother. 'I found a man in the Comité who knows of him.'

'And where is he?' Marianne demanded, springing to her feet.

'He is out east,' Antoine said.

Nicolas gave a contemptuous laugh. 'East! Well, that helps a great deal. My dear,' he turned to address Marianne, 'the man you seek is out east. Somewhere between Liège and *le Royaume d'Italie*.'

'I have it better than that.' Antoine was turning red. 'He is in the Swiss Confederation.'

'Ah, Switzerland,' Nicolas taunted. 'Well, that narrows it down. You may have to climb a few mountains to find him but I shouldn't let that worry you.'

'I can find him,' Marianne said. 'If I know he is in Switzerland, I can find him. Do you have a letter of introduction?'

Antoine scowled. 'What good would it do?'

'He is a secretive man. He won't see me without an introduction.'

The next evening Antoine climbed the staircase to the attic apartment bearing a letter. Marianne, Nicolas, and Madame Cachemaille were squeezed around the window in the apartment. Nicolas was absorbed watching a group of women in the street, remonstrating with a baker.

'Here it is,' Antoine brandished the paper as he came through the door.

'Let me see.'

The document was short, but to the point. '*This letter introduces Antoine Cachemaille and Marianne Muse who serve the Empire in Paris with the Comité de Sûreté and wish to continue their patriotic service.*' It was signed by Georges D'Oré.

Marianne read it twice. 'You've included your name,' she said. Her tone of voice betrayed her irritation.

'I shall come with you, of course,' Antoine said. 'Switzerland is a long distance away. This would be a dangerous journey for a woman.'

Marianne ignored this remark. 'It isn't addressed to Églefin.'

'It is addressed to whomsoever we choose.'

'And who is this Georges D'Oré?' she demanded. 'I've never heard of him.'

'He is the section leader of the Comité, a very important man.'

'So important, I've been here for four weeks and I've never heard his name.' She thrust the letter back into Antoine's hands. 'This won't do. This isn't even Jacques Renault and I thought he was supposed to be your friend. I need a name Églefin will recognise. Talleyrand or someone more important.'

'You're being stupid,' Antoine said. 'I can't possibly get Talleyrand. He doesn't have time to sign letters for silly country girls.'

Silly country girls.

'This is what happens when you beg a favour of my brother.' This comment came from Nicolas. His gaze was still out of the window. 'You should have asked me.'

'Oh yes,' Antoine snapped. His tone was sarcastic. 'Of course she should have asked you. A cripple with no friends. And I suppose you would go right to the top and ask de Cambacérès.' He twisted his knees inwards and hobbled across the room in a cruel mimicry of his brother, tugging piteously at his hair. 'Dear Monsiuer Jean Jacques, I am a humble soldier without a pension and I have an infatuation with my brother's mistress, please would you be so good as to write this letter

156

of introduction.' He sank onto a chair, amused by his own performance.

'Give me that.' Nicolas tried, but failed to snatch the letter from Antoine's hand. He leaned heavily on the arms of his chair.

'You shouldn't mock your brother,' Madame Cachemaille chided Antoine.

'He asks for it,' Antoine riposted, waving the letter as if it was a declaration. 'What does he know about the workings of the Republic? He only knows how to cut off his toes. And how to look down girls' dresses.'

Nicolas lifted himself up to a standing position. He stood unsteadily on his damaged feet. 'Give me a day,' he said.

'Nicolas, you don't have to do this,' Marianne said. 'You don't have to prove yourself to your brother.'

'No.' Nicolas limped to the door. 'Not to my brother.' He pushed the door behind him and they could hear the difficult sounds of his steps going down the staircase to the street.

5

Katya, 1980

So many years. So many memories. And now. After eight generations, it felt as if the wheel had turned a full circle. Here she was, Katarína Hasek, Katya, the first descendant of Marianne Muse ever to have the opportunity to step into the courtyard of Chateau Montbelliard-les-Pins, the first to lift the head off Neptune and to gaze into the deep well that lay beneath him.

Christopher, the vineyard manager, went in search of a torch. At the neck of the statue, Katya became aware of eyes watching from the courtyard windows.

'Is it really down there?' Milan asked her.

'Oh yes.' Katya could feel herself grinning.

'Will we be rich?' Milan asked her.

'We will be half rich,' she told him.

Christopher returned with the torch and a roll of rope. He passed the rope to Katya. 'I guess you're going first,' he said. 'Tie this around your chest. It's just a precaution. When you get to the bottom, untie it and we'll follow you down.'

The iron rungs looked unsafe. They felt rough and rusty to the hands.

'Take it easy.'

With the torch between her teeth, Katya started to descend. Heloise had never been down the well, she realised. She had no memories of this dark descent. How far did it go? She couldn't tell.

Above her the little circle of daylight was growing smaller.

'Are you OK?' Milan's voice sounded some way away.

'Yes.'

It smelled musty. Like old wine barrels.

Down it went.

Down.

'Any signs?'

She stopped and shone the torch downwards. 'Nothing I can see,' she said. She was suddenly anxious. She started going down faster.

And her foot hit water. A splash of water up to her ankle, and beneath it soft mud. Surely they wouldn't have left everything in the well to get wet? She shone the torch around and a sense of dismay started rising in her. There was a large chamber – hollowed out beyond the width of the well walls. It was large enough for her to stand in. At waist height there were stone shelves all around. The shelves were empty.

'There's nothing,' she called up. Her voice was quavering.

'Nothing?' Milan's voice. 'Send me up the rope.'

She untied herself, and tugged the rope. 'It's all yours.'

She spun around with the torch. The treasure had gone. Most of the shelves were broken and the gold was taken. A numb feeling was settling over her. 'It's gone,' she cried upwards. 'All gone.' Tears were beginning to well in her eyes.

'Let me see.' Milan dropped down beside her and took the torch. He swung it around, taking in the empty chamber. 'My God,' he said. 'So this is where they hid it.'

'Yes.'

'And someone found it. There's no secret hatches?' He inspected the walls. 'There don't seem to be.'

'We're too late,' Katya said.

'What's this?' The torchlight had fallen on an object squashed into a gap between the bricks. 'What is that?'

Katya moved towards it and put her hand out. 'It's a jar,' she said. 'A silver jar.'

'Whoever took all the stuff left it behind.'

Katya looked at it. It was a small silver vessel with a screw lid. 'Give me some light.'

159

Milan stepped closer with the torch.

Katya twisted the lid. It turned surprisingly easily. Inside the jar was a piece of parchment paper, with handwriting like a letter. 'Can you read it?' she asked.

'Not easily in this light.'

'Let me try.'

The writing was small, in wiry black ink, in an old-fashioned hand. Katya read it aloud. 'It's in French,' she said. 'I'll try to translate. *If you who read this note are a descendant of Heloise then I conclude you suffer the same affliction that possesses me and my daughter. I can think of no one else who could have found the coins in the vineyard, and so I must believe you are my sister, born before our mother met her fate. Half of the trove is rightfully yours.*' Katya glanced at Milan. '*I shall keep it for you. Find me at noon on Heloise's birthday on a year when her namesake reappears, at the place where Jacques-Étienne kissed her. Sylvie. 1830.*'

They sat on the marble steps of the fountain. Christopher returned Katya's coins. 'The well alone is a great discovery,' he said. 'I don't need paying.' He shook their hands. 'Whatever your next move is,' he said, 'good luck.' He left them sitting on the edge of the fountain.

'I don't understand,' Milan said, when they had read the note for the fourth or fifth time. He was still struggling with the French. 'When is Heloise's birthday? When do we have to come back? And who is her namesake?'

Katya took Milan's hand and squeezed it. 'It isn't bad news,' she said. 'Not altogether. So long as there is a descendant of Sylvie's left after all this time to carry out the rendezvous.' She looked up at the long white walls of the Chateau, at the steep roofs, at the towers. She could remember this place in Heloise's memory. At night the windows were lit with candles. Heloise would sit here. Here on this very step. She would sit and watch the shadows and listen to the voices and feel the warm breeze from the vineyards.

'Heloise was born on 10th March 1759,' Katya said. 'She was named after the comet. After Helios. Comet Halley. That's her namesake.'

This information was dawning on Milan. 'So we're too late?'

'In a sense, my love,' Katya said. 'We're a few years too late. The comet came back in 1835 and again in 1910 . . .'

'And the next time the comet visits . . . ?' Milan left the question in the air.

'. . . will be in 1986. We have six years to wait. I think we can do that, don't you?'

'So what do we do now?'

Katya rose to her feet and held out her hand. 'We go and get the rest of the coins,' she said, 'I don't think Sylvie's descendants need them anymore.'

'. . . and then?'

'And then . . .' Katya smiled, 'I think we deserve a holiday.'

'I'd love to visit London,' Milan said.

'I'll show you the sights.'

6

Marianne, 1813

Heloise once walked down Avenue des Champs-Élysées, Marianne remembered. It was the day of the balloon flight. She carried her parasol to shield herself from the sun. It was a bright day. An open carriage collected her, and Joseph Montgolfier, and two Montgolfier sisters, from Place Louis XV and took all four of them to Chateau de la Muette on the edge of the city, and there they joined a crowd in tense anticipation as the fire was lit beneath the balloon, and the smoke swirled, and as Pilâtre de Rozier and François Laurent, the brave aeronauts, rose steadily into the blue sky.

Today, as Marianne and Antoine picked their way through mud and horse muck across the very square where Heloise had boarded the carriage, Antoine told her it had been renamed Place de la Révolution; it was here, he explained, that the King had been executed, and Queen Marie Antoinette too; here Charlotte Corday lost her head – she who had assassinated Jean-Paul Marat, the leader of the Jacobins; and Madame du Barry, the King's mistress, met her death here, and many more. Very many more. All had been beheaded in this square. Antoine pointed out the place where the scaffold had stood. 'I was too young to see most of the executions,' he said, 'but imagine all that blood. Have you ever seen an execution?'

She had seen her own execution as Heloise. She had seen a dozen beheaded before her, and for every head the crowd had cat-called with excitement and shrieked as the blade fell. She hadn't struggled. Her ankles were broken. She couldn't stand. She was wishing for the blade. Yet she was numb with fear.

'It's thrilling,' Antoine said. 'It is the most exciting thing you

162

will ever experience. To see a person's head cut from their body as easy as slicing a sausage. If you get a good place in the crowd I swear you can see the very instant the soul descends on its journey to hell.'

'I have no desire ever to witness such a thing,' Marianne said.

'You will feel the fear in your liver for a week,' Antoine said. 'For those few seconds you imagine yourself on the scaffold facing the blade. You are willing it to happen, and yet as the blade drops your heart stops. People in the crowd piss themselves. They can't help it. You never feel more alive than the moment you watch someone losing their life.'

Nicolas had not returned by midnight. He had not returned by morning. 'You fool,' Madame Cachemaille chided Antoine, 'you drove him away.'

'He went of his own accord,' Antoine replied, sullenly.

'He can look after himself,' Marianne said. 'He survived the journey from Moscow.'

'Only just.'

'Well,' Marianne said. 'He can survive a night in Paris.'

But now it was the second night, and still no sign of Nicolas. 'Where is he sleeping?' wailed Antoine's mother.

'In a ditch, I hope,' Antoine said.

Antoine and Marianne were dispatched to scour Paris. There had been more rain and the streets were heavy with mud. They trailed down Avenue des Champs-Élysées to the Isle du Palais. In the bell tower of the cathedral a bell was tolling. 'News from the Peninsula,' a man in army uniform told them. 'Another victory.'

'*Vive la révolution*,' Marianne said, mechanically. She had learned the ritual responses of this capital city.

Antoine found someone he knew outside the *Armée* buildings near the river. 'Have you seen my brother?' he asked, but the man shrugged. There seemed to be high security. A full detachment of guards stood outside. 'The Corsican is in town,' the guardsman said.

'Nicolas may have come here to seek out Jacques Renault,' Antoine told him. 'Are you sure you haven't seen him? Nicolas? He walks with a stick now.'

'So does half of Paris,' the guardsman said.

They picked their way through greasy alleyways back to Rue de Sèvres. 'We searched the city,' Antoine told his mother.

'We asked just one soldier,' Marianne said, but she said it softly and the comment went unheard.

Nicolas returned just before midnight on the third day. The household was asleep but Madame Cachemaille rose when she heard the front door, and she wrapped her arms around her son. 'You came back,' she wailed. 'You came back!'

'Of course I came back, Mother. I said I would.'

'You said to give you a day,' Antoine said. He had appeared from his room. 'It has been three.'

'So I exaggerated.' Nicolas gave a shrug.

'Did you have any success?' Marianne asked. 'Did you see Jacques Renault?'

'If you stand in line long enough, he will see you,' Nicolas said. 'He will see anyone who served in the campaign. You just have to be patient.' From his shoulder bag he produced a document rolled up like a scroll, flattened, and sealed with a red wax. He passed it to Marianne. 'Don't open it,' he warned.

The document was addressed to *M.R. Églefin, Chevalier, Général de division, Chateau Montbelliard-les-Pins, Dijon.*

'Dijon?' Marianne said in some dismay. 'He left Dijon years ago. The Chateau Montbelliard is almost empty. I was there just a few weeks ago.'

'He has been sent back. You probably passed his entourage on the road. The Emperor is gathering troops for a war against the Austrian Empire. It will happen soon. Everybody thinks so. Napoleon's army will be led by Eugène de Beauharnais, but the divisions are already moving east, assembling in the eastern towns and in Switzerland and Italy. It will be bloody. Maybe the bloodiest campaign yet. Dijon will be a garrison town. Your man Églefin is heading up one division. He's in Dijon trying to drum up recruits.'

'Then it's either the worst possible luck or the best,' Marianne said. 'What does the letter say?' Her fingers were caressing the folds of the document as if this was a thousand-livre note.

'I will tell you what it says,' Nicolas said. He sank down onto the bed that Marianne shared with his mother. He was grinning. 'I know exactly what it says because I wrote it. All it needed was a signature and a seal. It says, *To our friend and ally in Dijon in all matters our love and respect.*'

'Good,' Marianne nodded.

'It says, *The bearer of this letter is Nicolas Cachemaille who served the Empire bravely in the Battle of Borodino and provided regular supplies to divisions along the Smolensk Road. He is no longer fit for military service due to injuries suffered on that campaign, but can provide a willing and trustworthy member of your staff, and I commend him for this purpose. His wife may travel ahead of him on account of his infirmity. She is Marianne Cachemaille née Muse hereafter representative of the Comité de Sûreté in Dijon. Afford both representatives all respects and offices.*'

There was a moment of silence after this, followed by a snorting noise from Antoine. 'This isn't a letter of introduction,' he scoffed. 'This is a proposal of marriage. How dare you!?'

Marianne ignored his intervention. 'I'm to represent the Comité in Dijon? Églefin will never allow it.'

'Exactly!' Antoine said. He clapped his hands to add the exclamation mark to this point. 'It's preposterous. Typical of my brother the fantasist.'

'It is not a proposal of marriage, and I have no plans to travel with you,' Nicolas said. 'Unless you would prefer to have me there. But you will have more credibility as a married woman than a maid. The letter goes on to provide details of your salary and requirements for staff and accommodation, all to be provided by Églefin.'

165

Antoine was on his feet. 'This is too much. He'll tear it up.'

'It has a simple signature,' said Nicolas, ignoring his brother, 'just an initial. But Églefin will be more than familiar with the seal.' He closed his eyes and recited. '*By the Grace of God and the Constitutions of the Empire, Emperor of France and its territories, King of Italy, Mediator of the Swiss Confederation, Protector of the Confederation of the Rhine, Co-Prince of Andorra,*' here Nicolas paused briefly for effect, before slowly articulating the final seven words. '*His Imperial and Royal Majesty, Napoleon Bonaparte.*'

7

Katya, 1986

'How is my English?'

'Improving.' Katya swung the Renault onto a country road and moved up the gears.

'Hey! Take it easy.' Milan in the passenger seat was struggling with a road map. 'Let's get there in one piece.'

'That's great English. Well done. An idiom.'

'An idiom?'

'One of those crazy things the English say that makes no sense if you're a foreigner. We don't really want to get to Annonay in *one* piece. That would be madness. Unless we're English, in which case we do. How far now?'

Milan consulted the map. 'I'm going to say . . . sixty kilometres. We should stop soon and take a break. It's my turn to drive.'

They left the main road at Vienne and drove into the town. 'Forty kilometres to Annonay!' Katya crowed. She pulled the Renault into a space and raised a fist.

In the Place du Palais they found a brasserie with tables in the square. 'It's too cold to sit outside,' Milan protested, but there were no empty tables indoors.

'We can stand it,' Katya said. 'We're tough.'

'I don't want to risk you getting a chill,' Milan said. 'What about the baby?'

Katya shrugged. 'For the baby the temperature is always the same,' she said. 'It could be a blizzard and she'd still be warm.'

'Or he . . .' Milan said.

'Or he.'

It had been a long drive and a rough sea crossing. Katya

167

was nervous. 'I want to get there at *least* a day early,' she had told Milan. 'Just in case.' They had left their home in Liverpool on 7th March, a Friday. Heloise's birthday would fall on the 10th.

'Don't panic,' Milan would reassure her frequently during the journey. 'I'll get you there.'

They had planned to take the hovercraft from Dover to Boulogne but the weather on Saturday had been too windy and services were cancelled. Katya grew increasingly anxious. They found space on an evening ferry to Calais. Milan spent the crossing throwing up. It was dark when they drove off the ferry in France. 'We still have all day tomorrow,' Milan protested, 'and we don't have to be in Annonay until midday on Monday.' Milan was keen for them to find a hotel for the night. Katya was determined to press on. 'I shall drive if you can't,' she insisted.

'It's OK. I can drive.'

They drove overnight towards Lyons, stopping only once for coffee and fuel. Katya slept on the back seat, curled awkwardly beneath a rug. She snored softly. Sometimes the white flick, flick of passing lights lit her face up like an old movie. Milan, checking in the mirror, smiled at the thought.

'We're back in Dijon,' Milan said, early in the morning when all his body ached, and the dawn sun was a faint glow on the eastern horizon. He wondered if Katya would appreciate a detour to the Chateau Montbelliard, but her snores suggested the diversion would be unwelcome. He drove on.

They took breakfast in Chalon-sur-Saône, overlooking the river. Milan tried to reassure Katya. 'We have twenty-eight hours to go two hundred kilometres,' he said.

She looked at her watch. 'We should get going,' she said.

'I need to sleep.'

'You sleep. I'll drive.'

It was a mad, foolhardy trip. No one would be waiting in Annonay to meet them. Why would they? Who would honour a promise made a century and a half ago? Who would willingly give away a fortune?

'Half a fortune,' Katya would say.

'Well, who would?'

'I would,' she would say, and Milan would close his eyes and sigh.

'Don't drive too fast,' Milan told her. 'Remember our baby.'

'Our baby will be fine.'

On the radio Katya found a French-language station playing American pop hits. '*I feel lo-o-o-ove.*' She tried to sing softly. Milan was trying to sleep. A newsreader told her that a Japanese space probe had flown past Halley's comet.

'Did you hear that?'

He hadn't. He wouldn't have understood it anyway. And so they drove.

They changed drivers and crossed the river bridge at Les Perrieres. 'We're nearly there,' Milan said.

Annonay. The town where Heloise was born. Katya could feel an overwhelming sense of longing.

'Do you recognise it?'

'No.' But it was still Annonay. The hills were familiar even if the streets weren't.

They were in a maze of narrow roadways. Austere, grey, stone buildings abutted the pavements. Cars were parked untidily. There was a bustle of traffic.

'Which way?'

'That way.' She had no idea. No sense of direction here. She had never driven through Annonay except behind a horse.

They swung onto another narrow street. Milan was following signs for the centre. But where were they? Katya was unsettled. A building looked faintly familiar. A church rendered in yellowing cement stood on a corner. Could that be a church from her memory? It wasn't a church she knew. It looked odd.

'Do you know where you are?' he asked.

'Not exactly.'

Annonay wasn't a pretty town. Not even charming. How sad to make that discovery. In Heloise's memories it was the prettiest place in France. But not today. Windows were shuttered closed. Concrete was breaking in patches from walls. There was litter on the kerbside, and graffiti on a wall.

It was a Sunday. Shops looked unloved and unvisited.

Katya felt weary. 'We need to find . . . where we have to be,' she said. 'And afterwards shall we find a hotel?'

They drove into a square and Katya consulted a map.

'How old was Heloise when she left Annonay?' Milan asked.
'Twenty-five.'

'1784,' Milan said. 'And this is the first time you've seen the town since that memory?'

'I see it in my dreams. I saw it just a few nights ago. It's a sharp memory.'

'All the same, it's little wonder you don't recognise the place. Almost every building will be younger than Heloise's memories. Where are we going exactly? Where did Heloise kiss Jacques-Étienne?'

'It was Jacques-Étienne who kissed Heloise.' Katya closed her eyes. She had never told anyone this. Not even Milan. 'We need to find Notre-Dame del'Usine. It's a church on a bend of the River Déôme.'

'A church?' Milan asked. 'They kissed in a church?'

'Don't sound so surprised. Notre-Dame del'Usine – our lady of the factory – was the Montgolfier family church. It was right alongside the paper mill. I think it was built by Laurent de Montgolfier. He paid for it.'

'That's where they kissed?'

Katya gave his arm a punch. 'Well, why not? Why not in a church?'

'Where did *we* first kiss?'

She slid an arm around him. 'On the doorstep of the farm in Nová Vyšný.'

'No!' he looked offended. 'It was in the drive.'

'Almost on the doorstep.'

'Twenty metres away at least.' Milan returned the hug. He looked at the map.

'Here.' Katya stabbed the map with her finger. 'Where the river curves around. There's a little hill, and the church stands on the top in a clearing of black pines.'

They wound their way back through the narrow streets and found a lane that led them away from the centre, through woodland, hugging the river valley.

'There!' Katya pointed. Through the trees a white spire rose upwards into the clear blue sky. The lane turned up the hill, and there it was, the church of Heloise's memory, pure and unchanged. '*Sacrebleu!*' Katya whispered, and her right hand crossed her chest. 'We found it.'

They stayed at the Hôtel du Midi in Place des Cordeliers, little more than two kilometres from the church. 'If the car breaks down tomorrow morning we can walk,' Milan said. 'Nothing can stop us from being in the church at midday. So long as you don't decide to have our baby early.'

They both laughed at this. 'You shouldn't joke about it,' Katya whispered.

'You told me our baby wasn't ready to arrive yet,' he said.

'It's eight months,' she said. She lay on the thin hotel bed-cover and looked out over the terracotta rooftops. 'Babies don't come at eight months.'

'Some do,' he said.

'Not ours.'

8

Marianne, 1813

She was in the Chateau Montbelliard-les-Pins. How odd it felt. The *Armée* had altered very little. The great oak doors were untouched. The long, cool hallway with its sprawling mosaics of Bacchus and the Satyrs amongst a harvest of grapes, was almost as Heloise had remembered it, as Marianne recollected it now, apart from a little fading and some damage from boots. There were paintings still on the walls. Marianne could remember the way Jean Sebastien hefted pictures from their mountings and slit away the canvases with a blade. Portraits he liked had been saved; others had been left. 'Not enough time to take them all,' he had barked at Heloise. Now here they still hung, those abandoned canvases, the rejected uncles and forgotten cousins of a disgraced family. Who would even know anymore who they were? Who would care? There above a fireplace in the atrium was Jean Sebastien's great uncle, François de Montbelliard-Tellier, duc de Troyes, who had fought the Duke of Marlborough at the Battle of Ramilles and who, as all the world had once known, lived for thirty years after the battle in a relationship with his estate manager. On a landing was a portrait of a woman. Who was she? She had flaxen hair and curls. An ancestor of Heloise, perhaps. She had a smile that curled at the corners the way Heloise had smiled. An ancestor of her own, Marianne thought.

Not every painting was old. In the centre of the great hall, facing the stairs, hung a portrait of the Corsican in his full army uniform. Behind him, a battle raged. 'Thank you, Monsieur Bonaparte,' Marianne whispered to herself. She patted her tunic to feel the reassuring contours of the picker's knife. If her luck was good, she would use it soon.

Through a window she could look into the courtyard and see the great stone statue of Neptune. 'Lift up his head,' Jean Sebastien had instructed Heloise and Sylvie. 'If anything should happen to me you must do it together. It will take two of you to lift it, but you can do it. You are strong. Go back when it's safe. Be patient. Be very patient. Maybe ten years. Maybe twenty. When the revolution is defeated and normality returns.'

When normality returns. But what was normality? Not a castle filled with blue-coated army officers. Marianne smiled. Neptune still guarded his secrets. She would be patient.

A door swung open and a portly aide-de-camp emerged from the room that had once been Jean Sebastien's private library. His braided jacket was unbuttoned. He waddled like a man with a painful liver. He waved a document with a red-wax seal. 'Mademoiselle Muse, I am Captain Moucel. Your papers seem to be in order,' he barked. His tone was petulant.

'Thank you.'

'Where is your husband? This letter makes mention of him.'

'He is unwell,' Marianne said. 'He will be here when his constitution allows.'

'You must forgive us for our caution. It is very irregular for a . . .' the man hesitated before finding the word, '*a girl* . . . to be assigned to such a role.'

'Do you question the Emperor's choice?'

'No, no. It is simply . . .' he waved a fat hand, 'we have had no representative from the Comité before.'

'You have no spies in the Bourgogne? No enemies of the Emperor?'

'None whatsoever, my lady.'

'I am not a lady, Captain Moucel. And I am not a girl. I am a spy catcher.'

'Indeed.' The captain appeared flustered.

'Are *you* a spy, Captain Moucel?'

The older man started a laugh, but caught himself. 'No, my lady.'

'We have no lords or ladies in the Empire.'

'No, my lady . . . *madame*.'

'Show me to General Églefin.'

The fat man coughed. 'There will be no need. You will deal with me,' he said, peevishly.

'I will deal with the General. Do I need to remind you where this order came from?'

The aide-de-camp waved the letter and passed it to Marianne. 'Yes, yes, yes. Very well, then. Be here tomorrow evening at six bells.'

They stood for a moment, toe to toe. 'Will that be all?' the man said.

'Not quite. I will need quarters in the Chateau.' Marianne had found a memory of Heloise giving orders to her footman. It helped to be reminded of the exact tone of voice to use, the level of confidence, the sense of entitlement.

The man exhaled. The frustration caused by this request showed on his face. 'We will find you a room in the north wing. In the cellar.'

'You will find me a room in the south wing on the first floor with windows overlooking the courtyard,' Marianne said. 'Not the room by the stairs. I don't want to be disturbed all night by comings and goings. Not the small room in the west corner, or the room above the privies. I don't like the smell of piss.'

The aide-de-camp looked as if he might be about to splutter.

'Not the room with the painting of Medusa above the fireplace. I would find her too disturbing last thing at night. Nor the room with the hiding place behind the panelling. I don't want anyone spying on me when I take my *toilette*.'

'How do you know these things?' the man demanded.

Marianne offered him a smile. 'I am a spy, remember. It is my job to know things. And I will need a maid.'

'A maid?'

'A maid.' Marianne let her eyebrows rise. 'Is that unreasonable?'

'No, *madame*.'

'Very well. You may show me up yourself.'

The maid's name was Alice. She dressed in a plain wool shift that fell to her ankles like a sack. She wore no shoes. She tip-toed wraithlike around the Chateau in stockinged feet, as if perhaps it might be an ill omen for anyone to catch sight of her, or speak to her, or to otherwise acknowledge her being. She knocked so softly on the door of Marianne's chamber, Marianne was fortunate to hear the gentle pad of knuckles on wood. Inside the room, the maid barely lifted her eyes off the floor. Marianne beckoned her to sit down.

'I am forbidden to sit,' the girl whispered.

Forbidden to sit? 'How old are you, Alice?'

'Twenty.'

'Well I'm nineteen,' Marianne told her. 'We could be sisters. We should be.'

For just a second the maid's face tipped and her eyes glowed, but as quickly she cast her gaze back down. 'Yes, *madame*.'

'Sisters call each other by their names. My name is Marianne.'

'Alice.'

'You should know, Alice, that until a few months ago I was a novitiate in the order of les Chanoinesses de Saint-Médrine in Quetigny.'

'You're a holy sister?'

'I was a novice. I don't think I was ever holy. And as for being a sister – well, I have a real sister whom I've never met. So I don't suppose I'm a good one. Sit down.'

'Mistress, I cannot.'

'If I say you can, then you can. Who gives you your orders?'

'Mistress Chevrolet.'

'And who is she?'

'She is in charge of the domestic staff.' A flutter of anxiety crossed the maid's face as she spoke these words.

'Is she cruel?'

A hesitation. 'No, *madame*.'

So she was cruel. 'Alice, you are to be my maid. The only person who should give you orders in this house is me. You will live here with me in this room. Do you understand? You will sleep here on the *canapé*. My mission here is of vital importance to the Empire. I need to know where you are at all times.'

A tear, Marianne noticed, had formed in Alice's eye.

'I will instruct Madame Chevrolet to send your meals up here. You will attend to my room, my *toilette*, my *vêtements*.'

'*Madame*.'

Marianne looked at the girl. She was poorly nourished. Her face was marked with spots. 'Do you carry a knife, Alice?'

'A knife?'

'To protect yourself? To protect your virtue? We live in a household of men, and most of them away from their wives.'

Alice shook her head, but there was a spark of fire in the way she did it. 'I can look after myself, *madame*.'

'Can you?'

'I keep my weapons hidden.'

'Weapons?'

Alice looked cowed. She had said too much. She drew her lips closed.

'Tell me. Your secret is safe with me,' Marianne said.

'A knife is no help,' the girl said. There was a sinister note to her voice. 'A man can take a knife from you with ease, and then you are defenceless. But if any man should try to get the better of me against my will, then I have my weapons.' She slid a hand into a thin pocket of her smock. When her hand emerged she was holding a pebble.

'A pebble?' Marianne said in surprise. 'Do you throw it at him?'

Alice appeared not to have heard this remark. She held the stone out between thumb and forefinger, looking at it this way and that. It was a tiny fragment taken from the carriageway. 'If they find it on me, I can say I picked it off the floor.'

'It's still just a pebble?'

A glance passed between them, and for the first time in the conversation, the girl started to smile. Her lips began to rise. 'I use it for sharpening,' she said, her voice almost a whisper. 'One hundred rubs a day is all it takes.' Her eyebrows lifted. 'One hundred rubs every day. You see, I really do keep my weapons hidden.' She blinked, amused now by Marianne's puzzled smile. 'It isn't always easy, but no one ever asks to see a maid's mouth.' With a grimace and a tip of her head she let her jaw drop and drew her lips apart, revealing the full extent of her weaponry to Marianne; like jagged icicles, her teeth were a ring of sharp and deadly spikes.

How strange it was to be in the Chateau. The nails on her boots clicked on the mosaic floor of the great hall like the tick-tick of a marching drum. Heloise would have disapproved. 'You will mark my tiles,' she would have said. But a scratch to the floor was of very little concern now. Some windows were broken. One of the portraits in the great hall had been defaced. A statue of a goddess on the east staircase was pockmarked with bullet holes; someone had been using her for target practice. Marianne made a mental note. Vandalism should not be tolerated in the Republic. She should speak to Églefin.

Before she killed him.

Églefin. She tasted his name in her mouth.

Églefin. Heloise had seen his face from the scaffold. He had stood beside the guillotine, enjoying the spectacle, his breeches caked in blood, his face flushed with pleasure.

Églefin.

Lewd laughter followed her down a corridor. She turned to discover its source. Four young men in light-cavalry uniforms and a fifth in a rolled greatcoat stood laddishly in the eastern stairwell.

'You have a pretty behind,' one called at her.

'It would be prettier with my dick in it,' said a second, and all five reacted with laughter.

She turned and strode towards them. Tick tick tick. Her boots on the tiles. The laughter subsided.

'I am with the Comité de Sûreté,' she announced. 'I will have your names.'

The young men fell silent. They were no older than she was, she realised. Boys. Nothing more.

'You!' she addressed a young man with corporal stripes who looked to be the most senior of the group. 'Write down all five names and bring me the list.'

There was a moment of tension. 'Yes, *madame.*'

'I will do nothing with the names,' she said. 'But if I should learn of any man on the list making an improper suggestion to a woman again, I will have that man arrested as an enemy of the Republic.'

A longer pause. 'Yes, *madame.*'

She looked at the boy. He had a curl of fair hair over his eyes. Nervous eyes. He had freckles around his nose. He spoke with an accent from the west. In another time, she thought, he might have been a farm boy. She might have danced with him at harvest time. She might have supped wine with him in the summer meadows. What preposterous twist of history had made this country boy an officer, and dressed him in a uniform that cost two hundred francs, and sent him east in search of men to shoot? How many battles would he survive before another farm boy in a different uniform shot him off his horse? 'What is *your* name, Corporal?'

He hesitated. 'Guellec. Loïc Guellec.'

A Breton name. He had marched twenty Roman miles every day for a month for this adventure. Would it be worth it? He would have to march another month to reach the fighting when it started. His feet were probably red with blisters. His pretty, curly hair was almost certainly full of lice.

'Are you married, Corporal Guellec?'

His nervous eyes flickered. 'No, *madame*.'

She found herself tugging at an unruly strand of her own hair. 'Would you do something for me?'

'Of course, *madame*.'

Why was she asking him this? She didn't know this boy. This Breton boy. But a voice in her head was urging. 'Would you keep a lookout for me?' she asked.

His eyes fluttered. 'What do you mean, *madame*?'

She gave the boy a smile, and tried to tuck the tress of hair back beneath her cap. 'I'm new to this Chateau, Corporal Guellec. I could do with a friend. Someone who might notice if . . . I don't know . . . if perhaps I was to go missing.'

'Missing?' He sounded alarmed. 'Are you in danger, *madame*?'

'Not that I know. But will you do it?'

He nodded his head. There was a curious look in his eye.

'Thank you.'

Alice woke her at dawn. She dressed in the only outfit she possessed – the cream shift from the dressmaker in Dijon. Alice helped her to tie on her boots.

She slid her picker's knife inside the calf.

Alice raised an eyebrow.

'It's a precaution,' she told the maid. 'I don't have sharp teeth like you.'

'I once bit a soldier's hand so badly, he wore bandages for a month,' Alice said.

'Really?' Marianne was impressed.

She would need to start work to establish her credentials as a spy catcher. 'Can you take me to Captain Moucel?' she asked Alice.

She met the heavy aide-de-camp in the courtyard. The square was bustling with young men – volunteers and conscripts for the Corsican's initiative against Austria. Whatever could have persuaded them, Marianne wondered. Had they not seen the wretched soldiers limping back from the Russian campaign? Was the lure of a blue suit and a musket so compelling?

'Every Frenchman is a soldier and owes himself to the defence of the nation,' Moucel said, as if reading her thoughts. 'It was decreed by the Jourdan Act in 1798. Every man over twenty has to serve for five years.'

Over twenty? This crowd were more like boys.

They sat together at a wooden table in the morning sunshine and watched the troops assembling. Moucel drummed his fingertips on the table as if it was a military drum. 'This will be an infantry regiment,' he told her. 'A quarter of them are volunteers.'

A high archway led from the south end of the great courtyard out to the carriage yard where soldiers were parading. A group of around two dozen men came marching through in perfect precision, all in full dress uniform, black boots buttoned to the knee, dark-blue breeches, blue waistcoats with white buttons, white diagonal belting from shoulder to waist, red-and-blue jackets, epaulettes, and high shako helmets bearing Napoleon's crowned eagle picked out in gold.

'Do you know the most powerful weapon we possess?' Moucel asked Marianne. 'More powerful than the musket?' He grinned and answered his own question. 'It is the uniform,' he said. 'No army in history has dressed so finely. What young man wouldn't want his moment on the parade ground dressed like that?'

They spoke for a while about spies. Moucel insisted, again, that there were no spies or traitors at Chateau Montbelliard-les-Pins.

'How would you know, Captain?' Marianne asked him. 'Do you imagine they would wear a badge?'

'Then how do you propose to tell?' the aide-de-camp asked, a dismissive sneer on his lips.

'Ask yourself, who are our enemies?' Marianne said. 'Austria. Switzerland. Spain. England. Imagine you are the English General, Wellesley. You have been routed by French armies in the Peninsula. But more battles are coming. You know it. You do not wish to be so easily defeated. So what do you need?' Marianne leaned forward. She had learned this rhetoric from the Comité in Paris. 'You need information. How many men does the *Armée* have? Where are they stationed? What arms do they have? How many horses? How well are they trained? General Wellesley would pay well for this information, would he not? It is worth more than the greatcoats of a thousand men. So yes, Captain Moucel, the uniform may be the most powerful weapon of the *Armée*, but information is the most powerful weapon of the English. See these men?' She gestured across the courtyard. The column of soldiers in dress uniform had broken up and were resting on the low wall around the statue of Neptune, unwitting guards of the Montbelliard treasure. 'Can you be sure that not one of them is selling secrets to England? Would anyone among them enjoy some English gold in his knapsack? Do you know all their names? Does any one of them have a cousin in England? An uncle in Zurich? A grandparent in Vienna?'

'We cannot be wholly sure,' the Captain agreed. 'But how can we protect ourselves against one rogue traitor?'

'Vigilance,' Marianne said, and she said it firmly. 'But if there are spies, Captain, they are unlikely to be among the men. The information they possess is too poor. It is the officers we need to watch.'

'The officers?' Moucel was becoming twitchy.

'Picture Wellesley for me in his tent. Does he not have his maps? Are they not spread out upon the tables? Does he not place a chess piece here . . .' Marianne positioned an imaginary piece on her imaginary map, '. . . and say, *Here are the French defences, and here . . .*' another piece, '*here are twelve hundred horses and forty cannons, and here . . .*' a final piece, '*here is the Emperor and his household, and his imperial guard.* Does he not do that?'

The Captain looked uncomfortable. 'Perhaps.'

'Good.' Marianne looked up at the courtyard clock. It was almost ten in the morning. 'And now, if you would be so kind as to escort me to the stables, I need to borrow a horse.'

She rode the ten kilometres to Quetigny, sitting astride her horse like a man. Marie Antoinette, Marianne reminded herself, had always ridden astride. So too, she had been told, had Catherine, the Empress of Russia. She wore a pair of men's breeches, borrowed from the stables, and she hoisted her cream dress up around her thighs. Heloise had been an accomplished rider, and even though she, Marianne, had spent very little time on horseback, she felt comfortable and confident in the saddle.

She arrived at the convent a little after midday.

Sister Agata with the smoky eyes was folding altar cloths in the needle room. She leapt from her stool and embraced Marianne. 'Look at you,' she exclaimed, 'you have grown taller than me.'

'It has only been a few months,' Marianne said. But it was true. She had grown. 'I have been in Paris,' she said.

'Paris!'

'And Dijon.'

Sister Agata clapped her hands together with joy. 'You must tell us all,' she said. 'Every adventure you have had. How I have prayed for you, Marianne. Every night and every morning to our Holy Mother and to Sainte Belina of Troyes, who watches over me, and to Sainte Médrine of the Rains.'

'Agata, your kindness is beyond compare.' Marianne took Agata's arm and steered her outside into the light. 'I have a horse here for you to feed and water, should it please you.'

Agata's smoky eyes blinked. She couldn't see well outside. She wrapped her arms around the horse's neck and sniffed for its smell. 'A beautiful horse,' she whispered. She planted a kiss on its brow. 'It will be my pleasure to groom him for you.'

'I knew you would enjoy it,' Marianne said. 'I'm here to see the Holy Mother.'

'Let me take you to her,' Agata said.

Mother Marie was in her garden on a bench. Once their greetings had been concluded, Agata left them. Marianne sat alongside the Holy Mother, and they looked out together at a fresh row of seedlings.

'New life,' the Mother Superior said. She was referring to the plants.

'New life for us all,' Marianne said. She drew an oilskin package from her waist bag. 'I have a gift for you, Holy Mother.'

'A gift?' For an instant, the older woman's eyes lit up and as quickly they faded. 'We have no possessions in here, my dear. You know this.'

'But I may give a gift to the sisterhood,' Marianne said, 'with my request that they be used by you whenever you need them.'

Curious now, Mother Marie unfolded the wrappings. 'Eyeglasses!' she said.

'Made by a lens maker in Paris,' Marianne said. 'Formulated for a person of years who can no longer read in candlelight. Try them.' She took the eyeglasses and wound the arms around Mother Marie's ears. 'Do you have your psalter?'

The abbess was shaking. She drew a small volume from a pocket of her habit.

'Try it.'

Mother Marie opened the book. '*Si ambulavero in valle mortis, non timebo malum,*' she read.

'Though I walk in the valley of death, I will not fear evil,' Marianne echoed.

The Mother Superior unwound the glasses and wrapped them carefully in the paper. 'Thank you, my child.'

'You will keep them?'

'I will look after them for any sister who needs to use them.'

From the chapel they could hear the choir rehearsing for evensong.

'Sister Nathalie still sings sharp,' Marianne observed.

'She is blessed with enthusiasm,' the Holy Mother replied.

'I have found the man,' Marianne said. She looked away. There was an austere beauty in the Abbess's garden. There were bees on the vines.

'The man from your dreams?'

'The same.'

'And what do you plan?'

Perhaps it was the solitude of the garden. Perhaps it was the path that wove between the rows of seedlings like an ancient trackway. Perhaps it was the voices of the choir. 'I don't know,' she found herself saying.

'*Mihi vindicta, ego retribuam, dicit Dominus,*' the abbess said.

'Vengeance is mine, and mine the act of retribution,' whispered Marianne.

'So says the Lord,' the abbess said, finishing the line. 'Vengeance does not belong to us, my child. Only to Him.'

Marianne could pick out the individual voices singing the *Te Deum*. Sister Agata was there. Her voice was like a bell. Clear. Resounding. Sister Marie France had a low voice. 'You sing like a man,' they used to say of her. Sister Marie Elizabeth had a tremble to her voice as if she was touched by an angel. Sister Edith had a bellow during the louder passages like a call to arms. 'I can hear all the voices,' Marianne said.

'They are not the same without you.'

Could that be true? Could a whole choir suffer from the loss of a single voice? 'I have something to tell you, Holy Mother. But the tale is a long one.'

'We have until vespers.'

'I must ride back soon,' Marianne said. But she relaxed and looked out over the garden to the grey hills in the east. This felt like home. How easy it would be to stay here. Never to face Églefin. Never to worry about her family fortune. Never to pretend she was someone she wasn't.

'Who cut me out?' she asked. 'Who cut me from my mother's belly?'

'It was the Abbess,' Mother Marie told her. 'The Abbess

before Mother Ruth, who was Abbess before me. Her name was also Marie. Marie Claude.'

Marianne nodded. 'My mother passed a message to her, to Mother Marie Claude, from her prison cell. She sent a servant girl to beg the Holy Mother to cut away her child.'

'I believe she did.'

'She did.'

So it was that Marianne told the story of Heloise Fouchard to Mother Marie of the Convent of the Rains. She told her the story of Annonay, and Jacques-Étienne Montgolfier, and the balloon which rose over the rooftops of Paris. She told her of Heloise's meeting with Jean Sebastien Montbelliard, of their extravagant Parisian wedding, of the Chateau near Dijon. She told her about the visit from the *comité* of the third estate, how the able-bodied men from the Chateau had marched away to serve the Republic, how Jean Sebastien, Heloise and Sylvie had ridden out with laden chests on board two open landau carriages, how coins were buried in the vineyard in case of emergency, how the little family had stayed hidden until they were unmasked by Roderique Églefin. She hesitated before detailing Heloise's treatment at the hands of Églefin; these were not the kinds of things you talk about with a holy sister. But without the detail her story would lack justification. 'Heloise was used by Églefin,' she told the older woman. 'Over and over again. Every day. She was violated and abused. Her bones were broken. She was barely fed. Her tongue was severed to prevent her calling out, to stop her telling anyone her tale. And when her pregnancy began to show, when a court would, by law, have spared her from the guillotine, then Églefin himself arranged for her transport to Place du Morimont and he stood beside the *bascule* as the blade fell. That is the man I want to kill, Holy Mother, and may God have mercy on my soul, I will kill him.'

They sat for a while in silence. 'Can you be sure?' the Abbess asked when the silence needed filling. 'These are only your dreams. They may not be real. They may be your imagination.'

'Then why do I know so much detail?' Marianne asked. 'Why do I know about the balloon, and the vineyards, and the great house? Why do I know about this?' She drew a hand from her pocket and opened her fist to reveal a gold coin. 'This was buried exactly where I knew it would be. Here.' She pressed the coin into Marie's hand. 'This is a donation to the convent.'

'You cannot buy my approval,' the Mother Superior said, quickly. She pushed the coin back into Marianne's pocket. 'Not with money nor with eyeglasses. You cannot buy God's approval. *Non occides*. You shall not kill.' Her voice was angry.

'*Non occides*,' Marianne echoed. 'The sixth commandment. But what about the fifth? Honour your father and mother? God placed it above the sixth commandment. Why would He do that unless He wanted it to take precedence? And how should I honour a mother I only know from my dreams when her murderer and abuser lives, and struts, and whores, and quaffs wine just an hour's ride away? Does it honour her to let him live?'

'It is God who lets him live, my child; God who lets each one of us live. The Lord knows the world is a dangerous place, we are only here by His mercy. No commandment surpasses another. Each one is absolute. You cannot break one commandment to fulfil another.'

'Then what should I do, Mother?' There were tears in Marianne's eyes. 'Why do I have these memories if not because Heloise demands to be avenged? Why?'

In the chapel the choir were singing the *Agnus Dei*.

'God may be testing you,' Mother Marie suggested.

'Then let me fail the test. It isn't a test I want to pass.'

'*Agnus Dei, quitollis peccata mundi: miserere nobis,*' the voices sang.

They listened to the chant as it faded away.

'If I don't kill him, I could report him as a spy,' Marianne said. She explained how she had come to Dijon as part of the Comité de Sûreté.

'And what would happen to him?'

'If the Comité believe me, they would execute him.'

'Then his death would still be on your hands.'

So it would.

'Our faith is never easy,' the Abbess said.

Choir practice was over. The holy sisters were trailing out of the chapel, still humming the *Agnus Dei*.

'We are not the holy convent of sunshine. We are not the sisterhood of contentment and comfort,' Mother Marie said. 'We are the Abbaye Sainte Médrine – the convent of the rains. We are les Chanoinesses de Saint-Médrine de la Pluie. We are a sisterhood born of grey skies and storms. We are born to face challenges. We are given the strength to bear the rains, however heavy they may be. And after every rainstorm there comes blue sky.'

Marianne sighed. 'Rain is no great hardship, Holy Mother. Rain is an inconvenience at worst. A blessing at best.'

'Then take away that lesson,' the Mother said. 'The same thing can be a hardship and a blessing. Every coin has two faces. We can never see them both at the same time. But God can. A man can be evil and redeemable. Maybe this is true of Églefin. Maybe you see only one face.'

The interview was over. 'I must fetch my horse,' Marianne said. She rose to her feet, crossed herself and kissed the Abbess's hand. 'You have been my mother,' she said, feeling the familiar ache in her side as she spoke the words.

'And you have been my daughter.'

'I will never forget you.'

'Nor I you.'

It was as close a declaration of mutual love as they could ever express.

9

Katya, 1986

Five hours until midday. Five hours had never seemed longer. They took coffee in a bar near the church. I haven't felt this nervous, Katya thought, since Záhorská Ves and the night of the balloon. Yet what was there to be nervous about? If Sylvie had a great, great, whatever, granddaughter, one who had inherited the same memories, and if she showed up, then they would hug, and cry, and share stories, and maybe discover if there was anything left of the treasure. And if no one appeared, she and Milan would drive to Paris and go sightseeing, and she would show him the Eiffel Tower and describe for him Rosa's visit there in 1900, and then perhaps they would visit the site of the old Chateau de la Muette where the great Montgolfier balloon once flew. In a few weeks' time they would be a family. Deep in her belly her infant kicked.

Milan squeezed her hand. 'Our lives are fine,' he said. 'You, me, and our new baby. I woke this morning a happy man, and if nothing happens to change it, I will go to bed tonight a happy man. We don't need treasure.'

'It has always been me who says these things,' Katya said. 'Never you.' Something was making her voice choke.

'It's true,' Milan said. 'I may not have a fortune but I'm the richest man in Europe.'

They parked near the church and sat in the car.

Nine o'clock. Three more hours.

'Do you see that house?' She pointed to a sombre grey building on the far side of the river, flanked from the road by a high, and rather forbidding, wall.

'Yes.'

'Heloise was born there. It was her family home.'

'Really?' Milan squinted at the house. 'It's quite grand.'

'Very grand. One of the best in Annonay. Or it used to be when the Fouchard family were there.' Katya sounded a long way off.

'What happened to Heloise's parents? What happened to the house?'

'Heloise's mother died the year after Heloise and Jean Sebastien married. Heloise never saw her mother after her visit to Paris to watch the balloon. She had no siblings. Her father was sent to the guillotine a year before she was. After that? Well, who really knows? In 1792, the Legislature passed a law confiscating the properties of enemies of the revolution. The house would have become a property of the Convention, and eventually it would have been sold to help pay for Napoleon's wars.' Katya was toying with her hair. 'That was how it worked. There were no bequests from the scaffold.'

'Shall we go and see the house?' Milan suggested. 'Let's do it. We have plenty of time.'

Katya shook her head. 'I don't think I want to.'

'We could knock on the door. We could pretend to be sightseers. We could ask them to show us around.'

Katya grimaced. 'I don't think I'm ready for that yet.'

'OK.'

Milan pushed open the car door and stepped out. The morning was cool, but the sky was clear.

'Don't leave me,' she said.

'Leave you?' Clouds were drawing pictures on the sky. 'I would never leave you.'

'I'm having a contraction,' she said.

The hospital in Annonay had white-tiled floors and a wheelchair with a wheel that squeaked. 'I don't speak any French,' Milan protested, rolling the squeaking chair down a long corridor. 'How will I explain what's happening to the doctors?'

'You won't need to explain,' Katya said.

In truth, very little needs explaining in a labour ward. An African midwife with dreadlocks in a bun did most of the talking for them. She took Katya's pulse, and timed her contractions, and tried to find the baby's heartbeat with a cold microphone that slid around Katya's belly, and when she couldn't find the sound she was seeking, she pressed a button on the wall, and outside they could hear feet running.

Should they be worried?

A doctor came in wearing scrubs. She whisked the curtain around the bed and Milan was abandoned on the wrong side. Voices were speaking fast in French.

Beep beep, *beep beep*. Was that a heartbeat? It sounded too fast.

'Let's go,' the doctor announced in English for Milan's benefit, injecting a sense of joviality into the process. The curtain rattled back and the bed was moving. Milan shot an anxious glance at Katya.

'Scrub your hands, please,' the doctor said to Milan. 'Are you the father?'

'Yes.'

'This way, please.'

And they were off down another white corridor that smelled of disinfectant. Double doors swung open and closed. A male doctor coming the other way with another patient on another trolley engaged Katya's doctor in an indecipherable conversation, and neither one stopped walking; words were gaily exchanged, as if they were lovers – an odd snatch of hospital communication on the move – their final remarks lost somewhere in the maze of rooms and walkways.

'Scrub now, please.'

They had stopped and everyone was scrubbing.

'Wear this.'

A blue gown was pulled over Milan's head.

'You should go back,' Katya whispered. Her face was drawn.

'Go back to the church.'

'No.'

'We won't have another opportunity for seventy-five years.'

'I don't care.'

And flip, flip, flip, doors swung behind them and bright lights clicked on. From somewhere a noise like the scream of a person being smothered.

It was Katya.

'Are you OK?'

'I'm having our baby, you ass.'

'Your timing has never been good.'

'Did you mean what you said about going to bed a happy man, whatever the day had in store?' she asked him.

Her eyes were closed.

'I think it might turn out to be the happiest day of my life,' he said.

A clock on the wall may have been a little fast. Already it was showing midday.

10

Marianne, 1813

'When you meet with the General, you must not approach him,' Moucel cautioned Marianne.

'Why not?'

'He is very protective of his person. He has a great many enemies.'

They walked along the central corridor towards the great atrium.

'I wish to meet Églefin alone,' Marianne told Moucel. 'I'm not a danger to him. I'm just a girl.' She could feel the weight of her knife beneath her waistband. She would slide it into his neck the way a butcher slices a pig. She would let him bleed out onto the parquetry.

'You may meet him alone only if he permits it,' Moucel replied. 'And I doubt if he will.'

They were standing before the high blackwood doors that had once guarded Jean Sebastien's library.

Behind the doors they would find Églefin.

The windows of the library, Marianne knew, looked over the front lawns, down the valley to the southern slopes where pine trees shaded the pathways, where the setting sun painted the hills red, and where the vines grew vigorously in the summer sun. Jean Sebastien had loved that view. He could see the fruit ripening and watch the weather changing. He could sense the arrival of autumn. He could almost smell the crop waiting for the pickers. If she was alone with Églefin, she could kill him with a single stab and run for a window, and from there she could sprint for the vineyard. It was two hundred metres – no more. By the time the alarm was raised she would be gone.

If she made it as far as the vines, then the task of finding her would be like tracking down a devil. She could slip between the rows of vines and reach the forests, and then who could find her? She could sleep in the branches of a high tree. By daybreak she would be ten kilometres away.

But first she had to do it. To get him on his own. To recover her knife from the seams of her shift. To find a moment. To put all of her weight behind the blow. Not to miss. None of these outcomes felt easy for her at this moment.

And when should she tell him? When should she confront him with his crimes? Not before she stabbed him – for then he'd be forewarned; he could cry for help; he could fight back. But what if her blow was too swift and too deadly? He should not die without knowing who she was.

This would be difficult.

There had been, she recalled, a Flemish harpsichord in the room – a delicate instrument, decorated in white and gold and inlaid with ivory marquetry, refashioned to suit the music of composers like Mozart. Heloise used to play it. Would it still be there? It had been far too large for Jean Sebastien to conceal in the well. Would Églefin play it? Was it still in tune? Perhaps she could lure him there. Perhaps she might encourage him to play a tune and stick him with her knife while the music filled his head?

There had been books too. Hundreds of books. They had covered one wall. Titles by Voltaire, and Descartes, and Molière, the maxims of François de La Rochefoucauld, a treatise on trade by Barthélemy de Laffemas, histories by Gédéon Tallemant des Réaux, Pierre Boaistuau's translations of Matteo Bandello's *Novelli*. So many books. A few may have been removed and hidden in the well, but most, Marianne suspected, had been left in the library. 'We can take nothing that will easily rot or perish,' Jean Sebastien had decreed when the treasures were hidden. She could, perhaps, lift a book down casually from a shelf. She could admire it. She could speak knowledgeably about it. She could show it to Églefin, and when he leaned in to admire it he would lean upon her knife.

But killing a man would not be so easy. Dear God, this was a world where death stalked daily, where countless afflictions could rob you of life in your sleep, and yet the human spirit wouldn't easily relinquish its hold to another human being. She could feel it. Églefin would be on his guard. That was certain. The words of Mother Marie of the Rains would be there to stop her hand. Years of reciting scriptures in Latin. The *Agnus Dei. Non occides.*

The fear of capture, too, would haunt her. Could she face the guillotine, the way Heloise had done? Could she turn her eyes to look at the blade?

There had been, in the room, when Heloise lived in the Chateau, a hand-painted beechwood globe showing the lands of the Americas and the Empire of China. Would that still be there? And Jean Sebastien's cherrywood desk and secretaire; would these have survived unharmed? She tried to picture the room. Knowledge of the space could help her. Could she stab him across a desk? Would the back of the neck be as effective as the front?

Églefin's secretary, a pale-faced man with a thin moustache, emerged from behind the library doors, consumed with his own importance. 'The General commands you to wait,' he told them.

'We act on his command,' Moucel said.

The secretary disappeared back into the library. Marianne and Moucel lingered in the great hallway, standing on the mosaic floor. A pendulum clock ticked out the seconds of their wait. 'Does he always keep people waiting?' Marianne asked.

'He is busy with responsibilities of the Empire,' Moucel said.

'Are we not part of those responsibilities?'

'We must be patient.' The aide-de-camp looked flustered. 'He is not a man who will accommodate an interruption.'

Clearly not. Tick. Tick. Tick. There was nowhere to sit.

After a very long wait, the high doors opened again and a guardsman in blue-liveried uniform emerged. He didn't even glance in Marianne's direction. He took up a position outside the door, glaring forward like a mannequin.

'Who is he?'

'He is a member of the General's personal protection detail.'

What a job. To stand outside a room and protect a man who sorely needed killing.

They waited. An infantryman with a shaking hand came around lighting candles. He drew new candles from a pouch on his belt and secured them in place onto the empty holders. He didn't speak a word to Moucel, nor to Marianne, nor to the protection officer.

The day was growing dark.

The secretary emerged again. 'Captain Moucel,' he barked.

'At your service.'

'Please fetch two officers from the Voltigeur company. The General would speak with them.'

'Of course.' Moucel clicked his heels. 'The company is billeted in the town. I will need to send a rider.'

'Then send one.'

'What about us?' Marianne demanded. 'We've been waiting for two hours.'

The secretary scrutinised Marianne as if this was the first time he had observed her, and her appearance was an affront. 'The General is busy.' He made a pout with his mouth.

'Well, so am I,' Marianne said. She marched forward towards the door.

'*Madame*, you cannot . . .'

The library was unchanged. The harpsichord stood beneath the window. The books still sat on the shelves. The shutters had been closed and a fire lit. A man lay on a *canapé*, his boots off, his bare feet sweating, his eyes closed. His wig was off his head, resting on a stand, and his head was as free of hairs as an apricot.

'*Madame*,' the secretary swept into the room behind Marianne, and with him the blue-uniformed protector. 'You must leave this instant.'

'Églefin!' Her voice startled even Marianne herself.

The man on the couch opened his eyes and blinked.

Sacrebleu! It *was* Églefin. It truly was. Roderique, *the haddock*, Églefin. Even now she could smell his stink. Even with twenty additional years on his shoulders, it was him. Even with no hair and no wig, even with pallid skin, even with his phallus stuffed in his breeches, even fat and bloated and larded with chins, it was him. Roderique Églefin. His eyebrows still met. His teeth were still gone. He still had a wart on his chin. His eyes still led to the dark pits of hell.

Églefin. She wanted to choke. To vomit. To piss down her leg. To shit. To run, and run, and run, and run, and never to see his face or hear his voice or to hear his name, or dream him in her dreams. How sweet it would be to tear him from her memories like leaves from a book and cast them onto the fire.

The guard in the blue uniform grasped her by the arm and began to pull her to the door.

'Get off me!' She struck him with an elbow.

'My apologies, Monsieur General.' Moucel was in the room now, fussing like a fat hen. 'I told her to wait. I commanded her. I—'

'Who *are* you?' Églefin's voice. His fishy, oily, haddock voice woven with his stench.

She drew herself up to her full height. 'My name is Marianne Cachemaille, representative of the Comité de Sûreté in Dijon by order of his Imperial Majesty, Emperor of France and all its territories, Napoleon Bonaparte.'

She was being restrained again. The guard had hold of both her arms.

'Let go of me!'

'You had better let her go,' Églefin oiled. 'She is sent here by *Napoleon Bonaparte*.' He lent the name a curious emphasis as if mimicking her delivery. 'Do you *know* him, *madame*? Do you know our Emperor so well as to call upon his name so easily?'

The guard released his grip and Marianne shook herself free. She drew the letter from the folds of her dress. 'Here,' she said, waving it. 'Here is my authority from the Emperor himself.'

'Put it away,' Églefin said. 'I have seen it.' He rose from the couch and reached for his wig, pulling it onto his shiny pate, and adjusting it for comfort. 'How do I look?' he asked his secretary, raising his double eyebrow. 'Magnificent?' He turned to a looking glass on the wall and made some small adjustments. 'Do you know. . .' he asked, still engaged with his own reflection, 'do you know how many forgers there are on the streets of Paris who could manufacture a letter of introduction like that, complete with the seal, and the signature, for . . . I don't know . . .' he waved a hand airily, 'half a franc . . . sixty centimes, perhaps?'

Marianne felt a pain in her chest. 'Are you accusing me of forgery?'

Églefin let his lips reveal his bare gums. 'Not necessarily. It may be genuine. But then again, it may not be. Maybe Monsieur Cachemaille wanted to rid himself of a troublesome wife.' He sat himself behind his desk. 'You do *not* know the Emperor, do you, *madame*? You have never met him. If you had, you would have protested at once. So someone else has arranged this letter on your behalf. This husband, I assume.'

'I worked for the Comité in Paris,' Marianne objected.

'Of course you did. I have no doubt of it. But so did a thousand others. Our Emperor fears spies, and he has every reason to do so. But he does not send a girl to Dijon with no retinue, no security detail, no gift or indulgence to prove his faith, no husband to vouch for her, no uniform, no family name that I might recognise, nothing. So I ask you again, Madame Cachemaille, who are you? You do not speak like a Parisienne. You speak like a Burgundienne. I should know. I have lived much of my life in this godforsaken province. I know the voices.'

'I was born near Dijon,' Marianne said. 'I went to Paris to work for the Republic.'

'Of course you did,' Églefin said, but his tone rang with suspicion. 'Are you even married, *madame*? What is your birth name?'

'My birth name is Muse. It says so in here.' She brandished the letter.

'Ah yes. Muse. Marianne Cachemaille née Muse. Born in the Bourgogne. Who did you lose, Mademoiselle Muse?'

'Who did I lose?'

'In the *terreur*? Come on. We all lost someone. Who did you lose? A father? A mother perhaps? A brother?'

'I am an orphan, sir,' Marianne snapped. 'I never knew my mother, nor my father. I am an unknown.'

'An unknown?'

'Yes.' This answer felt true. She held up her head. 'I am not ashamed. I am a citizen of the Republic.'

'Very good. Very good.' Églefin rose from his seat and slowly, with deliberation, he walked towards her. His back had developed a hunch. His shoulders rose up unnaturally high. He walked unsteadily.

Marianne found herself taking a step back. Her hand slid down to the seam of her dress where her knife was concealed. She could smell his ugly rancour coming closer.

'You look familiar,' he hissed.

'We have never met before.'

'But maybe I met your mother? Maybe I sent her to Madame Louisette? The barber? Do you know her?' Églefin pushed his face close to hers. He made a motion with his hand and the sound of a falling blade. 'Louisette, the mistress of princes. She can turn any head. She can cut your hair with a single slice. Did your mother have an appointment with Louisette, perhaps?'

'I never knew my mother.'

'A shame.' Églefin stepped back. The stink receded. 'But maybe *I* did. Hah! Have you considered that? Maybe I did.'

He stalked back to his desk and sat back down.

He walks like a man with the pox, Marianne thought. She had seen such men in Paris, hunched over, on the streets, swaying awkwardly, with their heads too far down and their knees too far apart. 'Look at him, his balls are infected,' Antoine used to tell her when such a man wobbled by. 'His dick will be covered in sores.'

'I am here to seek out enemies of the Republic,' Marianne said. She straightened up and looked defiant. 'I will report your lack of cooperation back to Paris.'

'Will you? Will you really?' Églefin asked, making no attempt to disguise the sarcasm in his voice. 'I doubt that, *madame*. You may continue your work here for the Comité de Sûreté but I will read each and every communication you choose to send to Paris, and so far as I can see, you have no friends in the Chateau, no way to send a letter without my approval. So write whatever you like in your communiqués, but be clear, I will throw on the fire any message that speaks ill of me or any of my officers, or any of the men under my command. Which does not leave you much to work on, Mademoiselle Muse. Maybe you can find spies among the local farmers. Who knows? Until I receive confirmation from Paris of your appointment, you and I will not speak again, and you will receive no special favours from the *Armée*. You will vacate your room. There is a servant's bedroom in the cellars you may use. You will be subject to a curfew. You will not leave your room after eight at night, or before eight in the morning. We will place a guard on your door for your own safety,' he gave a sneer, 'and to ensure our terms are met. Take her away.' He waved his hand and the guard seized her wrist.

'And have her washed,' Églefin commanded. 'She stinks of horses.'

She dreamed of Heloise's childhood. There was a tannery on the River Deume, on the far side of the river from the

Fouchard family home, and when the air was hot and still, on almost any day in summer, the smells of rotting sheep and cattle flesh and drying skins would carry over the wall, and Madame Fouchard, Heloise's mother, would send out an order to close all the shutters and seal all the doors. 'I cannot bear the stink,' she would say. But there was no escape from tanneries in Annonay. Along with papermaking, tanning was the business of the town. A dozen tanneries had a home on the rivers. Each one had a smell of its own. In Heloise's dream she walked the riverbanks at night with her father, the astronomer, he pointing out the stars and giving them names, while she, in her turn, identified tanneries to him by their smells. 'The corners of Orion are Betelgeuse, and Bellatrix, and Rigel, and Saiph,' he told her. 'And the tanneries on the River Cance are Segomas, and Oriole,' she said. They crossed, in her dream, the river bridge, and her father bent to pick up a stone. She smiled, for she knew what he was about to do. At the top of the bridge they stopped. 'Make a wish,' he said. 'Make a wish as the stone hits the water and the wish will come true.'

'Hush!' What is that?

Marianne was a light sleeper.

'Voices in the corridor,' whispered Alice. 'Perhaps they are changing your guard.'

Perhaps.

The bedchamber was a small one and the bed was narrow. 'There is no *canapé*,' Alice had said when first she saw the room. 'I will sleep on the floor.'

'You will do no such thing,' Marianne had replied.

'Shall I go back to Madame Chevrolet? No one else has a servant sleeping in their room.'

'When I was a girl at the Convent of the Rains,' Marianne had said, 'we would sometimes sleep end-to-end.'

She slept in her petticoat – her *corset et jupon* – with all the laces loosened. Alice's feet barely came to her chest.

'Hush!' she said. 'Lie down.'

Voices. Low voices. And then . . . silence.

The cellar room had a small window high in the narrow wall. By good fortune a bright moon and a clear sky lit the tiny chamber with a cold, faint light.

Voices outside too. Some way away. Soldiers talking. Timbers creaking somewhere above them.

'Hush.'

And silence again. Her dream had not dissolved. These dreams never did. Outside, for her, was Annonay, and the River Deume, and sheepskins drying, and her father walking with a stick. The gout was troubling him, but the stick was also useful for pointing to stars. She was in that world where the dream and reality coexist. She was nine years old and her name was Heloise. She was nineteen years old and her name was Marianne.

'Don't fear. The door is locked,' she whispered to Alice.

Alice disappeared beneath the covers.

'Hush!'

And then the unmistakable sound of a key. Alice slid noiselessly from the bed to the floor.

Marianne sat bolt upright. 'Who is it?'

'Who do you think?' A man crossed the room in less time than it took for her to reach for her knife and his hand was over her mouth almost before she could sniff his odour.

Églefin. In the moonlight she could see him clearly. His arm hooked around her neck and pulled back her head. She struggled with every shred of effort she possessed but his strength was formidable. He pushed something into her mouth . . . a rag . . . and pulled a gag tight around her face.

She was choking. The rag was too deep in her throat. She couldn't breathe.

He struck her on the face with his fist, so hard that for an instant she lost any sense of where she was. Her head spun. She choked again. Fell back on the bed. Tried to grab a breath, but breathing made her choke all the more.

How fast he was. He had done this before. He seized each of her hands and tied her wrists so quickly and so tight, her efforts to resist him were as ineffective as her attempts to scream.

She caught a breath. A partial breath.

He struck her again. Keeping her dazed was clearly part of his technique.

'I know who you are, you filthy bitch,' he spat at her. He drew his face right up to her and stuck his tongue into her eye.

She clenched her eyes closed.

'I know who you are!' He pushed her hard against the bed and punched her again, this time in the mouth. 'You fucking little assassin. You think you can swan in here and wave your forged authorities and do what? Poison me? Shoot me? Stab me in the neck?'

Her body felt frozen.

'You know your mistake, you silly bitch?' He put his hands on her neck. 'You told Moucel how well you knew the Chateau. You wanted such and such room or some such other room. Not the room with this picture or the room with that window. Who would know that? Who would know this house?' His fingers started to squeeze. 'And you look like your mother. She was a whore too.' He drew back and surveyed her. 'I should have known right away. You are Sylvie Mont-belliard, daughter of Heloise. A daughter of this very house. How ironic, eh? We searched hard for you, *mademoiselle*, and lo, you walk into our lair like a fly into a spider's web.' He released his grip on her neck and hit her again with the back of his hand, and now his other hand was on the skirts of her petticoat.

She was trying to scream. She sounded like a strangled animal.

'No one can hear you, you silly bitch. Why do you think I keep this room? Why do you think I have a key? I can at least fuck you before I kill you.'

He was the devil. In the clear white light he was a creature

202

from hell. He rose above her, and his moonlight shadow covered half the room. He pulled loose his breeches, and he was laughing. Laughing. There was a darkness in his eyes, the darkness Heloise had seen. He leaned towards her and ripped up her skirts.

Her head was swimming. Her ears were ringing. There seemed to be a noise. A great noise. A roaring. A bellowing.

She blinked her eyes.

It was Églefin. The noise was coming from him. His face had contorted into a dreadful expression of pain. His arms were flailing like a dying man. He was screaming. That was the noise. He was issuing a terrible howl.

She tried to move. To sit up.

Églefin was striking at something over his groin.

Sacrebleu! It was Alice. Her head was attached to Églefin's pelvis. He tried to pull away. To stand. But Alice was a limpet not to be shaken off. A leech. Her jaws were locked. Now, even as he rose upwards, so too did she, and the agonies of this enraged him more. He was shouting but Marianne couldn't decipher his words. He struck Alice with both fists.

Someone was beating on the door. Someone had heard the awful cries.

Églefin struck the maid again.

Her teeth, Marianne thought. Her sharp, vicious teeth. *I keep my weapons hidden.*

The door burst open and a soldier with a lantern stood framed in the darkness.

'Get her off me!' Églefin commanded. 'GET HER OFF!'

The soldier hesitated, but only for a moment. With the lantern still in his hand, he leapt forward to do his commander's bidding. He seized hold of Alice's arms. He pulled.

'Not like that!'

But it was done. Églefin fell backwards, and his roar was the frightful call of a wounded beast. Alice and the soldier fell back in the opposite direction.

'What in God's name were you doing?' the soldier asked. He scrambled to his feet.

In the light of his lantern, Alice's face was a morass of blood. And for a moment that was the tableau. The maid looked as if she had bathed in blood. But the expression on her face was one of triumph. She turned her head, and spat, and a tubular piece of flesh slid from her mouth to the stone floor like a slice of undigested liver.

'Kill them! For God's sake kill them.' Églefin, wounded, was weeping like an infant.

The soldier held up his lantern. He drew a short *briquet* sword from his waistband. 'Are you all right, *madame*?' he asked. He moved towards Marianne, the point of his sword towards her, and with a deft movement, he sliced through the ties on her wrists. A second slice cut away her gag.

Marianne spat the cloth from her mouth. 'Loïc?' she said. 'Loïc Guellec?'

'At your service, *madame*.'

Sainte Médrine was watching over her tonight. She threw a weak arm over the young officer's shoulder and kissed him on the lips. 'Thank you.'

'I promised to look out for you,' he said.

'Not everyone keeps their promises,' she said.

'We must make an escape,' he said. 'They won't let you rest for this.' He glanced towards Alice, who looked like a character one might pay two sous to see in a freak show. 'Either of you.'

'I can show you a tunnel from these cellars,' Marianne said. She was grabbing her dress and her boots.

'Then hurry. We must be quick.' Loïc looked at Églefin. He had collapsed onto the floor, sobbing. 'Shall I kill him?'

'*Kill him*,' hissed Alice. 'Kill him.'

Églefin's breeches were red with his own blood. Marianne felt strangely calm. She pulled her dress over her head and dropped to her ankles so her face was close to her tormentor's. The darkness in his eyes had been replaced by pain. She put her

204

mouth close to his ear. 'My name is Heloise Montbelliard,' she whispered, and in that moment, it was. 'I am the woman you abused, whose limbs you broke, whose tongue you cut, whose neck you severed. *Mihi vindicta, ego retribuam.* Vengeance is mine, and mine the retribution.' She rose back to her feet.

Églefin hid his face. He was still weeping.

'I came here to kill him,' Marianne said to Loïc. 'The vengeance must be mine, not yours.' She held out a hand and the solider passed her his sword. It felt heavy in her hand. An instrument of death should feel heavy. Death should not be trivial. It should not be rushed. She held the sword at arm's length and pressed the point into Églefin's neck. His eyes looked empty.

'Do you know what?' Marianne turned to Alice and Loïc. 'I rather like him like this.' She drew back the sword. 'I think the regiment may enjoy his story of being bested by a woman and emasculated by a maid. Besides, we have to remember God's commandment.'

'Thou shalt not kill,' whispered Alice.

'That one, yes,' Marianne agreed. But in her mind she was thinking of Commandment Five. *Nam Deus dixit honora patrem tuum et matrem.* She could hear the urgent voice of Mother Maria of the Rains, and now she understood what the commandment was asking of her.

Honour thy father.

PART THREE

The Comet

Take care of all your memories. For you cannot relive them.

Bob Dylan, 'Nothing Was Delivered'

1

Halley, 2061

'Where is my headset?' Halley calls. She loses it a dozen times a day.

'You left your headset on the dressing table in your bedroom,' says the voice in her ear.

She climbs the stairs and pulls the headset on. Blinks to get used to the darkness. Takes a deep breath. 'Call Dr Gray,' she says. She is feeling heavy today. Lethargic.

The room grows light.

'Good morning, Halley.' Dr Gray is always cheerful.

'Good morning, Dr Gray.'

Dr Gray is a simulacrum, of course. A computer-generated doctor living somewhere in the ether. She has grown older as Halley has grown older. When Halley was a girl, Dr Gray was young and bright. She had a head of wavy brown hair with red streaks, and she had a button nose, and freckles, and the kind of delighted expression you might find on the face of a children's television presenter. Over the years though, Dr Gray has become more sober. Once, beneath her white doctor's coat, she wore dungarees and a patterned blouse. Today she wears an olive suit with a shirt that buttons to the throat, and she has spectacles that hang around her neck on a chain. Her hair is grey. She has pens in her coat pocket. 'How are we feeling today, Halley?' she asks, and her tone is more serious than usual.

'Tomorrow will be my fortieth birthday,' Halley says.

'Forty!' Dr Gray says, as if the date wasn't programmed into her memories, as if this milestone in Halley's life was a complete surprise. 'And you don't look a day over thirty.'

'I'm feeling OK,' Halley says. 'A little sluggish.'

'Let's see then.' With the headset on, Halley's room has transformed into an antique medical consulting room. The doctor sits behind a desk. She picks up a paper file from the table and makes a show of reading it. 'Eight days since we last spoke,' she says. 'That's OK. We don't need to catch up all that often if you're feeling well. You've put on a quarter of a kilogramme since we spoke – so you're fifty-three and a half kilos – still a little light, but I'm happy with that. We're making some progress.'

'You haven't seen the price of food,' Halley says.

'Oh I have. I have.' She runs her finger down the sheet of paper. The sheet of imaginary paper. 'Watch the wine,' she wags a finger. 'Blood sugar normal. Hormone levels normal. No cancer markers.' She looks up and smiles. 'All good,' she says. 'Can I smell your breath?'

Halley blows at her screen.

'Fine. Fine. That seems to be fine. Any aches or pains?'

Halley says, 'I've been feeling a little lacklustre.'

'Just tired? Or fatigued?'

Halley considers the options. 'Just tired. Short of energy. Short of oomph.'

'Then I'll prescribe you a walk.'

Halley groans. 'Another one?'

'Eight kilometres, please. Brisk. A two-hour walk. You can walk to the park and back along the road past the school. You can stop for an ice cream. But not for a glass of wine.'

'I'll do it tomorrow. Is that it?'

'Do it today. No time like the present. Also the weather is better today. Tomorrow I'm forecasting rain.'

'Rain is no great hardship,' Halley says. 'This is Liverpool. I'm used to rain.'

'All the same,' Dr Gray says, 'a good brisk walk today will do you a world of good. Build up some wellness credits. Blow away some cobwebs. Give yourself a lift. I'm still concerned about your mental health.'

'My mental health is fine.'

'I'm pleased you think so.' The doctor simulacrum draws a pen from her imaginary pocket and runs it down her pad. 'You've had nine violent dreams this month, and twenty-one non-violent dreams.'

'That's normal for me, Doc. As you know.'

'Memory problems still?'

'They're not problems. How many times do we have to have this conversation?'

'OK.' The doctor is nodding, but an anxious look is crossing her face. 'Do you remember that cheek swab we did last month? We've had some results back from the genetics lab. Very curious.'

'Curious . . . how?'

Dr Gray gives a reassuring smile. 'I've uploaded your medical history to Professor White at Imperial College,' she says. She blinks. 'It's absolutely nothing to worry about, Halley.'

'What is nothing to worry about?'

'You have an unusual genotype. That's all. It's like having a rare blood type.'

'A rare blood type?'

'Humans vary,' Dr Gray says. She puts her papers down. 'There is no such thing as "normal", Halley. You know that.'

'Does my rare genotype have anything to do with my dreams? With my memories?' Halley asks.

'It's possible. Professor White would like to run more tests.'

'Is Professor White a real person?'

'She is an AI.'

'Well, she can whistle,' Halley says. 'I've had it with tests.'

'I've booked you an appointment at St Helen's Hospital tomorrow at three,' Dr Gray says. There is a soft *ping*. 'I've sent Jacob the details.'

'I need to be in France next week,' Halley says.

'I know, I know,' Dr Gray says. She has heard this before. 'This won't affect your trip. Talk to Jacob.'

'Jacob!'

The room changes. Away goes the old-fashioned consulting room with its couch and its posters of bones. In glides a young man with a clipboard, and the background of Halley's room is now a busy office . . . busy, busy, so busy . . . two dozen PAs on the telephone, on computer keypads scrolling maps of Asia and airline routes in Central America. 'Hi, Halley.' Jacob is tanned, T-shirted, well groomed. He is Halley's virtual personal assistant.

'How are the plans?' Halley asks.

Jacob looks poised. Cool. 'All tickety-boo,' he says. He flexes his virtual biceps. 'Although I'm still waiting for permission from the European Federation for you to travel . . .'

'I thought they promised us a decision by Wednesday!'

'And so they did.' Jacob looks rueful. 'But Europe always takes its time with travel visas. You know that.'

'They think I want to stay in Europe and never come back.'

'Well, of course they do. They've had three million immigrants from Britain in the last—'

Halley interrupts. 'My grandparents were born in Slovakia. My mother was born in France. That must help.'

'Not entirely. Your grandparents took British citizenship when Britain left the Union, and your mother was born on a holiday trip to France, which doesn't make her European, or give her any rights to live, or work, or visit in Europe. In a strange way, it could even be worse for you than if your family had been British for generations. It makes Europe anxious that you might be trying to use your grandmother's nationality as leverage to stay.'

'I don't want to stay.'

'You can always buy a resident's visa,' he suggests.

'Oh yeah,' she mocks him. 'Fifty thousand euros and I can stay as long as I like.'

'It is the only guaranteed way you can get permission to travel. Europe is under huge pressure to take more people from

Britain, especially since the floods and all the evacuations. If you can find the money, I can buy you a resident's visa. Otherwise you'll have to wait and hope you get approval for a visitor's visa.'

'Oh, for God's sake!' Halley says. 'I'll walk across the border into Ireland and get a boat from Cork, if that's what it takes.'

'Halley, I think you've been watching too many films from the forties. No one does that and gets away with it anymore. If you try it, you'll pop up on face recognition the first time you pass a camera. Also, every AI system you use will be obliged to report it to the border police. Including me,' Jacob says. 'And Dr Gray. And Shirley. And your tutors. And Professor Berry. You know I can't be an accessory to a crime.'

'Then get me a fricking visa,' Halley says. 'Jacob off.' A red light flashes on her headset and Jacob disappears. She has waited all of her life for this moment. Surely it won't be denied to her now? She does some mental arithmetic. If she misses the comet she will have to wait until 2134. She would be one hundred and thirteen.

'Shirley!' she calls.

Shirley slouches into the room. She looks much the same age as Halley. Perhaps a little over forty. She's chunkier. Not quite so pretty. Her hair is cut in an unflattering, pudding-bowl style. She wears dental braces. She too is a simulacrum, a *Bessie-app*, a piece of computer wizardry, but she occupies Halley's bedroom as if she was there. She sprawls out on the bean bag. She kicks off her heavy sandals and rubs her rather ugly toes. 'Hi Hun,' she says, glancing Halley's way. 'These shoes are killing my feet. I mean *killing* them. How do you wear them? They look great but they're giving me blisters.'

Halley is wearing the same shoes. 'Maybe you have the wrong size,' she suggests.

'Maybe I have awkward feet.' Shirley groans. 'I'm getting bunions. I swear I am.'

'Jacob is still stalling on my visa,' Halley says.

'The little creep,' Shirley looks at her. 'You want me to speak to him?'

'If you think it will help.'

'Does he know why you have to be there? Does he know how important it is?'

Halley shakes her head. 'If I tell Jacob then he'll tell the whole world. Next thing I know, I'll be a feature story on *Jane and John at Breakfast*.' She mimics a voice. 'A kooky girl from Liverpool claims to have a rendezvous for a meeting that was planned in 1850.' She exhales. 'I'll be a carnival sideshow. The girl who pretends to have memories from the revolution in France.'

'Jacob wouldn't tell,' Shirley says. 'He keeps secrets.'

'Except if I break the law,' Halley says.

'Then we're all obliged to tell,' Shirley says. 'But having crazy dreams was perfectly legal the last time I looked.'

'They're not crazy dreams, Shirley.'

'I know.'

'I need to be in France next week,' Halley says. Her voice betrays a trace of anxiety. She has just two weeks before Heloise's birthday. Two weeks to see if a message in her memory from seventy-five years earlier, a scribbled note left in a jar two centuries ago, might just have set in train an unstoppable sequence of events across the generations. The very idea seems to Halley the most unlikely suggestion in the world; and yet she has waited all her life for this. 'I'll come with you if I live that long,' her mother Kay used to tell her. But Kay had died in 2043 aged just fifty-seven.

Her headset pings. A message from Jacob. She calls his name and he reappears in view.

'Any news on my visa?' she asks.

'I understand you have a medical appointment tomorrow,' he says, ignoring her question. He nods his head almost imperceptibly. It is a technique to help her with the answer.

'I'm not going,' she says. 'They want to poke me and prod me.'

214

'Halley, you must go. You *have to* go.' A note of concern has entered his voice.

'I don't have to go,' she says. 'There is no law that says I have to submit to any medical procedure if I don't want to.'

'Not entirely true,' Jacob says, but he looks anxious. 'You will lose compliance credits.'

'Jacob, it isn't your job to look after my health. That's Dr Gray's job.'

'Halley, they want to speak to you,' Jacob says. His voice has suddenly dropped a tone, has become slower and more reassuring. 'That's all they want to do.'

Halley recognises the routine. 'Don't give me that voice,' she says.

'Which voice?'

'That dumbfuck AI voice. That patronising *I know better* voice. That *I'm smarter than you* voice. That creepy *just obeying orders* voice. That voice.'

There was a beat. Jacob came back with a modified tone. 'How about this?'

'You're still being creepy, Jacob. I can feel it.'

'I promise you I'm not being creepy. This is my down-to-business voice. They need to speak to you, Halley. I'm just passing on the message. This is an appointment with Dr Kareem Masoud.'

'And who is Dr Masoud? Another AI?'

'He's a human doctor. A graduate of Michigan State University. Aged forty-seven. Married with a son. He's an expert in genetic memory.'

'He's an American?' Halley asks, a little surprised.

'He was born in Chicago.'

Halley thinks about this. 'I don't need a doctor,' she says. 'I'm not ill.'

'No one says you are ill.'

'Then I don't get *why* they need to see me. And I don't get why they're sending you to speak with me instead of Dr Gray.'

'I manage your calendar,' Jacob says. He sounds hurt.

'So manage it. Tell Dr Masoud I'm busy tomorrow. And the week after that.'

'Halley . . . I'm not supposed to tell you this . . .' Jacob appears to be doing his best to sound uncertain.

'But . . . ?'

'But it could hold up your visa. If you don't see the doctor.'

She sits up at this news. 'Fuck you!'

'I'm only the messenger.'

'You're a piece of shitty software. You're a list of zeroes and ones.'

'And you're a list of nucleotides. It's against online guidelines to insult an AI, Halley.' His tone is sorrowful.

'Get me the visa and I'll see him.'

'See him and I'll get you the visa.'

Impasse. She gets up. 'Jacob off,' she says, and he is gone.

Shirley is still there on the beanbag, still rubbing her feet.

'Shirley off.'

She has a walk to complete. If she misses it, it will cost her wellness credits. Eight kilometres. Damn them. It's cold out.

She gets to the hospital at nine in the morning. The escalator isn't working. She climbs the stairs.

Dr Masoud is a genial man with hair like an ageing rock star. He fusses over her like a hen. 'Do sit down, do sit down.' He sounds reassuringly American. He sweeps across his consulting room and pulls a chair out as if she was an invalid.

'I'm not ill, Dr Masoud.'

'Good. That's good. That's very good.' He is beaming at her. He combs his fingers through his wayward locks.

'Will this take long? Only, I need to get ready for a trip away.'

A look of concern flutters over his features and is gone. 'No time at all,' he says. He makes a little flourish with his hand.

'We should be finished by . . .' he glances at his screen, '. . . early afternoon.'

'Early afternoon? I thought this was just an examination.'

'And so it is. So it is.'

His smile is so wide, she is drawn to forgive him. 'Get on with it then,' she says.

He comes around the desk with a stethoscope and a tricorder. 'Say *Ahhh*.'

'Ahhh.'

He checks her eyes, her knees, her ears. Click. Photographs her this way and that. 'Uploading,' he says. His screen fills with words. 'You're a picture of health,' he says, still beaming.

'Then why am I here?'

'We need to do a small procedure.'

He is good-looking, she realises. He is warm. He probably has affairs with his patients. He is married with a son. She remembers Jacob sharing this piece of information. Nonetheless, when his fingers touch her skin, pushing up her eyelids, moving her face as if she was a mannequin, she feels a tingle. A tiny charge of chemistry. 'I'm going to France next week,' she says.

'That's nice.'

She waits for him to press her for details. *Whereabouts in France? By yourself? Do you need a companion?* But the questions never come.

She is lonely. She knows this. She has an artificial best friend. She hasn't had a serious relationship for six years. Damn it, she's making up fantasies about a doctor she's only just met. What is wrong with her? She lies on the examination couch and closes her eyes. She is drifting somehow. Afloat with her memories on a dark ocean, on her back, looking up at the night sky, trying to count the stars. Heloise knew the names of stars, and so does she. Cassiopeia, Arcturus, Sirius . . .

'Are you working?' he asks her, instead. Perhaps he is interested after all.

'I do eighteen hours of community work each week to qualify

for the national salary,' she says. 'But I don't have a profession.' She tries to smile. 'Not like you,' she says.

'Work isn't all it's cracked up to be,' he says and he turns away to tap his screen so she can't see the lie in his eyes. 'Do you have a speciality?'

He's making small talk. That's all it is.

'I specialise in the social history of France in the early years of the First Republic.'

'Gosh.' His reaction seems genuine.

'If I publish a short paper twice a year I augment my national salary by ten per cent.'

'And do you? Do you publish?'

'Look me up,' Halley says. 'I've written sixteen papers and two books.'

'Excellent. Very good. On the social history of France?'

'In the time of Napoleon.'

'Aha.' He unsnaps the cellophane on a medical drone and touches it to her forehead. 'Stay still,' he commands. The drone attaches itself, leech-like, to her skin. She can feel it sampling her blood.

'Would you like a chaperone for this next bit?' the doctor asks. He lifts away the drone.

'Why would I need a chaperone?'

'I will need to ask you to remove some clothes.'

'What is this for, exactly?'

The doctor looks defensive. 'It's just a procedure,' he says.

Just a procedure. He makes it sound unutterably benign. Why then is she hesitating? Jean Sebastien was the first man to see her naked. There have been plenty since. She sighs, and with the sigh she knows she is providing her consent.

How easy it is to drown in memories. To let them overwhelm her. To become their slave. And yet what are they?

She sits up, peels off her jumper, and unclips her bra.

'I don't need you to do that,' he says. 'Just your pants.' Now his smile looks less sincere.

Perhaps she did need a chaperone. 'Explain it to me. Why are we doing this?'

He leans towards her and she can smell peppermint on his breath. 'Have you ever heard of junk DNA?' he asks.

'Junk DNA?' Was that an illness?

'The DNA in our cells is a long, long, string of letters,' he says. 'Each letter is called a nucleotide.' His eyebrows rise. His face glows. This is giving him more pleasure than the prospect of seeing her naked. 'Do you know how many nucleotides you have? In every cell?'

'Lots?' she says.

'Three and a half billion,' he says, very happy with this figure. 'Three and a half billion nucleotides parcelled up into twenty-three pairs of bundles, and we call those bundles chromosomes.'

'Yes. I know this.'

'But did you know that ninety-eight per cent of those nucleotides are junk? They don't do anything. They don't code for anything. They're just baggage.'

He turns away and starts to touch his screen. 'There is a woman in China,' he says, 'called Li Huiling, who claims to be a reincarnation of her mother. Have you heard of her?'

'No.' Halley shakes her head.

The doctor shows her his screen. A photograph of a Chinese woman in a headscarf.

'No.'

'Most of us have pretty much the same junk DNA,' he says, 'but not Li Huiling. She has around half a billion nucleotide bases that seem to differ from everyone else. Even from her own family, and it is dynamic. Ever-changing. Extraordinary. Test her DNA today and it will have some differences from yesterday. And more from the day before. Almost as if she is laying down a record in her DNA. Almost as if she is storing memories in her cells.'

'*Storing memories* . . .' The words strike Halley like a slap.

'Would you remove your underwear, please? I can call a

chaperone if you're uncomfortable.'

He is holding a colposcopy drone. She has seen them in pictures, but never thought to encounter one. It looks uncomfortably like a tiny white fish. He snaps it from its hygienic wrapper and shows it to her.

She blinks. Hesitates. 'Is it going to hurt?'

'Not in the slightest.'

'What will it do?'

'It will take a sample of your ovaries. A few eggs. That's all.'

'And if I refuse?'

His eyebrows flicker. 'You will need to have that conversation with your AI doctor,' he says. 'They did say something about a visa. I don't know. That isn't my sphere. But the health service operates on the principle of compliance. You know that, Halley.'

Memories. How curious they are. These faint ghosts from the past. These ephemeral night-time visitors. She tries to look for a memory where she can lose herself while the drone does its work. Katya's wedding at the little white church on the hillside, the Tatry Katolícky Kostol. And the memory is so easy to find. There it is. The sun shines. There are children in white tunics. The women wear embroidered bodices, some in red, some in blue. They sing the traditional wedding song and everyone claps the rhythm. Jaroslav looks so young. He wears one of his father's suits. Where is this memory? How could she find it so easily? Another one. Paris on the day of the balloon. She is Heloise. Jacques-Étienne Montgolfier kisses her on the lips. She can see the aeronauts waving. The King is waving.

'Do it,' she says. She slides out of her underwear and shuts her eyes. Somewhere, high above her, way beyond the bounds of Earth, the comet has arrived. Comet Halley. Her namesake. She has already seen it. A blazing streak in the night sky. For a few short weeks it will swing past the sun, and then it will be gone, off on its seventy-five-year journey. Heloise was born when the comet was in the sky; Sophia Leitner was born in

220

Vienna to Marguerita, when the comet appeared in 1835; Rosa Seifert and her stillborn child slipped away from this world in Paris in the year 1910 as the comet flew by; her own mother, Kay, made an unexpected early appearance in Annonay as the comet made a distant fly-past in 1986. Somehow the comet and its decades-long time signature had become a metronome for her many lives. For the first time in ten generations, Halley realises, there will be no event of particular significance to greet the interstellar visitor. Unless her trip back to Annonay qualifies. Or unless she dies on this doctor's table. Has she failed in some cosmic contract? She will give up some eggs. Maybe that will be enough.

'I'm ready.'

The doctor has his hand on her belly. Her eyes are closed. At the Tatry Katolícky Kostol they are still singing the wedding song. The children are clapping still.

2

Halley, 2061

France. The churchyard at Annonay. There is a faint smell of lilacs.

Curious, Halley thinks. Do lilacs flower in March? She searches her memories but finds no answer. All the same, there it is, a soft aroma, a gentle scent . . .

. . . it reminds her . . .

. . . she closes her eyes. It reminds her of Heloise. How fitting. Heloise wore perfume that smelled of lilacs.

No.

No she didn't. She wore *clothes* that smelled of lilacs. Halley can recall it now. Her Sunday dress was packed for the week in an oak chest and sprinkled with petals to keep it fresh.

So it was.

Find me at noon on Heloise's birthday on a year when her namesake reappears, at the place where Jacques-Étienne kissed her.

Some things are easy to remember. Your first kiss.

Here she is. Heloise stood here in this very churchyard.

Halley doesn't open her eyes.

It was her birthday. Heloise's birthday. She was seventeen.

Seventeen.

So long ago. So very, very long. But fresh in Halley's memory as if perhaps it happened just a week or so ago. So much of the little town of Annonay, and the church with its dusty car park and charging points and vending boxes and safety signs, seems unfamiliar. They don't fit into her memory of the place. They are interlopers.

Katya was here. Katya, her grandmother. Here in this car park. Seventy-five years ago. It's another fresh memory. She

222

dreamed it again just a month ago. Kay, her mother, was born just a short distance away. That was the day her memories of Katya disappeared into a tunnel. Here in Annonay.

There had once been, she can recall, a long row of black pines from the church gate to the road. Now there are just half a dozen trees, and where the avenue once ran, there are houses.

The churchyard is too small. Is it the same? Can it be the same?

But the gate is the same; an iron gate beneath a stone arch. Here at this gate, Jacques-Étienne Montgolfier touched Heloise lightly on her shoulder while their families were congregating in the lane, all ready for the walk home, and she had seen a fire in his eyes, and felt the heat of the fire in the touch of his fingers. 'I left my parasol,' she told him. She whispered the words as if they were a forbidden secret, looking for the reaction in his eyes. 'I left my parasol in the church.'

'Then I will fetch it,' Jacques-Étienne said.

Her father was talking to the priest. His arm was waving. Perhaps he was telling the priest about the stars.

Her mother was out of sight.

'I can get it,' Heloise said. Heloise aged seventeen. Heloise a ripe fruit, like a September grape ready to be plucked.

He held the church door open.

Heloise's blood was awash with sin. She could feel it like an infection, spreading out from her heart.

There was no one in the church. Just herself. And Jacques-Étienne. And Christ himself on the cross. And the fire in Jacques' eyes. And an irresistible force.

Three rows from the altar. Right in the centre of the row. That was where she sat. That had been her pew since she was old enough to walk into church on her own legs.

Halley Hasek pushes open the high door. A spear of sunlight floods through from the east window of the apse. 'Is anyone here?' she calls. Her voice echoes and vanishes into the stone walls. 'Anyone?'

No one.

The lines of seats are there just as they had been when Heloise and Jacques-Étienne had braved the church alone. One. Two. Three. Her heels clack on the flagstone floor. She stops at the end of the row.

Heloise had done the same. She had stood at one end of the row, Jacques-Étienne at the other.

'I don't see your parasol,' Jacques had said.

'Perhaps it's under my seat,' she whispered. She knew where it was. She had hidden it there. Her heart had known this moment would come.

And so they moved together along the row, he from the north and she from the south, and in the middle they met where the sunlight at midday shone like a heavenly warning. Together they bent, to peer beneath the pew as if the parasol was the only purpose for being there, him in his fine tunic and her in her Sunday dress that smelled of lilacs, and their faces were so close she could feel the sunshine reflecting from him.

That was when he whispered, 'If I kiss you here, in the sight of God, will I be damned forever?'

Two hundred and eighty-five years have passed since she heard those words. Halley eases herself along the row of seats and then, because she is alone in the church, she slides down onto her knees. How long since she has prayed?

She closes her eyes. The prayer won't come. Perhaps it is the damnation Jacques feared.

A noise startles her and breaks her reverie. She spins her head around.

An old woman in a black felt coat and a grey cotton headscarf is standing at the back of the church. Had she come through the door? Halley hadn't heard her.

For several seconds they survey each other. Halley's heart is beating unnaturally fast.

Then the older woman speaks, in French, and her voice fills the church and echoes off the roof beams. 'If I kiss you here, in the sight of God,' she says, 'will I be damned forever?'

'If you are to be damned,' Halley says, the words emerging from a deep well in her memory, 'then let us be damned together.'

There is the shortest moment of silence.

'What is beneath the seat?' the woman asks. She is still standing, immobile, at the back of the apse.

'A paper parasol,' Halley almost whispers. Uncertain.

'Take a look.'

She feels beneath the seat and her fingers touch it. 'The parasol?' She can barely say the word. She draws it out and holds it in her palms as if any touch might crumble it to dust. An ancient, fragile object. The paper has turned brown and brittle with age.

'If you were to open it,' the woman asks, 'what decorates it?' She looks at Halley, unblinking.

'Birds,' Halley answers. Songbirds of emerald and gold. She pushes the slider as gently as she can manage, and like a butterfly emerging, the wings of the ancient parasol unfold.

'I think this means I ought to kiss you,' the woman says.

'I think perhaps it does.'

Her name is Camille. She has a lined and furrowed face and a pinched expression. Her hair is white. But there is something in her still of Heloise. Of Sylvie. They sit together on a bench in the churchyard and contemplate the view through the trees across the river valley to the town. There is the smell of baking bread. Somewhere children are laughing.

'Tell me your story,' Camille says. They are sitting very close.

'How long do you have?' Halley answers, and they both laugh. They know how the centuries have overburdened them with stories. Their shoulders touch.

'Why did it take you so long?'

'To come looking for the treasure? I never quite found the moment. I fled from Napoleon to Salzburg. I rather upset a

Général de Division in Dijon so I had to steer clear of the city for a while. And in another life I married a Viennese doctor who wouldn't believe my stories, and in another life I lived in London and then in New York, and when I came to Paris in 1898 I didn't need the money, and by the time I did – another me, of course – it was wartime. And I ended up on the wrong side of the Iron Curtain.'

'Oh dear.'

'And in 1980 I escaped. I should say, my grandmother Katya escaped. She flew across the border to Austria in a balloon.'

'Gosh.' Camille is impressed. 'That must have taken some doing.'

'It did.' She remembers Katya's fingers releasing the ropes. She remembers dropping into the dark. 'Anyway, 1980; that was the year my grandmother found Sylvie's note.'

'But she didn't get here for the visit of the comet in 1986.'

'She did. She came with her husband and they waited in a car. She was pregnant. And as they waited, her contractions started and her husband took her to hospital. Just about the time she was supposed to be here, in the church, she was giving birth to my mother.'

'Ah,' Camille gives a knowing nod. 'We have a habit of being born when the comet comes.'

'We do.'

They sit and watch the town. 'Salzburg. London. New York. You've had some interesting lives,' Camille says.

'I have. Not always happy. But never dull.'

'For three weeks in 1830,' Camille says, 'the Chateau Montbelliard-les-Pins stood empty. The Bourbons put it up for sale. King Charles was a silly ass; he was running short of money. The estate sold for a ridiculously low price to a wine-maker from Macon. But in the weeks that the Chateau stood empty, Sylvie paid off the guards for two hours every night, from three o'clock in the morning until five, and in those two hours, over nineteen days, she and her daughter Louise

226

recovered every item from the well.' She nods her head and gives a smile of satisfaction. 'They packed the treasures into wine barrels – not the small *rundlet* barrels, but *barrique* barrels – large enough to hold a great deal of treasure. The barrels were too large to fit down Neptune's neck. Louise would go down the well with a dozen baskets; she would fill the baskets and tie them onto a rope. Sylvie would haul them up, stuff everything into barrels, and nail them down. They were living in a vinery near Fénay – close enough to the Chateau that they could ride home before dawn and not arouse any suspicion. No one knew Sylvie's identity. It was a small farm with just five thousand vines. Barely enough to support a family. But it had a house and deep wine cellars. They filled ninety-three wine barrels with Jean Sebastien's treasures, and they filled the cellars with the barrels.'

'Ninety-three barrels!'

'There was more treasure than even Heloise knew. Jean Sebastien had been squirrelling it away for years. I think perhaps he started moving his gold down there soon after the Bastille was taken. Anyway. Sylvie and Louise rode to the Chateau every night just before three in the morning, with five empty barrels on their wagon, and out they rode the next morning before cockcrow with the barrels filled.'

Halley shakes her head slowly. 'What a story,' she says.

'They finished the task without a single night to spare,' Camille says. 'On the hour they loaded the last barrel, Sylvie wrote her note, the one your grandmother found in 1980, and they rode away early with the final three barrels, and the new owners of the Chateau passed them just outside the gate in a dozen fine carriages and almost drove them off the road. If there had been just one more barrel to fill, they would still have been in the well when the party arrived.'

'Our lives have been defined by narrow escapes,' Halley says.

'Sylvie used to sell her wine in barrels to a merchant in Neuchâtel in Switzerland,' Camille explains. 'The wine she made wasn't special. Not as good as Jean Sebastien's wine had been. Her slopes weren't as good. Her soil was poorer. It was difficult to get a good price in Dijon for Burgundy wines. Even in the 1830s the markets were awash with barrels. So, Sylvie used to sell her wine to the Swiss. They were less discerning, and their own wine was even worse. It was four days' ride to Neuchâtel, and just down the road from the wine merchants was Petitmaître Bank, the first bank in the city. One day, on a visit to the wine merchant, Sylvie pushed open the big doors of the bank. She met with Louis Petitmaître and told him she had valuables she wanted to store. He showed her the bank's new vaults, cut into the rock beneath the building. "You can have one," he told her. "I want two," she said. And the next time she rode to Neuchâtel she took two barrels of treasures among her six barrels of wine, and she deposited them, one in each vault. A month later she took two more. And then two more.'

'Two barrels a time?'

'Two barrels a month. Yes. Any more would have been too great a risk. It took Sylvie and Louise four years to transport every barrel. By March 1835 it was done. Sylvie was fifty years old. When Louis Petitmaître closed the vault on the final barrel, Sylvie asked him, "Would you like to know what is in the barrels, Monsieur Petitmaître?" and he replied, "Madame, I would not. My job is to store them safely, never to look inside." Then he swung the door and turned his keys.'

In the square in Annonay a brasserie serves diners at circular bistro tables strung out along the pavement. A robot waiter in a white cap wearing a gingham apron carries trays balanced high on its fingertips. Halley and Camille pick a table.

'You look as if you need feeding up,' Camille tells Halley.

'My doctor tells me I'm too thin,' she agrees.

'Mine tells me I smoke too much,' Camille says. 'We have to ignore them. You and I have lived enough years without them; we can live a few more.'

'Do you have daughters?' Halley asks.

'Sons,' Camille says. 'Two.'

'Sons?' Halley looks surprised. 'There's never been a boy in my family. Not one in the years since Heloise.'

'Boys don't inherit the memories,' Camille says. 'Only girls.' She makes a rueful expression. 'I have a granddaughter,' she adds. She catches Halley's eye. 'No,' she says to the unasked question.

'Then . . .' Halley leaves the thought unspoken.

'Then it is just as well you didn't wait for the return of the comet in 2136,' Sylvie says. 'No one would be here to greet you.'

They think about this. Three hundred years of memories.

'So . . .'

'. . . it ends with me,' Camille nods.

They look down at the table and Halley absorbs this news. The robot waiter brings their meals and they pick at the food. Neither has much of an appetite. They share memories of Heloise. Camille's memories end when Sylvie was born. She knows nothing of Roderique Églefin. She knows Heloise faced the guillotine. She knows Heloise may have been pregnant. But little more. 'News would come back to us from time to time,' she tells Halley. 'One of the servants from the Chateau went to the execution. She saw Heloise's body being cut by an old woman in a headscarf, and she swore to us that a baby was delivered through the wound. We never learned what became of the child. Until today.' She offers a rueful smile.

Sooner than Halley expected, they are running out of stories. There are too many to tell. Or too few.

'Did you ever wonder why?' Halley asks, after a while.

'Why what?'

'Why it happens. Why we have the dreams. The memories?'

The lines on Camille's face are like a map, like contours that trace out the patterns of all her lives. When she moves her face, the lines move into new shapes. New patterns. She purses her lips and a map of rivers runs upwards towards her nose and down towards her chin. 'My dear sweet child,' she says, 'your question makes no sense.' The meal has finished. She taps a Gitane from a packet onto the back of her hand and offers one to Halley.

'No thanks.'

She rummages in a bag for a lighter.

'How do you still smoke?' Halley asks. 'Who smokes anymore?'

'I do,' Camille answers. 'It killed my mother, and her mother before her, and God knows we all die of the wretched habit in the end, but we can't give it up. None of us could. I bought a thousand packets in 2025 when it looked as though they might be banned, and now I smoke just one pack a month. I have around half of them left. When the last one goes, maybe I'll give up.' She rests the cigarette on her lip and clicks her lighter, drawing the smoke into her lungs with a groan of satisfaction. 'Who cares about dying anyway?' she says.

'I care,' Halley says.

Camille looks at her. 'Perhaps you do,' she says. 'Anyway. Your question is wrong. You can't ask *why* of anything in the universe. Why is this a hill? Why do magnets point north? Why do men have monstrous egos and tiny dicks?'

'You *can* ask why to all of those,' Halley protests. 'This is a hill because the weather and the geology have made it so. Magnets point north because the Earth has a magnetic field and—'

'Pah!' Camille brushes these objections away. 'This isn't what you meant when you asked *why*. Your question was deeper than this. What you want to know is *why* WHY WHY. WHY has the universe delivered up this wrinkle? What is its bigger purpose? What role are we to play in the master plan? Isn't that your question? Isn't that what you want to know?'

'Perhaps.' Halley can feel herself deflating from Camille's tirade.

'Then stop asking,' the older woman says. 'There is no

230

answer. Not because we don't know the answer, but because there is no master plan. No design. No grand intention. Do you have a speciality?'

'I specialise in the social history of France in the early years of the First Republic.'

'Of course you do.' Camille's answer sounds dismissive. 'My speciality, as it happens, is palaeontology – I study fossils.' She waves a hand. 'I don't do it to earn a government wage. I don't need a wage. But everyone needs to be an expert in something, and this seems to suit me. So let me ask you a question, Halley Hasek. What was the purpose of *Amphicoelias fragilimus*? You don't know this creature? Well, you're not alone. It's a dinosaur we only know from *one* fossil and that fossil has disappeared. It crumbled into dust centuries ago, and the dust has been swept up and consigned to the rubbish. So why did this poor animal exist? What purpose did the thousands of generations of *Amphicoelias* fulfil? They struggled to feed themselves, to lay eggs, to raise young, to fight off predators, and by God, they succeeded for who knows how long. Maybe a million years. We don't know. It may have been the largest land animal that ever existed. Maybe it was the largest animal in the entire universe, ever. I think perhaps it was. We will never know. But don't ask why. There is no why. It was here. It has gone. The same is true of us.'

Halley is silent. Something in Camille's answer irks her. But she doesn't respond. Of course the universe has no purpose. She knows that. But everything plays its part in the whole. She knows that too. If Camille's dinosaur hadn't existed, perhaps *we* wouldn't exist, she thought. The words are forming on her lips, but she bites them back. 'Memory, though . . .' she says.

'What about memory?'

'It has a purpose. Don't you feel that?' Halley can feel herself reaching for something, for an explanation, for an insight that is just beyond her reach.

'It helps me to remember where I left my keys,' Camille said.

'I can't see how it helps me to remember dying in childbirth, which I did in 1886. Or losing a child to smallpox. Which I did. Or losing two sons in three weeks in the Battle of the Somme.'

'I'm sorry,' Halley said.

'Don't be. I could say I'm sorry for all the foul and dreadful things that happened to you and your memory line all this way down the centuries – because I'm sure they did – but what good would it do?'

'I had an ancestor who used to say, *These things are past*,' Halley says. 'These things are past.'

'She was a wise ancestor,' Camille says. 'What was her name?'

'Frantiska Němcova.'

'You should listen to her. The moving finger writes, and having writ, moves on.'

'Is that a quotation?'

'It is.'

Camille draws deeply on her cigarette. 'Let me tell you about fossils,' she says. 'They are tiny shadows of the past. Echoes. Postcards from creatures we can never know, sent to us from a past so distant and remote we can't even imagine it. Not really. You and I have three hundred years of memories, Halley Hasek. More than any other persons alive – so far as we know. Imagine living one thousand years for every *day* of our remembered lifetimes. We would be over a hundred million years old. But *Amphicoelias fragilimus* is two hundred and fifty million years old. That's why I study fossils, Halley. That's why my speciality isn't the revolution, or the great war, or the films of François Truffaut. Fossils put my memories into perspective. They tell me, I too, with my centuries of memory, am no more than the faintest shadow on the landscape of time.' She reaches an arm out and touches Halley's hand across the table. 'Don't let recent history deceive you. The revolution, *la terreur*, the Third Republic, the great wars, the dust bowls, the great famine – all of these are grains of sand on a beach a million kilometres wide. A day will come when each one of them is forgotten, when the stories and memories have crumbled into dust like the bones of *Amphicoelias*.'

Halley nods. 'So all that matters is the present?' she says.

'Of course. There is no pain in the past. Only the present.'

'And the future?'

'It doesn't exist. This moment now. This is the only thing that is real.' Camille stubs out her cigarette. 'I must go,' she says. 'I shall keep the rest of my cigarette for later.' She pushes the stub into her purse.

So the future *does* exist, Halley thinks. Camille may deny it, but she keeps her cigarette stubs. She can hear, in her mind, the words of Mother Maria of the Rains. 'Give no thought for tomorrow,' she would say. 'Today's problems are more than enough for us.' Yet she too would store up coins from the poor plate against hard times ahead.

'Isn't there something you should ask me?' Camille says.

'Is there?' Her mind is somewhere in the distant past.

'Your share of the gold?' The older woman lets her lined face break into a grin. 'Isn't that why you're here?'

'I haven't thought very much about it,' she says, and the answer is strange but truthful. 'I think more than anything, I just wanted to meet you.'

'Of course.' Camille lowers her eyebrows. She draws an envelope from her bag and slides it across the table. 'There have been expenses,' she says. 'We have to make deductions every year for the cost of the vaults.'

'Of course.'

'One of my ancestors gave a barrel each, from your vault, to her sons.'

'I see.'

'All the same, I think you will be happy with what remains. Are you surprised? Did you expect anything still to be there for you?'

Halley shakes her head. 'It has been so long,' she says. 'I haven't allowed myself to think about it too much. I've thought

233

about *today* a great deal. I've thought about it for seventy-five years, you might say. Meeting a descendant of Sylvie. It never quite seemed real.'

'You have Sylvie to thank,' Camille says. 'When coins went missing from beneath the vine, she knew Heloise's child must have survived. She made provision to keep half for you. How could any of us let her down?' She taps her fingers on the envelope. 'The bank is now called Perigord et Cie. You will find it in Fauberg du Lac in Neuchâtel. A real, traditional Swiss bank. You will need to show the letter and the certificate of authorisation to Monsieur Gotthardt. Make an appointment to see him before you go. There are two passwords for the account. One is Heloise's birthday. The other is the line you gave me in the church. *If you are to be damned, then let us be damned together.* I open one barrel at a time if ever I need capital. I like the surprise when I break open the lid to discover what lies within. I haven't needed to open one for quite a while. I still have sixteen barrels that have never been opened.'

'Sixteen!' Halley is surprised.

'You have thirty-six.'

They walk towards Annonay together. 'This is my house,' Camille says. They have stopped in front of a grand building, partly concealed behind trees and a high wall.

'You live here?'

Camille's lined face pinches up. 'Where else would I live? Do you recognise the house?'

'Of course! It's the house where Heloise was born,' Halley says.

Camille is nodding.

'This is where she grew up. This is where she met the Montgolfiers. The walk we just did . . . the walk from the church . . .'

'Yes, my child. The walk home from church. They used to do it together. This is where our family belongs, Halley. Sylvie's daughter, Louise, came back to Annonay when Sylvie died,

234

and she bought this house with money from the bank vaults in Neuchâtel. You, Halley, you have had lives in London and New York, and who knows where, but we . . . well, we stayed at home. Louise, and all of her daughters ever since. Including me. Here.'

Sometimes Halley feels her lives like a maelstrom, like a storm at sea, and herself no more than a bottle afloat in the waves and the froth, fragile, immobile, subject only to the whims of the winds and the tides, flung from one far shore to another. But Camille has grown roots in the same small place that nurtured them both. Katya had pointed this house out to Milan. *Shall we visit?* he had asked. But Katya wasn't ready for it then. And her baby was on her way.

'Didn't you want to see the world?' Halley asks. She can, in her mind, see the great statue growing in New York harbour, can picture the elephants on Fifth Avenue for the Thanksgiving Day parade. She can feel the crowds in Oxford Street. She can smell the foul drains of Vienna. She can see the lynx in the High Tatras, its feathered ears gusting in the mountain breeze. She can hear the bells in Prague.

'Our little town is perfectly lovely,' Camille says. 'This is where I belong. You should pick a place, Halley. You have seen enough of them. Where is it you live now?'

'Liverpool.'

'Pah!' Camille mimes a spit at this. 'And what is keeping you in that big, unfriendly city? Do you have a crowd of friends?' She raises her eyes. 'I thought not.'

'You think I should move?'

'You're a rich woman now. Very rich. Find out where you belong. Go wherever your heart is. Maybe it's here in Annonay. There are some fine homes here. Buy one. Settle down.'

'I want to have a daughter. I don't want to be the end of my line.'

'Well, have one. Do you have a husband? A boyfriend?'

'No.'

235

'Then you had better hurry.'

They stand at the gate. There is no invitation to go further.

'We should stay friends,' Halley hears herself saying. Another vote in favour of the future.

'We should,' Camille says.

Halley touches her wrist. 'You are now friends with Camille LeClos,' the voice says in her ear.

'Does it bother you?' Halley asks. 'That you will be the last to carry your memories?'

Camille blows a lungful of smoky air in Halley's direction. 'Not in the slightest,' she says. 'My memories are too long. Too heavy. Too much of a burden. I shall be glad to see them go.' There is something in her eyes that tells Halley this won't be far off. 'Besides,' she says, 'everyone who dies is the last to carry their memories, and everyone dies. Eventually.'

'So we do.' Halley kisses her. Once on each cheek, and then, because it seems to make a difference, on the lips. Camille doesn't try to stop her. She smells of cigarettes and lilacs.

3

Halley, 2062

It was a splendid comet. Everyone said so. It was the highlight of 2061. The year itself was not so good. It was a poor summer because of the volcanoes. So much soot was in the sky, the sun barely shone. It was no one's fault. These things happen. The planet is a volatile place. There were people who blamed the fracking, but really? How could that be? The dust clouds led to a poor harvest, of course. Nowhere was unaffected. Everywhere was cold. The Alps had their first winter snows for a decade. But that had to be a good thing. In the dust-bowl states there was some hope of rain. '*God has sent us this cloud to cool the world down,*' said a maister on the sphere. Well, maybe She had. The war in China raged on. The newspheres lost count of the casualties. An earthquake in Chile shook a chunk of ice off part of Antarctica, and the ice was the size of Portugal, and this caused all sorts of problems in the Southern Oceans; coastal communities were evacuated all around the globe as the waters rose again. These things happen too. An infection with no cure started in Asia and spread into major cities. A *superbug* they called it. A travel ban came into force to keep it out of Europe. The bug wasn't fatal. It caused lethargy. Victims would be reluctant to move. *It's like a sleeping sickness*, the newspheres said. But it wasn't. Not really. Sufferers were wide awake, but they couldn't tell their muscles to move. A team in America were working on a new antibiotic. It looked promising but it could be years away.

It was one hundred years since humankind first went into space. Imagine that. One hundred years since they built the Berlin Wall. Almost a hundred years since The Beatles. How time flies.

And now it is a new year. There are parties. A new year is always something to look forward to. A time of hope.

There are floods in January. Rains like the rains of Genesis fall across Europe. Due to the volcanoes, in all likelihood. In the north of Slovakia, the Tatrzańska River bursts its banks, leaving a trail of mud and debris all the way down the track leading along the river valley from Stary Smokovec to Nová Vyšný. The autopods have difficulty with the road. They can't find a safe route between the puddles and the fallen branches.

'This road is blocked,' one autopod tells its occupant. 'I advise you to make this journey at another time.'

'It's OK,' the passenger says. 'I shall walk.'

Go where your heart is.

Halley Hasek steps out and into the mud.

'It isn't safe to walk,' the autopod advises.

'I can manage.'

How high the mountains look. Like a wall separating this world from the next. They are heavy with snow. The first snows, she has been told, since the dust bowls and the great heatwave. Here in the valley though, there is no snow. Only slush and mud. She hoists her bag over her shoulder and finds a route along the lane, following where other feet have walked.

There are red kites hunting in the river valley. One of them is calling like the wail of a baby. She can hear the echo of the cry from the mountainsides. Along the lane there are hawthorns and oaks, tall maples, and mountain ash. She can see the river. The waters have subsided but the stream is still a torrent. A haze of mist hangs over the valley.

The track down to the Němcov farm is almost underwater. She should have brought wellington boots. To hell with it. She rolls up her jeans, steps into the cold water and wades.

At the farmstead, the byres are dark and empty. She sits on a step, takes off her socks, wrings them out and hangs them on a wall. She pulls her shoes back onto wet, reluctant feet.

She peers through gaps in the timber wall into the dairy. The railings have rusted. The stone walkways have been ransacked for their blocks. There have been no cows here for years. Flecks of straw remain, and the memory of a time when this barn was filled with the groans of cattle at milking, and the stink and splash of manure, and the whirring of the milk pumps. An air of sadness hovers up there with the mist. The milking machinery has gone. Well, good riddance. It was a Soviet monstrosity. She remembers Katya boiling kettles to steam the pipes, Jaroslav talking softly to the cows, patting their flanks, old Krystof raking up the straw.

She can smell geese. There is a new goose barn by the field where the bullocks once were. It is empty. But it wouldn't take too much to restore it, she thinks.

She crosses the farmyard to the farmhouse, climbs the steps, and tries the handle on the kitchen door. It is locked.

No matter. She can wait.

It all looks smaller than she remembers it. More dilapidated. Everywhere always does. Memory is a magnifying glass. But the meadows . . . well maybe they look the same. There are snow-drops pushing up between the grasses. Late for snowdrops, she thinks. It will be the volcanoes. Nobody's fault.

It could so easily be improved, she thinks. Nowhere near as formidable a challenge as she had feared. New paving in the farmyard. The old cobblestones could go. She would need drainage for the fields. New fences. She would get a milking bot and house it close to the pasture. The cows would come and go as they chose. She would put water troughs into every corner of every field. She would lay new sand trackways to pro-tect the cows' hooves. She would build a stock bridge over the river and open up the fields on the northern slopes. She would plant hedgerows, build new gates. She would rebuild the byre with rubber mattresses for the heavy cows to lie on at night. She would have her own micro dairy on site to bottle the milk. She would make ice creams.

A heavy-built man is making his way on foot down the

trackway. She can see his felt hat appearing and disappearing behind the trees. He picks his way carefully to the gate. He has rubber boots, but he isn't dressed for this. He has a suit patterned with red and blue squares. He is too wide around the middle for the waistcoat. He is splattered with mud from the lane. He carries a folder underneath his arm. He is out of breath. 'Miss Hasek?' He waves.

'*Dobrý den, Pane Černý,*' she says. Good day, Mr Černý .

'You speak Czech?' He is pleased about this. He makes his way up to her and shakes her hand. 'I thought you were English.'

'I have Czech in my family,' she says.

'I'm sorry the weather has been so bad,' he says. 'I didn't really expect to find you here.'

'I like the weather like this,' she says. 'Rain is no great hardship. Rain is an inconvenience at worst. A blessing at best.'

'I'm glad you think so.' The rain is stopping anyway. There is a glow to the valley like stage lighting.

'Well, since we are both here,' he pulls keys from his pocket, 'let me show you around the house and the farm.'

'There is no need,' she says. She is looking away, watching the kites circling. 'I have already made my decision.'

His face falls. He has waded through mud for nothing. 'Really,' he says, 'you should look around. It might surprise you. The farmhouse is bigger than it looks. And it has been well maintained.'

She ignores his imploring. 'I will buy the farm, the farmhouse, the buildings and all the fields. There are disused fields I can see on the other side of the river.' She points to them. 'Please find out who owns them and offer them whatever you need to buy them. It's the old Svoboda farm. By the look of them, I don't think the fields have been grazed for ten years.'

'You want it?' He looks astonished.

'This little valley is perfectly lovely.' She touches her wrist. 'Make a payment in full of six hundred and sixty thousand euros to the Černý Land Agency,' she says. 'The proprietor is with me. I am under no duress.'

The agent's screen pings. He pulls it from a pocket in disbelief. 'Six hund—' he stammers.

'I'll take the keys,' Halley says. She plucks the key ring from the man's astonished hand. 'I shall stay here tonight.'

'I don't think it is fit to stay in,' Černý says. 'There is no furniture. No heating.'

'I can light a fire.'

He looks at her the way a man might survey a dangerous animal. 'It doesn't work like that,' he protests. 'These things take time. There are legalities to pursue. Papers to sign.'

'Then pursue them,' she says. 'Sign them.'

He is open mouthed.

'I have paid you ten per cent over your asking price, and in return I want a prompt and efficient transfer of title. You can find me a lawyer if you choose. Otherwise, we can do this the old-fashioned way with a handshake.' She holds out her hand.

After a moment he reaches out and takes it.

'You may continue with your day's appointments, Pane Černý,' she says. 'My goods are on their way from England. They should be here in a few days. Visit me again when there is paperwork to sign.'

And now she is alone again, on the doorstep of her house, with only the ghosts of her past to keep her company. Frantiska was carried over this hearth by Jaroslav. It was a day of perfect happiness. The sun shone. The village children were there to cheer. Katya was kissed goodnight here, on this step, by Milan Hasek on more occasions than she knew. She could remember his warm smell. His wire spectacles. The way his eyes would crease when he smiled.

In April the grass would start to grow. She would have a dairy herd by then. She would have Braunvieh cattle. They were more contented on the hills, and far less temperamental than Simmenthals. She would hang cowbells around their necks and they could graze the slopes. She could sit on her verandah and listen to the ding ding of the bells.

She would need a verandah.

'Jacob,' she says.

'Halley?'

'Find me a local house builder and a farm contractor. Find someone who has a bulldozer to clear the lane. Advertise for two farm workers.' She hesitates. 'Four,' she corrects herself. 'Experience of dairy farms an advantage but not a requirement. Must enjoy working with animals.'

'Is that all?' he asks. There is a hint of irony in his voice.

'I need someone who builds farm buildings. Soon. Get me quotations for a byre. Five hundred square metres. Well insulated and ventilated. I want a robotic parlour.'

'Yes, miss,' he says. 'Do you want quotes?'

'Yes. But the quicker they can start work, the better. Find me details of livestock markets.'

'Yes, miss.'

'I want a dog. Look for someone locally selling puppies. A Czech wolfdog. And a Bohemian shepherd. Two dogs.'

'Dogs or bitches?'

'I don't mind. And I want a horse. Better make that two horses, one to ride and one as company for the other. Make that one horse to ride and another to pull a cart. I need them both trained and broken. No more than five years old. Geldings, please.'

'Two horses,' Jacob echoes.

'And order me a bed. If anyone can deliver today, I will pay double.'

She stands on the hearth and collects her thoughts. *Find out where you belong. Go wherever your heart is.* She can close her eyes and imagine the kitchen on the other side of the door, with its long oak table, and its big iron range, and the smells of coffee and *kolaches*; it should have cured meats and sausages hanging from the beams. There should be a family around the table for breakfast: children, and farm boys, and elderly relatives, and hangers-on. There should be comings and goings and stories about what happened the night before. They should be complaining about the government, and the weather, and the food shortages. There should be teenagers having their first romance, and widows having their last. There will be kittens in the hay barn that no one will have the heart to abandon. There will be schnapps in an old clay ewer. They will walk out on Sundays through the forests to the waterfalls and they'll return exhausted.

It won't be like that, she tells herself. She knows it won't. Not yet. But in the distance she can hear the town hall bell and she knows how it will be. Faces she has yet to meet. Names she has yet to learn. Stories yet to tell.

There is a heavy iron key on the ring. It feels familiar in her hand. She pushes it into the lock and turns it.

'There was once a woman who lived in this house who was reincarnated a hundred times,' says an earnest young man from Poprad. 'It's true. My grandmother heard the story from her grandmother. The woman who lived here had memories that went all the way back to Noah and his ark. She was a daughter of Adam.'

'And she lived here in this house?' laughs Brooklyn. 'For a thousand years?'

'No.' The young man is so serious that Brooklyn's laughter hurts him like a wound. 'No. She didn't live here for a thousand years. But she did live here.'

'Then we should have a plaque on the wall,' Brooklyn says. She is sixteen. She has dark eyebrows and a Hungarian, gypsy complexion. She has no idea that the young man at the table is so infatuated with her that her every word, every shake of her head, every flick of her eyes, can injure him or lift him with ecstasy. 'The plaque could read, *Witches Once Lived Here.*'

'Perhaps they still do,' Babička Halley says. She rests her bony hand on the table. 'I've heard these tales too,' she adds.

'You shouldn't listen to stories,' Fan Li says to the boy, but she says it kindly. She reaches over and ruffles the young man's hair. 'This is a superstitious country,' she says. 'People here believe all manner of things. I always say, believe what you can see with your eyes and never what you hear with your ears.'

The boy's name is Khalid. He came from the dust storms in Syria when he was six and he didn't speak for nearly two years. He has been living with a family in a tenement in Poprad and when he talks about his grandmother he means the grandmother who raised him as a Slovak, not either of the grandmothers he left behind in Syria. Now he's seventeen and he's a Slovak, in everything apart from looks. He has been working for almost a year with the cows on the Němcov farm. He's overawed by it – by everything – by the landscapes, by the big compliant cows, by the cheerful family camaraderie on the farm, by the flurry of languages spoken, by the general absence of rules, by the undercurrent of love that filters into every conversation. He has stumbled accidentally into heaven. This is how it feels.

Brooklyn is Albanian, and Romanian and Turkish, and who knows what. She has been at the farm since she was five. She was in an orphanage before that. She too is a child of the great dust bowl. A survivor. There is wildness in her nature. She is stocky, and strong. She carries sacks of feed corn from the mill on her shoulders with the same ease and confidence as the boys. More, perhaps. She leaves her hair uncombed, but ties it back with coloured ribbons. She has the loudest laugh on the farm and the loudest cry. 'My father was a tempest,' she tells people, 'and my mother was a thundercloud. And I am lightning.' There are those, in the Tatras, who believe this tale, if only because there is something otherworldly about Brooklyn. That gleam in her eyes can only be lightning. That nature, that energy, can only be the hurricane. She wants to go to Mongolia where they are planting one hundred billion trees. There is plenty of space in Mongolia, and in Kazakhstan, for new trees. They need people. They are baking felled trees in stone ovens to make charcoal and burying the charcoal deep underground. It will take a thousand years to reset the balance but Brooklyn already talks of it with a passion that Babička Halley admires. 'Sometimes we have to make plans for a thousand years,' Brooklyn says, and Halley agrees. 'When you are eighteen,' Halley tells her, 'then you can go, with the blessing of all the family.'

There are other children. Some of them are at the table for breakfast. Others are about their jobs. Fan Li is as tall and slender as a tree. She is nineteen, the oldest of the group that Halley calls 'the grandkids'. When Fan Li arrived from China, spirited away from the wars aged only three, there were thousands of orphaned children seeking homes. Halley was sixty-four. 'I'm too old for you to call me Mama,' Halley had told Fan Li. 'Call me Babička – Grandmother.' They speak the Czech language at breakfast, French at lunchtimes, and English in the evenings. This has been the rule at the Němcov farm since Fan Li arrived and it seems to make sense to the children, who never question the curious regime, although the farmhands like Khalid, Miro and Andreas despair of the rule. 'I wish we could speak Chinese too,' Halley told Fan Li when she first arrived at the farm. 'I would love you to keep the language you learned as a child.' But Halley has no words in this tongue. Instead Fan Li visits a Cantonese family in Poprad once a week for language lessons. She is comfortable now in four tongues. She wears narrow glasses on the end of her nose, and she looks like a young lawyer in her tailored black skirt and leather boots. She helps with the cows, but only when required to do so. Otherwise she is an artist. She makes artworks from local stones. She paints them with scenes from the Tatras and sells them in Poprad in the markets. She has a girlfriend from Prague who is a nurse. They have been dating for a year.

Milan is only ten. He was on a boat from Libya when he was rescued and sent to Poprad. He still speaks very little Czech and even less English or French. But he's learning.

Morriz is Russian. He is fifteen. He has brooding eyebrows. He thinks about girls. He hums tunes from Italy. He cries easily. 'Try not to upset Morriz,' Halley will tell the family. 'He is easily wounded.' But fifteen is an age for wounds. He shovels food into his mouth, anxious to finish first. 'Not so fast,' Mamma Sarah tells him. 'You will make yourself ill.'

Shilling is English. She is as pale as paper with hair as red as autumn. She is twelve. She is reading *Wuthering Heights*. For the third time.

And there are others, too, at breakfast. Miro the stockman

who acts like a member of the family, and Andreas with one arm who runs the dairy and makes butter and ice cream, and Mamma Sarah Willis from Belfast who came here as a nanny to Fan Li and who now looks after the house and pretends to be a mother to all the children, and Pane Černý who comes once a week to do the accounts. Sometimes there are more. Sometimes fewer. Breakfast is a dynamic time on the Němcov farm.

It is a year since Carlo died. He was Halley's sort-of-husband. They never exactly married. But why would that matter? She was forty-four when Carlo came to the farm. He was some way past fifty. He had a son and daughter of his own but they're in the cities now. One of them is a doctor. One isn't.

Halley has a seat at the end of the long table, beside the window. This has been her place for as long as anyone can remember. She has her own cushion, worn flat into the shape of her backside. She has armrests. She can sit here for hours some days. Every now and again a newcomer might settle down, unsuspecting, into the chair (if Halley is out of the room) and all eyes will look their way. 'I wouldn't sit there,' the family will say. 'That's Babička's chair.'

Halley doesn't speak about her gift. Why would she? What good would it do for all the world to know? When she dies the grandkids will each inherit a barrel from the bank vault in Neuchâtel. The rest will go to an organisation that helps to protect wild places. The world needs more wild places.

The farm will never be sold. It belongs to a trust that will look after it in perpetuity. Anyone in the family and their heirs and descendants may live there. They have two thousand hectares now. Halley has bought every farm in the valley. 'There are plenty of houses for you to live in,' she has told them. But still they all live in the Němcov farmstead. That won't last. Fan Li has her eyes on the Svoboda farm. 'Move there when you're ready,' Halley tells her. And soon, perhaps, she will.

'I'm going for my walk,' Halley tells the family after breakfast.

'Shall I come, Babička?' asks Shilling.

'You should stay and do your schoolwork.'

'Someone should come with you.'

'I will have the dogs. I shall be fine.'

It is autumn. She loves this time of year. Old Krystof used to say the trees were packing up their bags to go home. They are golden and cream and all the colours of the earth. She kicks through leaves the way the girls do. The dogs run in circles.

The path leads over the old stone footbridge and into the woods. It's a climb, but she can manage it. Carlo built a bench for her on a rocky promontory. It's a favourite spot, and there she stops to look out over the valley and the farm. Most of the cows are in the meadows. She can hear the ding of cowbells. She knows the name of every cow.

Today, perhaps, she will climb further. She walks with a stick. It's her hip. They used to give old people new hips, she reflects, but not so often these days. The bugs have become too strong, and the drugs too weak. It is dangerous now, to cut people open.

A pity. She could do with a new hip.

She braves the path upwards. These are trails she has walked for forty years, and in her memories Frantiska walked them, and Katya too. The views will be breathtaking if she can get beyond the treeline. She pushes her stick into the ground. Presses on.

It is cooler than she had expected. Perhaps she should have worn her scarf. There is the promise of winter in the north wind.

Up she climbs. Clack, clack goes her stick on the rocky path.

There are mushrooms growing in a glade. She collects a few, but she hasn't brought a basket. Sunlight is streaming through the trees. Autumn leaves are falling like confetti.

She sits on a fallen tree and pulls a small white box from her pocket. 'Shirley,' she says.

The daylight is too bright for Shirley to be seen clearly. But she is there all the same. A faint hologram of a very old lady. She joins Halley on the log. 'My legs are aching,' she says.

'Mine too.'

'We shouldn't be climbing all this way at our age.'

'Maybe not, but here we are.'

They sit and watch the view together. 'How is your hip?' Shirley asks.

'Awful.'

'You should speak to Dr Gray.'

'I try to avoid her. She has turned into a nag.'

The sunshine makes patterns on the forest floor. They are shadows and blocks of light like the shapes of countries on an unfamiliar map. 'Is she coming?' Shirley asks.

'She'll be here soon.'

'How can you be sure?'

'Because she's never let us down in six years,' Halley says.

She is not comfortable on the log. She moves to find a better spot. 'Move along,' she says. She is telling a hologram to move. It amuses her. She laughs and the sound disturbs an animal. There is a rustling in the bushes. They both fall silent. One dog barks in alarm.

'What if it's a bear?' Shirley whispers.

'Don't be soft.'

What if it *was* a bear? Would it matter all that much? There are worse ways to go than being eaten by a bear.

'Babička, you've climbed high today.' It is Fan Li. She has scaled the hill and emerged into the clearing, not even short of breath.

'I wanted to see the view,' Halley says.

Fan Li slides onto the log, ignoring the hologram, and she rests her arm on Halley's shoulder. She plants a firm, uncompromising kiss onto Halley's cheek. 'You must take care, Grandmother,' she says, in English.

'What do I have to fear?'

'Falling. Breaking your ankle. Running out of breath.'

'There is only so much breath in a body,' Halley says and she returns the kiss. 'We all run out one day.'

Shirley has repositioned herself onto the forest floor. Fan Li rests her own screen down and a second hologram appears. A much younger woman, a girl, studious in appearance with a neatly trimmed bob of hair.

'Hello Julia,' says Halley.

'Are we ready?' Fan Li asks.

'Recording,' says Julia.

'When Katya was sixteen,' Halley says, 'there was a short period of enlightenment in Czechoslovakia. It was a time that would become known as the *Prague Spring*. One morning, I think it was in August of that year . . .'

'In 1968?' Julia suggests.

'Yes. 1968. One morning in 1968 Otillie's mother wakes us all, pounding on the door. *We are all free*, she is saying. *We shall all be free.*'

'One August morning,' Fan Li echoes, 'in 1968, Hana Anya woke up the whole house with her knocking. "We shall all be free," she was crying.'

'She was. She tells us Mr Dubček had taken over the party. "I shall go to America," Hana Anya says. "I shall go to London."'

'Why would she go to America?'

'We had no freedom in Czechoslovakia. We couldn't even travel to Prague without arousing suspicion. Hungary would have been difficult. Western Europe was almost impossible. America was a dream.'

Halley is unravelling her memories to Fan Li. She has been doing it almost every day for six years.

Fan Li nods. She repeats the words that Halley says. Her head bobs slowly as if the movement helps to cement the memories.

'Krystof comes downstairs in a lather,' Halley says. '"What is all this fuss?" he asks. "It's Mr Dubček," Hana Anya says. "He is going to free us all."'

Words. Words. Words. Her memories are distilling into words. She has to pick them. To find them. They filter through her mind and emerge onto her tongue. And they don't do the job at all well. In her mind she can see the big farmhouse kitchen from the summer of 1968, she can smell the bread baking, she can hear the commotion, can see the faces, can recognise the voices. But flattened and converted into words, the kitchen loses the aromas and the colours and the sounds. Memory is reduced to snippets of half-forgotten conversations. He said *this*. Or something like it. She said *that*. Or words to that effect. It isn't memory. It's a kind of fiction based on memory. It's a shorthand. But it is the best she has.

'You're doing fine, Grandmother,' Fan Li says, and she squeezes Halley's wrist.

She's doing fine. She tells Fan Li the story of the demonstration on the Prešov-to-Poprad road. When she reaches the part where Jaroslav lay dead in a pool of his own blood, she is weeping. This isn't the first time. Fan Li hugs her. 'I think that's enough for today, Grandmother.'

Perhaps it is.

'They took away my ovaries,' Halley says. It isn't what they have been talking about, but it is on her mind. She isn't looking at Fan Li. She is looking out over the endless plain.

'You didn't know they were going to take your ovaries, Grandmother. They lied to you.'

'I could have walked away, but I didn't,' she says. 'I swapped my family memories for a ticket to France.'

'And a vault full of treasure,' Fan Li says. She says it kindly. 'And the family you have now, the family you love, a family who loves you. And the chance to meet someone else who shared Heloise's memories.'

Wisdom from a teenager.

'Yet where is Camille now?' Halley asks. 'She is long dead and her memories with her.' Camille is dust, she thinks, like her ancient fossil.

251

'I am your memories now.'

'I know.' Halley gives the girl a kiss. She feels the familiar ache of love. 'And I can't thank you enough for all the hours you've given to this. But I think it may be time to stop.' She wipes a tear from her eye. It's a tear for the long-lost Jaroslav Němcov. 'You will never remember all my stories. It was foolish of me ever to imagine that you would.'

'It isn't a chore,' the girl says. 'It has never been a chore. I love to hear your stories. And Julia will remind me if ever I forget.' She squeezes Halley's wrist gently. 'And Shirley is writing it all down.'

'No one will ever read it,' Halley says. 'Why would they? There are better memoirs than mine.'

'None that I have ever read,' Fan Li says. 'One day it will all be published and you'll be famous. So we shouldn't stop until it's done.' She touches Halley's hair, the way a carer might, brushing it away from her eyes. 'What is your happiest memory, Grandmother? What was your happiest day?'

'I can tell you my *worst* day,' Halley says. 'Not the guillotine – that was a blessing; not Lidice – I didn't learn about the horrors until later. Every day that Heloise spent in her cell. Every one was a terrible day.' She closes her eyes. She is travelling somewhere, in her mind. 'But maybe not the worst.'

'Don't dwell on the bad times, Grandmother,' Fan Li says.

'A snowstorm,' Halley says, 'in the mountains. So cold. So very cold. We hid in a shepherd's hut – me, when I was Marianne, Loïc my protector – darling, sweet Loïc – and Alice, little Alice, my friend and my rescuer. Napoleon's army was at our heels.'

'I think you told me this,' Fan Li says, but Halley seems not to hear.

'We hid in a shepherd's hut. The wind was so cold, I swear it blew right through our bodies. It froze our bones. My fingers turned to stone. It was painful even to breathe. The snow became a blizzard. Down the hill, Alice had seen men with lit torches. She had heard voices. "We should press on," Loïc said. "We're not safe here." And so we did. But further up the mountains the wind was even stronger. "We should look for a cave," I said. But there were no caves. Loïc had an infection in his foot. He could barely walk. Yet he carried Alice over his shoulders, the way Brooklyn carries corn. We stopped in a valley. We couldn't go any further.'

'Babička,' the girl cautions her.

'We all took cover under a single coat. Loïc's coat. We huddled into a ball. But it was dark. We had no warmth in our bodies to share.' Halley is crying now. Fan Li can see the trail of tears.

'The shepherd found us in the morning,' Halley says.

'I know.'

'Marianne was the only one alive.'

Fan Li takes her hand. 'And the happiest day?' she asks again.

'That's an easy question,' Halley replies. 'Today is the happiest day. It nearly always is. Do you know the funny thing about my memories?' She doesn't expect an answer. 'Not one of my ghosts ever grew old. No one passed me a memory in their forties. Yet here I am. I'm eighty-five. I am the only one to grow old.'

The dogs have found a scent in the trees. They are chasing something. A squirrel perhaps.

'Take the dogs with you,' Halley says. 'I should like to sit here for a while.'

'Are you sure, Grandmother?'

'They pester me. They won't let me sit peacefully.'

She closes her eyes. There are memories playing out on her eyelids. Dreams from another time. Voices of children. Cries of pain. Laughter. There are lights. Movement. She is at a great party in New York. Chandeliers are swaying. Otto's enormous statue is holding up a flame. She is on a tumbril. Tied. Crowds are jeering. There is the smell of death. They are lost in a snowstorm. Down in the well and the gold has all gone. '*Run, you silly fools.*' It's the old soldier in Lidice. The grandfather. She runs until her heart bursts.

She can hear the sounds of Fan Li and the dogs descending the hill. Fan Li is used to this. She knows Grandmother Halley likes to sit, when the day is clear, alone with nothing but her memories.

Halley can see, looking out over the plain, the paper mill where Milan Hasek once worked before he and Katya moved away to Záhorská Ves. It feels so close and yet so long ago. The mill has been closed for years, but the building still stands. There are families living there now. They are converting the factory into dwellings.

Did she do the right thing coming back to the Tatras? She hasn't asked herself this question in decades. But today the thought is in her mind like a mosquito in a dark room. Did she know they were lying about her ovaries? *We just want to take a sample, a few eggs. That's all.* That was what Dr Masoud told her. She learned the truth four years later, after Carlo moved in, when a fertility clinic in Košice ran some tests. Had she suspected this truth when she lay on the table in the hospital in England? Had she willingly exchanged her reproductive rights for a visa?

And anyway, did it matter? Fan Li was right (she usually was). She, Halley, had a family she loved, a family who loved her. She wouldn't turn back the clock, even if she could. What did it matter? What difference could it make if one old woman was to die? Would the Tatrzańska River dry up? Would the wars in Asia end? Would the glaciers refreeze? Would the seas fall? Would it rain in the dust bowl?

No. There would be no earthquakes. The sun would rise and set. Humankind would go about its business, some people wrecking things, and others fixing things, and all anyone could hope for was for the fixers to be more successful than the wreckers. There would be tears shed, to be sure; but every tear would fall here on the Němcov farm. The people who would weep would be the people she loved.

Funny how the clouds roll off the mountains. Like a

lugubrious waiter pulling down a tablecloth. Funny how some leaves drop so slowly and others dive. She can feel a heaviness in her feet. *Feet of clay*, she thinks. *Hliněné nohy. Pieds d'argile.* It is the uncomfortable log on which she sits, interrupting her circulation. She tries to move, but the heaviness is growing.

'Halley,' says the voice in her ear. 'You are experiencing a cardiac episode.'

A cardiac episode.

'I am calling for help. Can you reach in your pocket and take a white pill?'

Can she? For a moment she isn't sure what a pocket is. What a pill is. What an episode might be.

'Halley, I need you to lie down. Can you do that, please? Lie down on your back.'

How cold it has become. Once, in New York, Rosa stayed out nearly all night when the snow was so deep and the blizzard so wild, no one from Brooklyn could make their way home, and her hands were so frozen, she thought she would die, and she nearly did. And then there was the night she lost Alice and Loïc. It isn't that cold. But something in this cold is the same.

'Halley! Halley! Lie down please, Halley. The pill. The white pill.'

Once Marianne was forced to beg on the streets of Salzburg in January. January, when there is never any charity to be had. A man went past and she looked away to avoid his eye, ashamed to be squatting with a baby on a snowbound corner, angry at his disregard. In a short while the man returned with a blanket. Never underestimate humanity. It will always surprise you.

'Halley! Halley!'

There is movement. The bilberries are swaying. She feels eyes watching.

'Jaroslav?'

Why Jaroslav? Dead for more than a hundred years.

'Loïc? Milan?'

Like a slow ballet, all legs and flowing motion, a lynx is

255

emerging from a bush, his paws precise and practised, his ears sharp, his eyes agleam.

There are no lynx in these mountains. Not anymore. Not since Katya. Not since Frantiska. Yet there he is. The lynx is fluid. His head extends on a cautious neck. He flickers his ears. He sniffs.

He is the most handsome thing Halley has ever seen. His eyes are gold. His legs are ermine. He has fawn fur on his snout and whiskers like quills, and his face says, *I am king of these mountains. I stalk these cold peaks. I walk these hills and I take what I need.* He has no fear. He knows if a mouse stirs, even a hill away.

'I'm here,' Halley says.

He is smaller than Halley has remembered. Everything is. But he is death if she chooses. Catch the eye of a lynx and there *will* be a death.

'I'm so glad you came back,' Halley says.

There are voices in the valley. The lynx pays them no heed. He knows where they are. He has time.

'I remember you,' Halley says. 'I have seen you before. I was just a girl.'

The lynx has come to see her. He steps onto the log where Fan Li had sat. He balances with no effort. His eyes look into Halley's heart. Halley can smell his breath on her face.

'I'm not afraid,' she says.

Once on a dark, black night she, as Katya, dangled from a rope high above the world, swaying this way and that way, and the lights and voices and gunshots far below felt like the distant displays of irrelevant bees.

There is a voice in her ear but she can't tell what it is saying.

Yet the time will come when you have to let go of the rope and trust the darkness to catch you. She has always known this. Everything matters until it doesn't.

Down below in the dark people are calling. Dogs are barking. She has been here before.

It is time to release the rope.
She is falling.
Falling.
It's a long way down.

Part 2

Our Environment

PART FOUR

Our Little Island

It's a poor sort of memory that only works backwards.

Lewis Carroll

Our Little Island is Perfectly Lovely

Our little island is perfectly lovely. There are dew-apple trees growing all the way along America Lane from New York Heights to Tokyo Bay. I wish you could see them. They are the most beautiful trees you could ever imagine. They have high canopies of lime-coloured leaves and long, snaky coils of ribbon flowers. I wonder if you have dew-apple trees on your island. On our island, they flower seven times a year, once with every season. Each season the blossom is a different colour, so if you were to awaken from a very long slumber you could look out of your window and straight away know it was second spring because the flowers would be ruby red. Or else it might be harshest winter and the flowers would be blue like the ice on the top of Canada Hill, or it could be summer and they would be yellow and gold like tiny paper strips of afternoon sunshine.

'Our little island is perfectly lovely,' Jennis and Metthew tell me, and they say it every day at bedtimes, and lots of other times besides. We go for walks down America Lane and Jennis takes her parasol. We collect dew-apples for stewing, and strawberries for eating, and we catch crunch flies, which are perfectly delicious. All along the seashore there are people gathering pound crabs, mussel shells, and flatfish. It's prettiest at sunset when Canada Hill glows in the light of the evening, sea breezes shake the branches of the dew-apple trees, and the blossom drifts down like a colourful rain. Gentleman Marker rakes up fallen flowers for the farm fields, and Metthew helps him pile them onto the carts. One day Metthew will be a farmer. He loves raking, shovelling and forking. He might go and work for Gentleman Marker if Gentleman Marker will have him.

Metthew likes pigs best of all, although he couldn't do the killing. I couldn't do the killing either. Jennis once slit a pig's throat with a minnow fin and it bled enough blood to fill a bucket. I don't think she will ever ask to do it again. Mother had to wash her tunic three times before all the blood had gone.

Our island is lovely. Perfectly lovely. 'If only the seas weren't so fierce.' That's what Father says. My great-great-grandparents were founders and I can remember one, Founder Angelo. It's true. I was four years old and I remember him holding me on his knee, singing me a very strange song. He was one hundred and three. The oldest-lived of all the founders. 'It's a historical link,' Father says. I have to hold onto that memory of Great-great-grandfather Angelo. One day, when Mother and Father have gone, and when Grandmothers Katya and Nura have gone, I might be the only person left alive to have seen a founder with my own eyes. It will make me special.

Grandmother Nura says our island is lovely. When she was a girl she had prickle flowers all around her house in Little Portugal. It took twelve years to rid her land of the spines, and another ten years before the last prickle flower was gone from the island. Grandmother Katya used to say destroying the prickle flowers was a sin. She would say, 'How do we know they weren't essential for the balance of life?' That was the kind of thing Grandmother Katya would say. 'We're all part of a web of life,' she would tell me. But Grandmother Nura says it was us or them. She says prickle flowers were put here to keep us out. 'Be happy they're gone,' she says.

I've never seen a prickle flower. I wonder if you have them on your island. One jab from a prickle thorn can send you to sleep for a year. Grandmother Katya slept for four whole years after she ran into a prickle bush when she was just nineteen, and when she awoke her sweetheart, Ben, had married Gentle-madam Esla and they had a child called Tom who grew up to become Gentleman Tom, the captain of the island. 'That's what prickle flowers do for you,' Grandmother Katya says. 'They set you loose in time.' In Little Portugal there is a man called Farm-hand Fallow who is still asleep in a box in his bedroom after falling into a prickle patch forty-five years ago. No one knows when he will wake. Maybe he never will. They feed him with soup down a tube. 'He will wake up,' Grandmother Katya says, and she ought to know. But won't it be strange when he does? Everything will have changed. He won't recognise a single face.

I'm going to tell you about the ship, even though you must have learned these things from your own founders. Mother says I should write everything down. You never know what they might have missed on other islands. If there are other islands.

Father says we shouldn't call it a ship. Not really. Not if you're imagining the sort of thing you'd read about in science fiction stories. He says it was a missile. Sometimes he says it was a bullet. It was far too small to be a spaceship – barely bigger than a football. A feat of micro-engineering, Father says. It was Carrier 1309. That was its name. It was one of a swarm of eleven thousand Carriers made in a place called London where Great-great-grandmother Eliza's biological mother lived. It rode away from the sun on a comet, and carried on going. That's what Father says.

On Day One of Year Zero, as we count the days, Carrier 1309 entered our atmosphere several hundred miles east of here, unfolded a parachute, and drifted with the winds all the way to a landing spot on the southern slope of Canada Hill.

Another Carrier, called 1740, washed up on a beach near Tokyo Bay around forty years ago. It didn't work. Father says it failed to activate. It was at sea for too long. You can still see parts of it in the Island Hall on America Lane. No one has ever managed to fix it.

Carrier 1309 took nineteen thousand seven hundred and one years to get here. Space is very big, even when you're a bullet. It took six thousand and eighty more years, after Day One of Year Zero, to prepare the island for occupation. A long time, Grandmother Nura would say. But there was so much to do. The first printer bots were tiny – no bigger than a baby's thumb. They used the power of the sun, and they used water and air, to collect the materials they needed to print things, and the things they printed first were more printer bots, which is funny. Some of the printer bots were hundreds of times larger than the first ones were. And then, when there were plenty of printer bots, they all started making ant bots. The ant bots built things. They quarried tiny bits of rock, each piece no bigger than a grain of rice, and they carried these fragments of rock into the places where the towns would be, and they glued them together, slowly, over a great many years, to build houses, and schools, and farms, and roads. They cleared fields. They created water courses. They dammed the Nile River. Father says there were millions upon millions of ant bots. At one time, Father says, the whole of our island was covered with a swarm of tiny ant bots. I like to imagine them like a shiny blanket smothering the south of the island all the way from Canada Hill to the bays. Everything we see on our little island was built by them. Even the statues that line America Square. It is why our island is so lovely. The ant bots made it lovely.

Three thousand years after Carrier 1309 landed, the ant bots began to plant the fields. They used frozen seeds from Home. Most of the plants we grow on the island – the grains and the fruits – strawberries, potatoes, beans, soya, rice, sugar sticks – all of these came from Home as seeds. Space was so limited on Carrier 1309 that there were only six seeds for every type of plant, so the bots had to be especially careful. They had to be sure that conditions were right, and they must have been right, because most of the plants grew. The ant bots cultivated them, and harvested them, and in time the second generation of seeds was planted, and then the third, and before long the island was the way we know it today.

The first animals were goats. The bots grew them from tiny frozen embryos. Mother bots incubated them, and gave birth to them, and suckled them. After the goats came sheep, pigs, and then dogs. Then they grew chickens, and ducks, and all the other animals we know. There were flying birds too, and fish, and bees, and earthworms, and butterflies. All creatures that would make our island more perfect.

None of the goats survived. They were all destroyed by prickle flowers. I've never seen a goat, but the fate of the goats is recorded in the island archive, and of course I've seen goats in films and books.

They started to grow people six thousand and eighty years after Carrier 1309 landed. Father says that humans can't survive interstellar space travel. In some of the films I've seen, people are frozen in glass coffins for long space journeys, like Gentleman Fallow in his box. But Father says this would never work in practice. Humans don't survive freezing, he says. And even Gentleman Fallow is ageing as he sleeps. Besides, the ships would have to be too huge, Father says. Each ship would need to be the size of Founders' Hall. It would take an unbelievable amount of energy just to get them up into space, let alone to send them all the way to another star. And radiation would cook everyone on board long before the ships could reach a destination. The only human you can freeze, Father says, is an embryo – an embryo just one cell big. So that was how we got here.

All of the sixteen founders were frozen embryos. They were defrosted, grown in artificial wombs, and raised by care bots. All sixteen of the founders were great-great-grandparents of mine, which is amazing when you think about it.

Great-great-grandmother Eliza was the first founder born. She never saw another flesh-and-blood human being until she was nearly fourteen. She never saw a grown-up person until she herself was fully grown. She was raised and fed and washed and clothed by care bots. The bots tried to teach her to speak, but they weren't especially successful. She learned how to understand language, after a fashion, from the bots, and from films. Thousands of films.

I find it difficult to imagine how it must have been, but Grandmother Katya says Eliza never thought it in any way strange. It was the only world she knew.

Founder Eliza was on her own for the first thirteen years of her life. She enjoyed her childhood, Grandmother Katya says. But it was lonely. She spent her life learning. Bots printed books and taught her to read. Now we have thousands upon thousands of books in the libraries of Founders' Hall and the reading rooms in Little Portugal. We have more books than anyone could read in a lifetime.

The bots did everything for Founder Eliza. They made meals. They cleaned up behind her. They printed clothes for her to wear (but she rarely wore them). They played music. They told stories to send her to sleep. They made repairs when she had a tantrum and broke things. They weighed her and measured her, and tested her water, and kept her safe. They did everything.

Almost everything.

All the same, Founder Eliza was an unusual child. Of course she was. I have seen film of her childhood. It's all part of our island archive. She slept a great deal. She had an odd way of walking. She made foolish noises. She rarely spoke. Once, for a week, she sang the same song to herself, over and over, and the words she sang were, '*bum bum bum bum bum.*' When she was ten, Eliza began to cut herself. She cut marks into her hands and her arms. The bots took away everything that was sharp and so Eliza stopped talking to them. She only used words for things she needed. Water. Food. Lights. Dark.

The bots would do her bidding. What else could they do? But for a while she barely ate. She would lie on her mattress and hum tunes.

And then, when she was twelve years old, something happened.

She started to remember.

For several weeks, night after night, she suffered violent

dreams. These were her memories coming back. Some nights she screamed so loudly, the walls of Founders' Hall would shake. Sometimes the bots would wake her, but after a while she began to stop them. 'Leave me be,' she would say.

She began singing different tunes. Using different words.

'Print me some books,' she told the bots, 'on French history.'

'What year?' the bots asked.

'From 1759,' she said, 'until Waterloo.'

On the morning of her thirteenth birthday, almost a year after her dreams had started, Eliza rose up and she spoke to her bots in a voice, and in a manner she had never used before. She walked into the great atrium where every bot could hear her, and she stood on the mosaic star in the centre of the vaulted chamber, and she looked up at the roof, and she spoke. 'I know who I am,' she told the bots. Her voice echoed in the open space. 'I know who I am, and why I'm here. I understand it now. It has taken me a while, but now, today, it makes sense. You may start to incubate the next children.'

'Are you sure?' the mother bot asked.

'I'm sure.'

'How many?' the bot asked. 'How many children?'

Eliza thought about this. 'Five,' she said, after some reflection. 'Three boys and two girls.'

When she had spoken in this way to the bots, Eliza walked to the door of Founders' Hall and she spoke to the bot on the door. 'I am thirteen years old,' she said. 'I am no longer a child. You may open the door and release me.'

According to the legends, for they are legends now, the bot hesitated for a very short time. The door of Founders' Hall had never been opened, not once, in all the years that Eliza had been alive. She had lived her short life within the walls. She had never seen the sky.

'Open,' she commanded again.

And this time the bot obeyed her instruction. The doors of Founders' Hall rolled open, and the light of the sun shone

267

down through the atrium and lit every corner of the great hall. Eliza, the only living human on the island, stepped outside for the very first time.

What a day that must have been. On our island we remember that day with a ceremony whenever a child reaches thirteen. We call it *the releasing*. It has become our tradition. All the doors in the town are symbolically opened, and the thirteen year old is sent out to walk alone, from one end of the island to the other. From the top of Canada Hill, as the sun sets, the new teenager sends up a huge balloon made from the dried leaves of tiger palms. The balloon rises and rises, its flame burning in the darkening sky so everyone on the island can see it. The winds sweep it away, over the oceans to who knows where. Our hope is that it will find another island, if there is one. It reminds us of Carrier 1309. We send it off, but we never know its destination.

In every balloon is the story of our island, written in the hand of the child who released it.

And this is my account of the island, ready for my balloon. My releasing is tomorrow.

All of the first sixteen founders were my great-great-grandparents. I share a little piece of each one of them. But my matrilineal line goes back to Eliza. That makes me special.

All five infants in the first family were healthy and strong. They were born nine months after Eliza's releasing. Eliza raised them and fed them and taught them. She told them stories. She dabbed their eyes when they were tearful and kissed their bruises. She brushed their hair. She helped them in and out of clothes. She made them meals, and washed them, and played games with them, and these were things that had never happened to her in Founders' Hall.

But she knew these things from her dreams. She cuddled the children, and she kissed them, and she told them they were beautiful, and she told them they were loved. She sang lullabies in French, and German, and Czech, and English. She made a big, wide bed where all six of them could sleep if they wanted, and she made individual bedrooms as they grew. When ten years had passed, when all five children were tall and strong, she told the bots to defrost the final ten embryos, and they too were nurtured successfully, and they too grew vigorous, and full of health and life. One of these infants would become my great-great-grandfather, Founder Angelo, who sat me on his knee when I was four and he was one hundred and three.

In time, Founder Eliza made a home with Founder Dan, a tall boy with dark skin and with features she would describe as *African*, and they moved to a homestead on the slopes of Canada Hill and they grew soft fruits like grapes and raspberries, and Eliza became the first captain of the island, and so she was until her heart gave in when she was eighty-two; and now she is part of the island, and a stone covers the spot where her body lies. It's a place I will visit tomorrow on my tour of the island. I will put a stone onto her grave, just as every child must do on the day of their releasing. Grandmother Katya says that one day there will be a mountain of stones. Already there is quite a pile.

When the time was right, Founder Eliza told her daughters, Marianne and Esme, about her memories. She warned them to expect the same dreams that she had had. Sure enough, Marianne and Esme had dreams too. Marianne was my great-grandmother. In her turn she warned her three daughters and her sons Milan and Jaroslav to expect the dreams.

Every girl experienced them. But not the boys.

It seems that the dreams may be more than dreams. Today there are eleven people on our island who have had the dreams. All are girls, and all descend from Founder Eliza. They share the same stories. They are capable of curious things, these people. They can talk to one another in different tongues. They have a knowledge of things that no one should know. They sit together sometimes, and they tell each other tales that seem to be tales of Home.

Mother tells me my own dreams will start soon. I'm nervous. But I'm excited. Mother tells me I will have some of her memories. She says that when I do, I will understand her better. She says this is what happened between her and Grandmother Katya.

Our little island is perfect. It feeds us and it clothes us. There are three hundred and twenty-one people here now. We are all descended from the original sixteen founders. We still have technology from the printer bots, although the ant bots have long gone. An ant bot only lives for a few months before it wears out, and then it rots away quite quickly. Father says the ant bots were made of sugar. 'They dissolved in the rain,' he says. When our island was fully built there was no need for ant bots any longer. 'Ant bots are a very slow way to build a world,' he says. 'It takes thousands of them and they take centuries to do their work.' When they were gone, the printer bots turned their attention to building care bots, and mother bots, and all the other devices that would be needed to incubate and grow all the embryos and seeds. We still have some of these bots, and we have screens and a picture house in Founders' Hall. There are lots of useful things the bots can do. They can source minerals from seawater. They can print their own replacement parts, and they can make all manner of devices and things they have been programmed to make. They can make dinner plates, and shoes, and tunics, and shovels, and nails; but you can't ask them to make anything that isn't in their catalogue. You can't tell them to build an airship. They don't know how.

This world is not an altogether friendly world. Even without prickle flowers it isn't the most hospitable of places. The seas are too fierce to sail, the rocks are as sharp as knives, and if you try to build a boat, the *gila* fish will eat it. Twice people have tried. Founder Lucien died when he went out to sea in a dugout canoe. He paddled out on a misty day when the seas were far less violent than they usually are, and he vanished into the fog. No one saw what became of him, but most people think the gila fish were to blame. Then there was Farmhand Enda; she made a raft, many years before I was born, and she tried to sail it into the bay, but a swarm of gila fish found her and they ate both her and her craft before they could even reach Staten Rock. Father says we're stuck on this island until we can fly.

Here's another thing. The atmosphere on this world isn't especially good for us. The oxygen is thin and the CO_2 is high. We're a little lighter here than we would be on Home, apparently. But our bones grow brittle and we run short of all manner of minerals. There is very little natural calcium, for example. The bots built devices to extract tiny quantities of calcium out of huge volumes of seawater, and this is added to our food. It was one of the reasons the bots had to wait so long before defrosting any embryos. There are similar problems with magnesium and zinc. On the other hand, arsenic is a fairly abundant metal here and it's dangerous for us. 'This isn't paradise,' Grandmother Katya says. But then she says, 'I've seen a lot of places, and none of them were paradise. This is as good a place as any.'

You might think this would be a funny thing for Grandmother Katya to say. After all, she was born on the island, and she'll surely die on the island, but you see, she has Founder Eliza's memories, and memories of Home. She is quite the wisest person I know. I talk to her about all the places she has seen, all the things in her memory, and she says to me, 'You will know it all one day.' She says human beings can be the cruellest of creatures, and also the kindest. She says we can be the smartest of beings and also the most stupid. She says we have the capacity for the most love, but also for the most hate. She says that people are the most beautiful things in all creation, but also the most ugly. 'Who would choose to be cruel?' she asks me. 'Who would choose hate? Who would choose stupidity? And yet we can,' she says. 'And yet we do.' I'm not sure why she says these things, or how they can all be true, but when Grandmother Katya tells me things, I know they are important because she sits beside me and she squeezes my hand, and sometimes I see tears in her eyes. She says we can know everything there is to know about the past, yet still be taken by surprise by the future. 'Nothing is written,' she says. 'We make our own destinies. We choose.'

One day, she says, I will understand.

On the top of Canada Hill is the radio dish. It is the biggest feature on the island. It was built by the bots many centuries ago. It is supposed to bring us messages from Home. It listens for signals from Home and from a thousand other systems where people might be, worlds where other Carriers might have gone. But in all the years it has been there, the radio dish has never heard a peep. Grandmother Nura says perhaps it isn't working. But Father says it's working fine. The reason it hasn't heard a peep, Father says, is because no one has ever sent us a message. We can send messages to Home but they take ninety years to get there, so we don't send many. All the same, I will walk to the radio dish tomorrow on my releasing, and I'll send a message. I will type it out onto the keyboard one letter at a time and when it is done I shall press 'Send', and off it will go on its ninety-year journey.

This account will be my message.

I think my mother's dreams may be starting. Last night I dreamed of a huge balloon. I hung beneath it on a rope. The dream was so sharp, and I remember it so clearly, I think perhaps it was one of mother's memories. I let go of the rope and fell into a river, and four men I had never seen before pulled me out, laughing loudly and cheering, and telling me, 'You are free now. You are free! You can be whomever you like. You can do whatever you choose. You are free.' It was a happy dream. I could feel the joy in my chest like a bird escaping from a cage.

*

Our little island is four miles long and two miles wide. I know every inch of it – every bay and every hill, every lane, every field, every tree, and every home. But I have never walked all around it by myself. It takes a whole day to do that. I will do it tomorrow. At dawn the bell will ring in Founders' Hall, and all the houses from New York Heights to Tokyo Bay will throw open their doors, and I will step out on my own. I will call 'Hello,' into every open door I pass. I will dip my toes into the ocean at Little Portugal and then I'll walk all the way to Tokyo Bay and I'll do the same there. People will come out of their houses to give me food and drink, and to wish me well. They will clap and sing to me as I pass. Finally, I shall climb Canada Hill and I'll send the radio message, and when that is done I will seal these pages into an envelope and I'll tie it onto the balloon.

The tradition of the balloon goes all the way back to Great-great-grandmother Eliza. It was her idea. There will be a big crowd. Most of the island will be there to watch. I shall light the fire that will send the balloon upwards. I'll stand and watch it growing smaller and fainter until it disappears from view. And then my childhood will be over and my adulthood will begin.

And maybe one day you will find this note. Maybe one day we will discover a way to communicate. Maybe one day we shall be friends.

My name is Heloise Starchild.

It's a pleasure to meet you.

Hello.

ACKNOWLEDGEMENTS

This has been a work of fiction, and wherever I have made mistakes with historical details, this will be my defence. No character is based upon any real person, living or dead. All anachronisms are the faults of my imagination.

Halley's comet was famously seen over England at the time of the Battle of Hastings, and it appears on the Bayeux Tapestry. Edmond Halley sought out historical records of the comet and these enabled him, in 1705, to predict its return in 1759 – which it duly did. (A good account of the 1759 appearance can be found in *When Computers Were Human* by David Alan Grier.) The comet reappeared in 1835 and made a spectacular visit in 1910 when the Earth passed through the tail. The 1986 appearance was disappointing. The comet and the Earth were on opposite sides of the sun. Most people never saw it. The next appearance, in 2061, will be a lot more exciting.

On the night of 20th–21st August 1968, armies from the Soviet Union and its allies invaded the ČSSR (the republic of Czechoslovakia). In a single night, 200,000 troops and 2,000 tanks entered the country. Czechoslovakia's own forces were confined to barracks. It was a swift and brutal occupation.

Readers may be interested in this account of an incident on the Prešov-to-Poprad road. It comes from *Shli na pomoshch' druz'yam. Voenno-istoricheskii zhurnal 1994* and is the first-hand account of General Semyon Zoltov. He writes:

On the first day of our march along the roads of the CSSR, a tragedy occurred. En route between the cities of Prešov and Poprad, the path of a tank column was blocked by a group of women and children. As was later revealed, they had been planted there by extremists, who were hoping to provoke an incident involving a huge loss of human life. To avoid running over the people, the mechanic-driver of the vehicle at the head of the column swerved sharply to the side. The tank overturned from the sudden movement and, having fallen on its turret, caught on fire. Two soldiers serving in the tank received severe injuries and one of them died as a result.

A sculpture by the Czech artist Marie Uchytilová-Kučová now overlooks the site where the village of Lidice once stood. The sculpture is entitled *The Memorial to the Children Victims of the War*. It consists of eighty-two bronze statues of children (forty-two girls and forty boys) aged one to sixteen, representing the eighty-two children murdered at Chełmno in 1942.

Escape by balloon from Iron Curtain countries to the West was rare, but not entirely unknown. In one of the most notorious escapes, two families fled East Germany in September 1979 in a homemade hot-air balloon made from taffeta. They took off from a forest clearing ten kilometres from the West German border. The plot took a year and a half to plan, and the families made several unsuccessful attempts before their successful flight. There were eight escapees: Peter and Doris Strelzyk with their children Frank and Andreas aged fifteen and eleven, and Güenter and Petra Wetzel with children Peter and Andreas aged five and two. The balloon's volume was four thousand cubic metres.

Among the many books and websites I found helpful, I ought to single out *Journal of My Life During the French Revolution* by Grace Dalrymple Elliott. Grace Elliott was an Englishwoman, a courtesan, who was arrested in Paris as a spy in 1793 and was sentenced to be guillotined. Remarkably, she survived, and her memoirs, written in English, provide a rare insight into life in France during those tumultuous years. Like most old books, the text is freely available online.

Another helpful book, bristling with details, also available online, is Thomas Carlyle's *The French Revolution: A History*, published in three volumes in 1837. Volume Three is called 'The Guillotine' and was the source for many of the descriptions of Heloise's execution.

I need to say thank you to a lot of people. Thank you Sue for your endless positivity and support, and for putting up with me. Thank you Stan for your patience and perseverance. Thank you Fede, your insight and advice has been amazing. Thank you Kirsty for convincing me that the story wasn't completely crazy. Jon, I absolutely couldn't do this without you. Thank you to the brilliant and diligent Simon Fox who spotted all my inconsistencies and awkward turns of phrase, and to Lucinda McNeile who turned the rough hewn manuscript into a beautiful finished thing.

Thank you to members of the French Revolution Enthusiasts group on Facebook who were always ready to answer my idiotic questions. In particular, I need to thank Tyree Simonich and Stijn d'Hondt who trawled through Heloise's and Marianne's stories, helping to spot historical glitches. Thank you to our good friends Monique and Michel Segalen for fielding questions about France and the French language. Thank you to Dr Jon Bloor for insight into the behaviour of an AI doctor.

Thank you to the brilliant teams at Weidenfeld & Nicolson, Orion Books and at the North Literary Agency. You have been awesome. Let's do it all again sometime.